A Very Reluctant Lady

A Novel of Regency Romance

Teresa Sweeney

Courting Romance Publishing
California

Published in the United States by Courting Romance Publishing

ISBN 978-1-940319-05-6

First Edition

Cover Photography by Christina Brusaca
Cover Model: Alicia Floyd

By Teresa Sweeney

To my beautiful and amazing daughter Alicia and her extraordinary husband Kevin.
Generous, smart, strong, together they make an unbeatable team.

And to their beautiful children:
Harrison and their soon to arrive baby boy.

A Very Reluctant Lady

Chapter One

Mayfair, London, England
October

"Watch your mount, Donahue!" exclaimed the Earl of Felton as a loud crash resounded. Kevin's spirited animal pranced and shook his head from side to side trying to break free from the firm grip Kevin had on his reins. The beast wanted to bolt and escape the danger he feared until Kevin brought him to heel with a tight squeeze of his thighs and a stern shout commanding obedience. Settled, yet uneasy, his superior horse tossed his head and snorted at the nearby workhorse as if the animal was responsible for the frightening disturbance.

The long thoroughfare of Piccadilly was a bevy of industry filled with carts and laborers polluting the air with the smell of sweat and horse. Everywhere they looked crates were being slid, slapped, and dropped as carters unloaded and carried goods from delivery wagons to the shops and inns waiting to receive them. Dust motes rose from the wagon beds and floated aimlessly until they resettled back upon the wagon, the cobblestone street, or on the laborer, whom more times than not, wiped the bothersome dust from his face with his shirt sleeve.

Kevin was annoyed at being cautioned like a greenhorn and gave his concerned friend a steely-eyed look as he nudged his horse to fall back in step. Felton's chuckle did little to alleviate his perceived affront. He grew up riding horses, breaking wild ones, too, and no one had ever doubted his horsemanship skills. Some say he learned everything he knew about horses from his grandfather Sean Donahue, even his innate ability to calm the most restless horse, which he felt he just proved.

Born in America, Kevin came to London nearly six months ago as an agent for his family's tobacco exports and to purchase certain goods requested of him by his family and friends. Upon his arrival, he looked for amusement in one of London's gaming establishments and spent the evening playing cards. The British with their accent and manners intrigued him, so his eyes drifted from his cards to the other men in the room.

A young man's gleeful shout over his winning hand of cards made Kevin grin until he heard the young man's opponent profuse congratulations and then in the same breath, order another round of drinks. Kevin noted the numerous empty glasses were on the young man's side who the cheat revealed in his accolades as Crawford.

Kevin doubted the acclaimed loser drank anything. The cheat's glass remained full even when his drink was brought to his lips. The man was clearly a card sharp, a gambler who manipulated his skill at cards to set up his prey. The sharp expounded on Crawford's good luck and pushed the young man to drink, while suggesting they up the ante on their next hand before his luck changed. Kevin did not hesitate to intervene knowing Crawford's luck would change once the pot was at a size to satisfy the cheat.

Kevin quickly threw his cards down and pushed them forward to the center of the green baize table to quit his play and rose. He strode over to where Crawford sat and called the young man by name. Crawford stood, looking bewildered to be addressed by a stranger and even more surprised when Kevin, with a firm grip on his shoulder, led him over to an empty table.

The card sharp immediately rose and exclaimed his outrage at Kevin's interference, but the scathing squint Kevin gave made him sit back down. The villain might have feared to create a scene, but most likely his self-preservation motivated him to find another victim and he quickly turned his eyes elsewhere.

Kevin returned his attention to Crawford and quickly introduced himself. The young man responded in kind with his name, William Crawford. The jerk of William's head when he gave his name, the supposedly aristocratic nod of greeting, lacked distinction but amused Kevin into revealing another grin at the young man. William, high in his cups, returned Kevin's grin and then mirrored Kevin's movements and sat down at the card table.

Kevin immediately picked up and opened the fresh box of cards from the center of the table. He was sure William was about to ask why he called out to him, so to distract the young man he poured the cards into his hand and began to shuffle them.

Kevin dealt out the cards for play and watched over William until the wee morning hours when Lawrence Cowper, Viscount Atwood came looking for him. Kevin never expected his simple act of kindness to benefit him more than the pleasant evening of banter he enjoyed, but William's family insisted on thanking him with a dinner hosted by their good friend Edward Brentwood, the Earl of Felton. He was introduced to a number of titled persons and through the course of dinner revealed what brought him to England.

Felton was a wealthy man and made much of his money through importing and exporting goods, so the knowledge of Americans looking to England for certain items peaked his interest. He wanted to learn more about American needs and quickly invited Kevin to be his houseguest. It was not long before Kevin, Atwood, and Felton became good friends and the earl suggested a business proposition to Kevin.

The earl was keen on starting a new venture in America and offered Kevin a commission for every contract he acquired, not just for securing the new business, but a percentage of the products sold. Kevin agreed to the terms and recently returned to receive a substantial payment for his efforts. Now, thanks to Felton again, he had a place to live at The Albany.

He pressed his leg against his horse to steer him around a conveyance being unloaded for the high-end grocery store Fortnum and Mason and followed Felton. They passed in tandem between the same two stone pillars that once welcomed royalty and the upper echelons of society into the Great Court when the estate belonged to Baron Melbourne.

The mansion was set one hundred feet from Piccadilly and those who attended Lady Melbourne's entertainments boasted of a Great Stair and magnificent reception rooms. The Duke of York was a frequent guest at Melbourne House and admired it so much he purchased the highly-mortgaged home from the baron. In 1803, he sold what was now known as York House to Mr. Copeland, an enterprising businessman who transformed the classical three-story red brick and stone grand mansion into twelve bachelor apartments. Mr. Copeland renamed the newly structured building, The Albany, after one of the duke's titles.

Kevin and Felton entered the gravel u-shaped courtyard and rode straight up to the ten steps leading into the central part of the apartment building. They dismounted clear of any fool who might gallop into the courtyard without caution and held out their reins for the attending ostler to collect. The stable lad replied with a "yes, milord" when Felton instructed him to keep their mounts at hand. The boy tipped his woolen cap and led the horses far enough away so as not to hear his betters' conversation, but remained close enough to return their horses when summoned.

The friends began to talk the minute they were assured of some privacy. They stood tall, over six feet and looked quite distinguished in their gentleman's attire. They each wore a multi-caped tan greatcoat which made their shoulders look excessively broad and their waists narrow. Their tall black beaver hats added inches to their six foot one heights and their black riding boots were as reflective as a still lake. Kevin's blond hair contrasted against Felton's black; otherwise, they were equally handsome, fit, and blue-eyed.

"Thank you again, Felton, for securing the bachelor apartment for me," offered Kevin. "I shall deliver a voucher by tomorrow to your man of business for the rent you obligingly paid on my behalf if that is acceptable to you."

"As I mentioned before, Donahue, there is no rush or need for that matter. If I had my way, you would be residing with me. My lady wife Anne has already chastised me for failing to convince you to call Beaumont Manor home."

"I could not reside indefinitely as your guest, Felton. It was good of you to invite me to stay with you when we first met, but now that I plan on making England my home, I must see to my own residence. Besides, with the stake my father gave me and the tidy sum I earned for negotiating your export contracts, I am well-funded to purchase a place of my own."

"Well, I know you want a piece of property in the country to start a horse breeding farm, so I might not have acted in your best interests when I asked Rodchester to sublease his son's apartment to you. The moment I heard his son left England as an aide to our Russian Ambassador, I instinctively sought out Rodchester to make him an offer on the apartment. I knew he would not have need of it and would soon be overwhelmed with offers the minute the apartment's availability became known. What single gentleman would not want to live here? The Albany is within walking distance to the clubs on St. James Street and is only a hundred feet from Picadilly where our *bon ton* like to shop and eat. I hope you are not disappointed with my interference."

"I feel very much indebted to you for your foresight, Felton. The fully-furnished apartment is more than I expected to contrive. Are you sure Rodchester had no qualms letting to an American?"

"How could he?" countered Felton with surprise. "He would be a fool to instigate my disfavor."

The Earl of Felton was remarked to have the Midas touch and was sought for his business advice. His peers hounded him with requests to invest in his enterprises. No one with any sense intentionally sought his displeasure. He asked, "The apartment suits you?"

"Indeed," replied Kevin cheerfully, "the apartment is nicely decorated with colors and furniture very much to my liking. I have no wish to make any changes. Once I purchase my own mount I will feel quite established."

"You will need to hire a valet and staff. As for your mount, you may continue to use the horse I lent you, Donahue."

"I have no need for a valet or any staff. I have managed to bathe and dress myself since I was in short pants. As for your loan of your horse, as much as I appreciate your generosity, I must decline. I am going to Tattersall's today to purchase a good mount, maybe even a thoroughbred. I see no reason not to start acquiring my stock for breeding if I can find a horse with some good bloodlines."

"I disagree with your need for a valet, though will defer to your decision not to hire staff. The Albany probably has maid service you can subscribe to clean your apartment, but you really must have a valet to see to your attire. We British are fastidious when it comes to our clothes, unlike you Americans. Besides, if you wish to sell horses to our elevated society, than you best dress as one, or else no one will bother to do business with you. Allow me to ask my own valet for a recommendation."

"Very well, I will consider it, Felton, but only because these tight-fitted clothes considered the height of fashion are too difficult to get into and out of without assistance."

"Excellent. As to your visit to Tattersall's, I understand Sterling's heir is selling off some of the horses from his father's stable or his stable, since his father has passed. The new earl has no interest in animal husbandry. There should be some good stock from which to choose. It wouldn't surprise me if there were some thoroughbreds in the sale. The new Sterling has no notion of what his father owned. I caution you to not buy any horse without its papers."

"Of course," stated Kevin a bit vexed. "I am not as naive or young as you like to think me."

"No," replied the earl, grinning at having annoyed his friend once again. "I guess the protectiveness I have for Atwood just rolls over to you as well."

"I am glad Viscount Atwood secured the hand and married Miss Deneham. I thought they were a lost cause when I departed for America to acquire those contracts for you. I expect they will be quite happy. I am only sorry I was not here to witness the happy event."

"You shall see them over the holidays for Meg is anxious to introduce you to her cousin Alicia. Her father, Baron Deneham, breeds horses and sits on many racing committees. You would benefit if you could call him 'friend.'"

Felton's soft chuckle had Kevin inquiring, "What is so funny, Felton?"

"I just remembered a wager recently placed in the betting book at White's. Seems Deneham wants to secure a husband for his daughter and is forcing her to take part in the Little Season. Odds are being placed on whether she can bring a gentleman up to scratch or not."

"Is that not the way for all daughters of the realm. What makes Meg's cousin different? I cannot believe she is an antidote with Meg for a relative."

"No. In fact, she is quite beautiful and smart like Meg, but she is also too independent and used to running her father's household. Even Deneham agrees he allowed her too much freedom. He admits to having let her learn and take part in his horse breeding business which is quite improper behavior for a lady in our elevated society; even so, there are many who would be pleased to call her their own. It is not so much who will have her as who will she have. She has been known to say, "None.""

"While I look forward to an introduction to Deneham, I have no interest in his daughter. My only thought at present is in buying a mount which speaks to my knowledge of horses. Do you wish to accompany me to Tattersall's, Felton? We can break our fast first. My stomach is begging for substance."

"No, thank you, as tempting as a hearty meal sounds, I must decline, Donahue. I promised Anne I would not dally in Town. Besides, I am anxious to return to Beaumont Manor to spend time with her and my new son."

"I am happy for you, Felton."

"Thank you, Donahue."

A thump and a curse turned Kevin and Felton to see who ran into Kevin's backside. The collision proved insignificant to Kevin, but the offender sat on the ground cursing his ill luck. Kevin watched the agile slender young man with unruly brown hair jump to his feet with no concern for whom he collided. The lad set himself to rights with a tug first to his yellow brocaded waistcoat and then to his dark purple tailcoat. He checked off each item of his apparel and then straightened his black beaver hat, before looking up to see a tall broad shouldered man slapping a riding crop against his thigh.

Kevin waited for the dandy to make his apology and was about to lose his patience at the young man's lack of manners when the lad's light brown eyes widened in fear.

"Egad!" he cried out as if he expected retribution for his clumsiness. "I do beg your pardon. I was not watching where I was going. You will excuse me as I am in a bit of a rush and must be off."

Head down, he quickly circumvented an astonished Kevin and then in his haste, had the misfortune to slip on a horse's leaving. The young man's boot heel slid forward on the slick mass causing him to ungraciously fall to the ground again. This time, his rump landed on a foul mound of waste.

"Damn! Damn! Damn!" he cried while quickly righting himself to march back into the Albany leaving the much forgotten Kevin and Felton astounded.

"Charles," informed Felton of the young man's identity. "He is Lord Deneham's presumptive heir after his brother."

Surprised, Kevin asked, "Related to Miss Margaret Deneham?"

"They are distant cousins. Baron Deneham is his guardian. He established Charles here at The Albany with hopes of gaining his ward some Town *bronze*. He just recently graduated from Cambridge and while I do not think him dull-witted, he is surely untried. With no world-experience or father to mentor him, he is a bit lost among our prodigious society, especially since he has no wealth to call his own. His only opportunity to engage with the aristocracy has been through Deneham's benevolence. I believe since the boy is willing to be guided, Deneham hopes to bring him up to snuff."

"I expect I will meet him again," remarked Kevin.

Felton laughed. "Indeed. It should prove amusing to see if the young pup remembers you."

Chapter Two

Piccadilly's multi-storied shops were opened in earnest by the time Kevin broke his fast and stepped back onto the popular avenue. The public scene would draw the interest of any people watcher, even Kevin's, if his mind was not preoccupied on his hopes and dreams of owning a horse breeding farm.

Kevin wanted to work with horses ever since he was a boy and saw his grandfather Sean Donahue settle a most ornery beast. His grandfather was born in Ireland and at five and ten years of age, made his way to London after he lost his family to illness. While looking for work on the docks, a press gang captured and immediately forced him onto one of His Majesty's Ships headed to America. Once onboard, he took the king's coin preferring to be paid for his service than not. He reluctantly followed the drum for two years, until the night his unit billeted at the Osborne Tobacco Farm and he fell ill with camp fever. His commander left him to recuperate, then ordered him to rejoin his unit if he did not die. Osborne's daughter and only child nursed him back to health and in the process the young couple fell in love and married. He never rejoined his unit. Instead, he spent the rest of his life raising a family, growing tobacco, and earning a reputation as the man who tamed horses.

The Osborne Farm passed to Kevin's parents and became the Donahue Farm. The farm was intended to pass to either Kevin or his brother Ryan. Unfortunately, both sons had other aspirations. Ryan went away to school and became a doctor. There was no chance he would return to manage the farm since he lived and worked in Boston. Kevin, on the other hand, had yet to save the funds he needed to realize his dream and was prepared to let go of it if necessary. He respected his forefathers and all they accomplished, too much, to let the farm pass out of his family.

His grandfather used to thank the wee folk, fairies, for bringing him to the Osborne Farm where his life changed for the better. If Kevin was a fanciful man, he would have believed he was gifted with the same Irish luck. First, his sister fell in love with a man who was more than happy to run the Donahue Farm once he married into the family and then, Kevin was asked to accompany the family's tobacco export to England because their agent refused to leave his expectant wife. In England, Kevin met Lord Felton and through him earned the substantial commission he needed to fund his dream.

The crowded Picadilly sidewalk was filled with people from all stations of class intent on shopping, serving their masters, or selling their goods. Footmen carried packages; maids walked discreetly behind their employers' daughters to protect their reputations; grooms and street urchins alike, watched over the aristocrats' horses and conveyances. Peddlers called out their wares and ragtag boys anxiously waited for a gentleman or lady to offer them a coin to sweep the dung away from where they wanted to cross the street.

Kevin took little notice of the morass of people or the coaches and curricles clogging the street and impeding his steps. He was excited to purchase his own mount. He had declined the continued use of the horse the earl leant him. He did not want to deal with stabling two horses when he returned from Tattersall's. Only time would tell if he had any horse to stable. He suffered the crush of people and maneuvered briskly through them to get to the renowned horse auction house located at Hyde Park's southwestern border.

He left Picadilly and crossed the street to enter Hyde Park and let his stride lengthen now he was through the crush of people. He began to slap his riding crop with each step and swing of his arm against his long greatcoat. He was too preoccupied to get to Tattersall's to marvel at the thick verdant lawn or hear the plane's rustling tree leaves. Nor did he hear the wary jaybird, perched and hidden on a branch screech at him or the nesting group of small stout-chested sparrows chirp anxiously as he passed.

Any other time, Kevin would acknowledge the park's beauty and breathe in the sweet smell of dewy grass. He would stop to look at the mother duck gliding across the glistening Serpentine with her ducklings following in her wake and grin at the grey herons standing near the water's edge as if on stilts. The scene of children romping about the lawn before setting their toy boats onto the water under their nanny's care would amuse him, if he was not thinking how the founder of Tattersall's with a bit of savvy and a thoroughbred horse made his fortune.

Richard Tattersall was described as tall and good looking, owning an amiable personality that drew people into his company. He was an adventurous sort and found he could improve his situation in the elevated male racing community where one's horse knowledge took precedence over one's class of station. He mingled and cultivated relationships with princes, dukes, and lords, of which the Earl of Grosvenor was one. In 1766, Richard asked the earl to lease him the five fields on the corner of Hyde Park where a turnpike separated the park from the open country to build his auction house. Thirteen years later, Richard purchased *High Flyer*, the thoroughbred which ultimately made him a wealthy man from Lord Bolingbroke.

Kevin dreamt of owning his own horse breeding farm and racing his own horses. He was a capable man and had no doubt he could find success, much like Tattersall, who with one great horse made his fortune. If he was lucky, Kevin would find his prized horse today.

The remnants of a quarrel brought him to an abrupt stop right when he entered the Tattersall's graveled courtyard. A lady's raised voice instinctively diverted his attention from the stables where he was bound to the outraged woman. He thought he might have to come to her rescue, until he recognized the man at the end of the lady's frustration was no other than Richard Tattersall: proprietor, grandson and namesake of the man once called "Honest Tatt." Whatever the quarrel, he knew the lady was in no danger. Richard, like his father and grandfather before him, was an honest man.

However, the lady was clearly outraged. She stood as stiff as a board with her arms straight and tight by her sides; both of her fists were clenched. Her deportment marked a tempest, but her rising blush over her unseemly outburst contrastingly made her appear more sweet than thunderous. She looked the height of fashion wearing a small hat adorned with a curved ostrich feather perched at an angle on her head of rich brown hair. She was quite attractive in her fitted cobalt blue riding habit made of fine Merino wool. The short-waist jacket accentuated her figure boasting of curves that made Kevin grin in appreciation. He quite enjoyed his inspection of her until his eyes returned to her beautiful oval face and found her light brown eyes smiting him. She deliberately snubbed her perfectly straight button nose up at him and turned her features away from his scrutiny. He wanted to laugh at her affront. *Did the lady think her little snit would offend him?* Hardly, his skin was too thick and his self-assurance too strong to be affected. If anything, he was amused and tempted to seek an introduction with the beautiful termagant should she still be around when he finished his business.

He waited until she reengaged her discourse with Tattersall before making his way to the stables. The image of Richard's head shaking from side to side, obviously denying his vixen her request had him releasing the chuckle he could no longer control. He entered the stables smiling and then stopped to take in the scene of horses and buyers. There seemed to be more grooms than gentlemen taking inventory of the stock if one was judged by the clothes they wore. Coarse wool jackets and caps of men jotting down their observation onto a tablet outnumbered the fine wool tailcoats and tall hats of their betters. Kevin guessed the common men were head grooms since stable lads usually could not read or write. Most likely, the grooms were ordered to assess the horses and report back to their lords who were still abed after a late night of carousing. The grooms' findings would determine whether their masters attended tomorrow's auction.

Kevin advanced forward and took his time to inspect the horse listed in each stall, examining the caliber of every mare and stallion. He thought his quest was lost for finding a prime breeder until he came upon Maximilian. He recognized a thoroughbred, a horse built for speed when he saw one. He knew he found his prize unless the stallion was injured. He could barely contain his excitement. The black bay stallion clearly had Arabian features. He stood seventeen hands tall. His build was sleek with very muscular hindquarters, sloping shoulders, and a deep barrel of a chest. He almost danced a jig in his excitement until he realized how quickly the bidding would soar once Maximilian was placed on auction. There was no way he could compete with the wealthy lords whose money seemed bottomless.

Reconciled to disappointment he was about to take his leave when a disturbance caught his attention. A man clumsily entered the stables almost as if he had been pushed from behind. He was quite possibly pushed for two large men following close behind him looked more like ruffians intent on trouble than members of polite society. Kevin could tell the aggravated man was a gentleman or at least looked like one because his suit bore the mark of London's renowned tailor, Weston. Kevin had no interest in interfering in another man's affairs, but he hesitated to leave another man outnumbered. He waited to see what would come. He unconsciously tapped his thigh with his riding crop and watched. His scrutiny brought the gentleman's attention to him and to his surprise the man approached him with a smile.

"He was my father's favorite. What do you think of him?"

Kevin was surprised by the gentlemen's relaxed demeanor and remark. He had to ensure he heard the man correctly and asked, "Do you mean Maximilian?"

"Yes. He has fine blood lines. You interested?"

"I expect he will draw a fine crowd and good bids tomorrow."

"Indeed, but you see I am having a bit of a cash flow problem at the minute and would be happy to part with him if you have the funds to give me today."

Kevin was sure the man was crazy or making a jest, but he was not about to walk away from what might be one of life's lucky gifts. He knew what the horse was worth, but had no wish to start the bidding so high. In jest, he offered, "I'll give you two hundred pounds."

"Make it five hundred and the horse is yours."

Simply out of habit, Kevin countered, "four hundred."

The man bit his bottom lip and replied, "I can take nothing less than four hundred twenty-five. The horse is yours if you can give me the funds now."

Kevin almost gasped before reason set in. He realized this could be a ploy to finagle funds from him and then be accused of horse thievery without any respectable gentleman to bear witness to the sale. He said, "I'll pay you once I see the horse's papers and you contrive a letter of sale, witnessed and dated by Richard Tattersall himself."

"Done," replied the Earl of Sterling.

"Done," echoed Kevin, doing his best not to grin like a fool.

Alicia walked away and mounted her horse thoroughly frustrated and angry. She was ready to ride to

The Albany to confront Charles until common sense prevailed. Such action would draw scandal and might even ruin her reputation. Besides, she did not even know if Charles was at his bachelor apartment. Still bristling with anger, she headed home to wait for him to call upon her.

She was not sure where to direct her fury: at Mr. Tattersall or her cousin Charles. In fairness, she admitted Mr. Tattersall had been more than courteous to her. He agreed the moment her absent cousin arrived to present Lord Sterling with her offer to buy Maximilian. Until then, Tattersall gently reminded her how his hands were tied for the law forbid him to enter into a contract with a lady. With remarkable forbearance, she managed to hold onto her rising temper when Tattersall asked again why her father was not to conduct the business for her.

"Why, indeed!" she grumbled as she huffed away knowing she could not keep the man from his business any longer. She could hardly answer how all of a sudden her father thought horse breeding was no activity for a well-bred lady, so he was unlikely to purchase a horse for her for that purpose. After seven years of learning and helping her father with his horse breeding, he decided it was time for her to marry.

He said he wanted to see her days filled with ladylike interests; such as, embroidery, fashion, dancing, and serving tea. She practically rolled her eyes when he mentioned that activity. *Who did he think has poured his tea for the past seven years? Or stands as hostess to all the guests who visit their home?*

Perhaps, if her mother lived she might feel differently about the social scene and behave as a demure young debutante should. She had been entering womanhood when her mother fell ill to influenza and passed away. After the funeral, she sought out her father for support and comfort, but found him sharing his grief with his brother who kept to his side. Her disappointment in not being able to grieve with him was evident to her Aunt Alexandra, whom quickly rectified the situation by taking husband in hand and departing for home.

However, no sooner did they leave than Alicia found her home invaded with neighbors offering their condolences. Once again, the constant flow of visitors diverted her father's attention and she despaired of ever being alone with him. She felt invisible to the matrons who sat in her parlour, pouring tea from her mother's fine floral china, speaking among themselves as if she wasn't there. She only needed to hear one lady talk about how her father needed someone to manage his household and more importantly, produce an heir with which to pass his title to become alarmed her father might remarry. Alicia had no desire to be under the thumb of a stepmother willing to barter the birth of a son for a marriage of convenience; especially one who could so easily dismiss her presence. She feared the ambitious lady would send her away. The lady could convince her grieving father she needed a finishing school to round out her education. Alicia just lost her mother. She had no desire to lose her father as well and decided the risk was too great not to do something.

She informed the staff they were no longer "at home" to visitors and set to learning what she needed to know to become mistress of her father's household. She met with the housekeeper and quickly learned her worries of her father remarrying were not unfounded. Her wise housekeeper told her she should seek her aunt's support to take on the role of mistress because even at the age of five and ten years old, her father still saw her as a child. The housekeeper said her aunt was the only lady, aside from her departed mama, with any influence over him.

Alexandra returned immediately in answer to Alicia's call for help. Between Alexandra's guidance and the staff's support, Alicia soon became competent to manage her father's household. She no longer worried her father would remarry for convenience sake.

Her concerns now centered on her own need to marry. She could not fault her father's motivation in ordering her to enter the marriage mart. What parent does not want to see his child settled and secure? However, the whole idea of a lady becoming her husband's property made her balk at the idea of marriage. She was too independent to be submissive to a husband's wishes. Her father nurtured her to think for herself. He applauded her ideas when they were sound and encouraged her to ask questions when they needed more consideration. She never silenced her voice or opinions. However, polite society did not favor a lady who felt equal to any man and

Alicia did not think any man could accept her belief she was.

She had spent almost all her time shadowing her father after her mother died. Almost immediately he noted her keen horse sense, her innate ability to discern what made a horse skittish and what calmed the beast. He had encouraged her to cultivate her gift and to learn his business. She loved the challenge of working with him for he shared his knowledge of bloodlines and breeding with her. Over time, she became as passionate as him to make Deneham's Horse Breeding Farm the finest in England, even if she could never inherit it.

The law of primogeniture made it impossible for her to inherit the property belonging to her father's baronship. The land was entailed and would eventually pass along with her father's title to her cousin Charles. Then she, instead of Charles, would be at the receiving end of the Deneham benevolence. Alicia did not worry her cousin would cast her off from the only home she had ever known. She and Charles were the best of friends, but one day he would marry and she would be supplanted in her role of manor mistress. She had no wish to be a burden or worse, useless with no duty to perform. She had dreams and she was determined if she could not inherit her father's horse breeding farm, then she would build her own, which is why she wanted to purchase Maximilian.

Alicia kept a constant eye on horse auctions, looking for those thoroughbreds whose lineage could be traced, but were often overlooked when sold. Normally, her efforts were for her father's benefit, but this time she searched for a thoroughbred to breed with her own mare. She wanted to breed a racehorse as good in their day as the coupling of *Eclipse* and *High Flyer*, but that was before she came home from Tattersall's and heard her father's alarming news.

She still had trouble understanding how her father's approaching financial ruin descended upon them. She helped keep her father's books and never saw the possibility for the disaster they now found themselves. A decade ago, her father reluctantly took a substantial loan from his good friend and neighbor Squire Bigsby to grow his business. They settled on a monthly interest payment and a six month period to repay the principle whenever Bigsby decided he needed his money returned. Deneham was confident he could easily get a bank loan and Bigsby's assurance he would extend the repayment period if needed made the loan from his friend easy to accept. The arrangement proved beneficial to both. Deneham built a bigger stable, fences, and grew his stock, while Bigsby gloated among his peers how Deneham paid better than the funds.

The root of their disaster came in the form of the squire's son William. The naive boy was gulled by a card sharp into betting more than he owned and rather than ask his father for the money and suffer embarrassment, he secured a loan from a moneylender. Each day the loan passed unpaid, the interest grew exponentially. William, in an attempt to raise the cash, fell deeper into debt with more losses at the gaming table. He suffered terribly at the hands of the moneylender's brutes when the grace period to repay the loan passed. He was deposited, bloodied, bruised, and broken on his father's doorsteps with the moneylender's message: "Choose." William could barely move his jaw or speak the words to explain his father's choice was between his life and the money owed.

Squire Bigsby did not have the money readily available and came to London to turn his assets into cash. He called on Deneham and took the baron by surprise when he called in his loan. Deneham quickly explained his tenuous situation once he realized his friend was in earnest. His assets were in the breeding and selling of horses which required subtlety and negotiations to garner the highest price. He reminded his friend how he used his annual hunt to show off his best stock. Any sign he needed to sell his horses for ready cash would plummet his sale prices. Gently, he reminded his friend of their six month agreement. Bigsby left shaking his head in sorrow.

Two hours later, Deneham received a note from his friend. Only one word was inscribed, "Sorry." Alarmed, he raced from his townhome without a word of leave for his daughter and rushed to locate Bigsby. Deneham searched the hotel his friend favored when he visited town only to discover the squire was no longer a guest.

Deneham returned to his townhome, gut-wrenched and worried, *what has Bigsby done?* The answer arrived through the post. Mr. Jones wrote requesting a meeting with Lord Deneham to discuss the repayment of his IOUs. The IOUs bearing his signature for the money once leant to him by his friend Squire Bigsby. Deneham knew before he even met with Mr. Jones the man would not honor his six month agreement and worried how he would raise the substantial funds to settle his debt.

Chapter Three

Deneham Manor, the Midlands
November

Alicia stood at her window overlooking the gravel drive and the number of carriages and gentlemen riders approaching her home. Since early morning she came to the window whenever she heard the sounds associated with arriving guests. Carriage wheels and horse's hooves crunched the gravel, leather ribbons slapped against horse flesh, horses neighed and coachmen called out their arrival. The first wave of carriages brought the servants, who once situated, worked diligently to organize and ready the room assigned to their masters. Valets hurried to unpack and press clothes, arrange toiletries, and order boiling water for the warm baths their masters expected when they arrived.

Alicia escaped the swirl of male activity by keeping to her room. She kept busy throughout the day from writing letters at her pedestal writing table to spying on the arrival of her father's guests.

The mahogany desk where she wrote once belonged to her mother as did several other pieces she cherished. There were two Queen Anne gilded wing chairs with cabriole legs ending in claw and ball feet situated near her fireplace with a small pedestal table of the same design placed between them. A mahogany tester bed with acanthus leaves carved into its cornice was on the opposite side of the room with a small pedestal table that matched the one by her wing chairs. Displayed on top of her mahogany chest of drawers with brass fixtures were two miniatures, one of her father and one of her mother commissioned shortly after they married. Also on display were her mother's sterling silver brush, comb, hand mirror, and an assortment of wood horses handsomely carved and sanded by Charles. A full length cheval mirror, an embroidered desk chair, and several brass sconces furnished the rest of her room.

Everything from her Damask bedding and drapery to her silk floral-patterned wall coverings were a shade of pink, popularly known among the *ton* as Peach Blossom. Two framed shire landscapes full of blue and green hues and an Aubusson floral carpet boasting of pink and green shades provided subtle and pleasing accents for her beloved room.

Alicia watched from her window as the Earl of Belcrave and his son descended from his carriage to be greeted by her father, aunt and uncle, and then herded into the manor. The scene was familiar to Alicia as her father hosted a fox hunt every year to showcase his stock of hunters. She and Charles were both excellent riders and rode those horses in the hunt her father wanted to show and sell. They knew how to bring their mounts to top speed and coax them to jump any barrier they came across. Alicia enjoyed the hunt for it was the one place she could best a man without censure. She was too admired for her horsemanship skills for any gentlemen to call her a hoyden; especially when they discovered she was far more interested in horses than in courting. She was no shy miss, but an intelligent and beautiful lady who could enliven any conversation with her vast knowledge and amusing wit. Men enjoyed her company too much to risk her displeasure by criticizing those daredevil skills to which she adeptly displayed during the fox hunt and to which they each aspired.

She was equal if not better than the average man, outriding and outjumping her father's guests. She only came in second to her cousin Charles. Of course, she and Charles knew the land better than anyone else. They grew up in the shires and ever since Parliament passed the 1770 Enclosure Acts, allowing common land to be divided into tracts and sold, landowners have been converting the tracts into pastures which made excellent ground for the seasonal fox hunt. The hedgerows and fences dividing the tracts of land were the perfect challenge for the daredevil sportsman and the plush grass was the best surface for a group of horses to gallop and reach top speeds.

Alicia and Charles were experienced fox hunters and knew better than to let the fox lead them on a merry chase. They often crossed over the land to where the fox generally headed, rather than follow the hounds and field of riders. More often than not, they intercepted their prey before the other hunters caught up to them.

The knock on Alicia's door drew her attention away from the gravel drive and her meandering thoughts. She turned her body towards her door and gave permission for her visitor to enter. Her cousin Charles tentatively entered as if he expected to come under attack. When no assault, either verbal or tangible flew at him, he strode forward and asked, "I am forgiven?"

Alicia pressed her lips together in regret before admitting, "It is not your fault our English Laws prohibit me from entering into a contract without benefit of a man, nor is it your fault Lord Sterling sold Maximilian before my offer was made. Undoubtedly, an offer that was too meager for him to accept. I was wrong to rant at you. Forgive me?"

"Always," Charles grinned.

"Did you ever learn the gentleman's name with whom you collided?"

"Yes," he replied. "And it is my ill luck the man resides at The Albany. I had a devil of a time keeping out of his sight; especially since he always seems to carry that riding crop with him. I have no wish to remind him he wanted to use it on me!"

"I doubt he would assault you at The Albany, Charles. Surely, you misunderstood his intent," reasoned Alicia.

"You did not see his face, Alicia. He was quite put out. Plus, I learned the man is American. Who knows what rules they follow? We Brits consider them uncivilized, do we not?"

"He must be quite alarming for you to judge him without knowing him. It is unlike you to be biased, Charles. I dare say he is a gentleman to have the cachet to live at the Albany. Who was the other gentleman you said was with him?"

"I did not notice once I took in the size of the man I accosted and the damn riding crop he slapped at his thigh. Once I apologized, I kept my head down not to offend him anymore than I did. Word is the Earl of Felton subleased Rodchester's apartment for him. His name is Mr. Donahue."

"Donahue?" gasped Alicia, bringing her hand to her chest as if to settle her heart. "Oh, Charles," she explained with a chuckle, "Unless I am mistaken, you will no longer be able to avoid coming face to face with this American. I believe he is to be Papa's guest. Lord Felton is bringing an American friend with him."

"It is not funny, Alicia," chastised Charles. "I ruined my favorite purple tailcoat with that fall. Besides, I am not sure Mr. Donahue will not use his crop on me once he sees me!"

"Nonsense," argued Alicia. Her cheerful demeanor turned harsh at the idea of any man hurting her beloved cousin. She fiercely added, "Should he even look at you with ill favor I shall take my own riding crop to his backside!"

Charles laughed and said, "I bet you would."

Calmed after expelling her diatribe, Alicia grinned and said, "You should probably thank the man for relieving you of that monstrous coat. I do not know why you subscribe to dressing like a coxcomb."

"You just have no sense of style, Alicia," he retorted. "If you visited Town more often, you would know my attire is *all the crack*."

"Well, I have no wish to reside in Town so I will take your word for it, but really Charles, I do think a more sober dress is more appealing to a lady."

Charles had no wish to engage in an argument over his fashion choices and changed the subject. He asked, "Why are you not greeting your guests?"

"Technically, they are my papa's guests. Aunt Alexandra stands in my stead. Have you forgotten my papa does not like me to make my appearance until the next day? He does not like presenting the gentlemen to me, even though I know most of them, until they had a chance to refresh from their journey."

"Then, do you wish to ride with me? I have no wish to mingle with those who think little of me."

"You make assumptions, Charles. You are superior in character and in horsemanship to any man; especially those dandies you try to impress with your attire. You should not worry yourself with what others think. Trust me, papa's peers will come to call you "friend" once they get to know you and discover how well you ride. You can outrace anyone and though most of the men my father invited are indeed *high in the instep*, they will easily seek your company when they witness you in the saddle."

Charles shrugged his shoulders.

Rising, Alicia put a shoulder around her younger cousin and said, "Go get our horses saddled and I will join you as soon as I change into my riding habit. A ride will do me good. I have no desire to remain in seclusion until tomorrow. Do you prefer to dine in my room with me this evening or join papa and his guests?"

Charles' mouth spread wide in a boyish grin. Alicia laughed and pushed him on his way, saying, "Grab some bread, cheese, and a couple of apples from Cook. We will break our fast when we reach the river."

"Thank you for garnering this invitation to Deneham's hunt for me, Felton," said Kevin. "I really appreciate the introduction."

"You need not thank me. You have been good company for what could have been a tedious journey."

"Is there anything I should know or be wary of in my manner? I am an American, after all."

"Do not harp on your nationality unless you wish to defend it," laughed Felton. "With your love of horse flesh, you need have no concerns of fitting in. Besides, Deneham's is the tamest of all the hunts. With his sister-in-law and daughter in residence, the gentlemen tend to watch their drinking and their speech, though Deneham does give his guests the first evening to unwind before asking them to behave. You will find the evening unfiltered in conversation and manner."

"Then, his sister-in-law and daughter will not join the festivities this evening?"

"Deneham always has his brother Sir Marcus Deneham and his wife Lady Alexandra in residence to protect his daughter's reputation. Society would besmirch the Honorable Alicia Deneham if she was the only lady present, so Lady Alexandria will play host and greet us when we arrive, but will retire after dinner. The Honorable Alicia will not be introduced until tomorrow for the hunt. She will ride with us. Both she and her cousin Charles are exceptional riders."

"Indeed?"

"Indeed!" bellowed Felton with a laugh as his eyes caught the indomitable lady and her cousin rush a hedgerow to cross it to the other side.

"Who was that?" asked a wide-eyed Donahue.

Felton grinned at his friend.

Surprised, Donahue asked, "That is the Honorable Alicia and Charles? The same coxcomb who ran into my backside?"

"Yes, and close your mouth Donahue, lest someone see you and think you witless."

"Well, I daresay, the lad presents a different impression on a horse. He rides like the wind. Do you know I have not seen hide or hair of him at the Albany since our unfortunate meeting?"

Alicia bit down on her green apple and savored the tart juicy chunk while she breathed in the fresh country air and admired the panoramic view of the shire's landscape. Fluffy white cumulus clouds drifted across an expansive cerulean blue sky and a verdant grassy flatland was broken only by a hedge, stream, or wood. The hedgerows quartered the land into sections and these natural fences kept the fattening cattle, when present, in their pastures.

The hard riders loved the challenge of jumping these barriers and were what enticed them to the hunt. Low quickset hedges provided the easiest jump for the field of riders to cross having short rails on each of its sides. Riders were challenged with hedges supported by a rail on one side and a ditch on the other, but the most difficult hedge to conquer was the tall untrimmed and bulky bullfinch. The tall hedge was considered the bane of the hunt. Riders were forced to either push through their coarse thickness or lose time to find another way around to follow the fox running wherever it could to evade the hounds fast on its tail. Even seasoned riders were led on a merry chase.

Alicia loved to compete with Charles for the lead, but thoroughly disliked the grisly end and always left the field before the hounds captured the fox.

"What will you do now Alicia?" asked Charles from where he sat on the grass, pulling the green blades without thought from the earth while he spoke.

Alicia looked down at her cousin. She was woolgathering and realized Charles probably asked his question after noticing.

"You mean my plans, Charles?"

"Yes, your plans now Maximilian is no longer an option."

"Who says he is no longer an option?"

"I did. I told you he was sold."

"Yes, sold, not gelded."

Charles said nothing, just shook his head at his cousin whose response would have shocked all of polite society had she uttered it in their presence.

Alicia blushed at the silent rebuke and retorted, "It is a perfectly clinical term. I see no reason for you to look at me as if I did something wrong."

"Do not be obtuse, Alicia. You know very well ladies do not mention such things."

"But," she replied. "Breeders do."

Charles shook his head again and waited for Alicia to answer his question.

"I don't know what I will do, Charles. I was all set to prove I could manage quite nicely, earn my own income and take care of myself, but that was before I knew what might be our financial ruin. I cannot waste the funds I have on a horse I cannot stable or feed. My dream of independence is undone. Papa wishes to see me settled and secure. I can't help wonder if I do as he wishes, then perhaps my husband could pay this debt of his that keeps increasing. I should think the growing interest illegal, but papa will not fight it in the courts. I think he believes it will bring us social ruin. I offered him my dowry but he will not touch it! He says it is secured in a trust for this very reason. Nobody can get their hands on it until I marry or turn five and twenty years."

Charles kept his head down and continued to pick the blades of grass and drop them down onto the pile he was forming. Alicia thought how this affected him and asked, "Are you worried you shall inherit nothing but debt, Charles? Papa and uncle have many years to live, plus Papa will come about. He is too smart to let this villain be our downfall."

Charles' head bobbed up; his eyes wide in surprise. "Alicia, how can you think me so shallow? If I worry, it is for you and uncle, not for me."

"I am sorry, Charles." She opened her mouth to say more and then stopped.

Charles pushed her to speak, "What is it?"

"How in the world am I ever to become a demure debutante? Most gentlemen know me to speak frankly. They will not be fooled by me holding my tongue or fluttering my eyelashes."

"You do not have to fool them, Alicia. Not all men desire a timorous miss. You have your admirers. All you need to do is offer some encouragement."

"Now who is being obtuse, Charles. Do you really think I would encourage any gentleman who has admired my fine eyes?"

Charles laughed. "No, I expect not, but Alicia, if your Aunt Alexandra can find a man with her *joie de vivre* and loud laugh, surely you can find a man who appreciates your animal husbandry."

"We shall see," grinned Alicia as she recalled the tale her aunt loved to tell. Aunt Alexandra was quite fond of describing her wretched debutante season and how in spite of her common face, figure, and unladylike laugh, she married the most handsome man she had ever met, thereby creating a tremendous amount of speculation about their union. Even today, with her uncle still greatly admired for his good looks and charm, the gossipmongers continue to wonder why he married his wife.

"Now come on," rallied Alicia. "We have rested enough. Let's give our mounts their heads before we go home."

Chapter Four

Alicia's eyes were bright with laughter when she spurred Cleo past Charles to enter the stable first. She wasted no time to pull up in front of him and tease him with a wide grin. The brisk ride back to the manor improved her spirit and she chuckled at Charles with wind-blushed cheeks.

The long brick stable could hold up to forty horses and was kept clean by a dozen stable lads. The ostlers daily swept and shoveled each stall while the horses roamed and grazed in two separate pasture fields. One field was allocated for stallions, the other for mares. There was little to offend the senses since the horses were brushed and washed regularly.

The familiar scent of sweet hay and oiled leather reminded Alicia of all the wonderful times she spent by her father's side, learning about horses. The memory broadened her smile until she heard a heated argument where one of the people involved was her father. She immediately turned and sought him out. She was surprised to see him quarreling with a man she did not know. Usually, her father kept her apprised of all his guests; especially those visiting for the first time. She knew Lord Felton was bringing the American and the hefty and robust Earl of Belcrave was bringing his youngest son Lord Harry. However, she did not know the man with whom her father attempted to soothe, nor did the stranger distinguish himself as a gentleman or anyone hospitable. He was loud and overbearing, almost vulgar in his manner as he waved his hand and pointed vehemently at her father's chest. The scene angered her. Her father looked as if he was under attack and she impulsively heeled her mare forward to come to his aid. Charles mirrored her actions and immediately brought his horse to her side.

Their actions caught the baron's attention and he quickly delivered them a stern expression which halted their approach. Alicia and Charles kept their horses in place, unsure what to do, until the baron's head groom came to assist Alicia to dismount. The groom deftly lifted Alicia from her sidesaddle. Charles dismounted in tandem and gave his reins over to the ostler who ran up to retrieve them.

Alicia waited for her father to acknowledge her and when he did not, Charles tugged on her arm for them to leave. She started to oblige her cousin and fall in step with him until she heard the stranger exclaim how much he liked the pretty filly. Outraged to hear her exquisite mare denigrated, she opened her mouth to chastise the man but was stopped when her father remarked, "She's not for sale." She saw the man sneer at her father and reply," Ah, Deneham, you have much to learn. Everything is for sale for the right price or in your case to repay a substantial debt. We shall barter later."

Too stunned to speak, Alicia closed her mouth and looked at the man who she now knew was the villain behind their troubles. He was younger than her father but not by much. Her father still had two years before he turned fifty. This man had gray filtering through his overgrown and oily black hair. He might have been considered handsome before a rough life broke his nose and prematurely aged him. He did not stand straight, nor did he hold his head high. He was of average build and to a passerby might be taken as a tradesman in his coarse wool attire hanging loosely on his body.

However, he seemed to grow in stature and in strength as Alicia stared at him. Her blatant inspection did not go unnoticed by the moneylender. He turned his body to glare at her and returned her assessment in kind. Alicia trembled when his black and soulless eyes roamed slowly all over her body and scrutinized every ounce of her flesh from head to toe. It was as if he could see through her layers of clothing when he licked his bottom lip with his tongue like a predator. A leer grew from his frightful stare.

Alicia had never been treated so vulgarly and knew the nausea overwhelming her was rooted in fear. A frigid chill coursed through her veins and she crossed her arms over her chest as a way to ward off the evil she faced. Her survival instincts moved her to run out of the stables as fast as she could and find sanctuary. She ran harder when she heard the villain chuckle and feared he might give chase. She never looked back, so she did not know Charles followed her until she slammed the door of her room and he called out in pain. Aghast, at seeing him holding his hand, she profusely apologized and tried to look at his injury. Charles waved off her concern, entered her room and shut the door behind him.

Distraught, Alicia walked over to the two gilded embroidered upholstered chairs by the fireplace, sat down in one and tried to catch her breath. She beckoned Charles with her hands to take the other chair and then asked between gasps, "Is it him, Charles? Is it the moneylender?"

"I expect," he replied sadly. "No doubt, your father will come to you and explain. He did not look happy to see you upset or under the man's scrutiny."

With her fear still resonating inside her, Alicia practically whispered, "Did you see the wickedness in his eyes, Charles? He scared me out of my wits. No man has ever looked at me like that." Then, recalling her earlier promise to Charles, her eyes widened and her voice rose in volume, "I feel utterly foolish remembering how easy I thought to thrash the American if he hurt you, but the idea of retaliation never occurred to me. Perhaps, because I expect a gentleman's code of conduct, regardless of how unmannerly I might be. I would not want to find myself alone with Jones. I do not think he is a gentleman."

Charles' jaw dropped at the absurdity of a moneylender being a gentleman, but restrained from correcting her other than saying, "No, not a gentleman."

"Why is he here?"

Charles looked despairingly at Alicia, and then answered, "He cannot take the property for it is entailed, but everything else is up for grabs. Be prepared, Alicia. If he chooses, everything dear to you will be gone."

Alicia's eyes widened in astonishment and asked for clarification, "You speak of our livestock, Charles?"

"Yes! Everything in the stables and in the house: furniture, paintings, silverware, china, jewelry. He could even take your clothing if the scoundrel wished. Every item on your property has been inventoried."

Alicia's eyes darted around her beloved room until her search landed on her keepsakes displayed on her bureau. She stood and shouted, "How?! How is this possible? Are you telling me the law permits it?"

"Yes. But do not despair. He might not be as cold-hearted as we make him. Wait to see what your father says."

"I do not feel well, Charles. Do you mind taking your supper in your own room?"

"Not at all, Alicia, get some rest and I will see you tomorrow for the hunt."

"Oh, I totally forgot about the hunt. I don't know if I will feel up to riding."

"You must not falter, Alicia. I expect your father is depending on us to show his horses well to get some high bids. He needs us, so rest well and be ready to ride."

Alicia's fearful departure gave Jones the idea to suggest, "I will take your daughter to settle your debt, Deneham."

Enraged, Deneham grabbed Jones' collar and seethed, "You are not fit to say her name, much less marry her. Treat her like a doxy again and I will have your head."

Jones growled, "Who said I wanted to marry her?" Then, with surprising strength, he turned out of Deneham's grip and twisted Deneham's arm behind him in a brutal hold. He scoffed, "I have been fighting since I was a waif on the docks. Do not underestimate my strength or my wits."

Jones released Deneham and pushed him towards the stable doors. "Go on. Show me your assets, unless you wish me to continue to carry your debt with interest."

Deneham sighed. He let his pride keep him from asking his brother and sister-in-law for the money when it was within their means to pay it off for him. Now, because of the daily interest expounded on the principal, even with their help he would still lose everything of value he owned.

With deep regret, he groaned, "Come, I inventoried all my worldly goods. Your solicitor and mine agreed on its value."

Jones rubbed his hands together in excitement.

Dressed in her fine white cotton night clothes, Alicia stood at her window again. This time instead of spying on her father's arriving guests, she looked out upon the green pastures rolling over the land for miles and found comfort knowing Deneham Manor and its lands were entailed, therefore safe from Jones' greedy hands. Her room faced the front of the house, as did seven other bay windows. Each lookout provided a view of the long gravel drive leading to the manor, bordered with trees so tall she always thought they were centurions guarding and directing visitors to her home. Her three-storied red brick home was built in the mid-1700s to replace the original manor and looked rustic with its tiled roof and stone dressings.

The soft knock at her door turned her attention from the manor's land to her unknown visitor. She bid enter and then ran into her father's welcoming arms the minute he entered her room. She had a multitude of questions weighing heavy upon her, but her father's troubled face stopped her from asking them.

"Come sit, Alicia," he said.

Alicia sat and waited for him to speak.

"As you know, Mr. Jones holds my IOUs in payment for Squire Bigsby's debt. He is a man who preys on the vulnerable and takes advantage of them. Unable to pay my IOUs when he first called, he carried my debt with an extraordinary daily interest. I agreed to the terms believing I could secure a bank loan within the day. Unfortunately, I harshly learned my reputation is not enough collateral for a bank."

Her father paused for breath. His haggard and downtrodden features spoke of the burden he carried. She pressed for him to continue and asked, "I know all this, Papa. Can you tell me why he is here?"

Deneham looked at his daughter in surprise. He thought the reason was obvious, but confirmed for her benefit, "He is here to collect, daughter. He prefers money to horseflesh, so will wait until after the hunt to see what we sell. He has his own auction house where he sells those household goods and personal items he takes in lieu of cash. It sorrows me I had to ask my brother for the remainder of the balance and the burden it placed on him and Alexandra. I cannot blame Marcus for chastising me for not coming to him sooner. I know my pride caused our ruin. I may have been able to keep some personal items for you had I approached Marcus sooner. Now, everything we have of value is gone. I am sorry, Alicia. You understand the staff will be let go for I have no income to pay their wages."

"What will we do? We can live off my dowry until we come about."

"You will go and live with your aunt and uncle. They agreed to sponsor you next Season and I hope you will engage seriously in finding someone worthy to marry."

"Is that why you pushed me to attend the Little Season? You want to marry me off?"

"I wish you would not put it as though I want to get rid of you. I want to see you happy. There is a difference, but yes, I asked you to attend the Little Season in hopes you would find someone to wed. Little good it did, since you would not attend any of the galas. I don't know why I even bothered."

"Did you lose any money on my not bringing a gentleman up to scratch?"

"How could you think such a thing? And more importantly, how did you hear of that disrespectable wager placed at White's? I took umbrage and gave Stantonhill's son a good tongue lashing for his idiocy."

Alicia smiled at her protective father and heard his voice crack when he said. "I would see you happily settled, Daughter. I will not be here forever and it would break my heart to leave you alone without protection."

"I have Charles, aunt and uncle. I would not be alone."

"It is not the same, Alicia. The death of your sweet mama and then the demands of our business have kept you distracted from what a young lady aspires. In time, you will hunger for hearth and home. I want you to open your heart now while you have options."

"You mean while I am young and can breed."

"Don't be coarse, daughter. Do you not want a child, someone to give to you the joy you have given me?"

Her father's sadness made her want to cry; especially at the idea of a world without him. He must have known how the reality of her tenuous world hit her for he opened up his arms to comfort her. She stayed against his chest until her tears finally stopped and then she looked up and asked him, "What will you do?"

Sighing, he said, "I am going to find me a wealthy wife."

Alicia began to weep all over again.

Chapter Five

A cold overcast November day greeted the hundred riders who gathered in front of Deneham's red brick manor. The brisk air chilled their exposed faces, but their excitement and the glasses of champagne they earnestly drank anticipating the fox hunt kept them from feeling any discomfort. They sat tall in their saddles, moving their horses next to whom they wished to keep company. Only a few were Deneham's personal guests, everyone else were either locals and their guests or the Corinthians staying at the nearby inns. They were part of the avid huntsman crowd, the regulars who traveled the fox hunt circuit each season and paid a subscription to ride with the pack. James Quimley, *Master of the Hunt*, brought his forty hounds and stood out in his scarlet "pink" riding jacket amid the men who wore tall black beaver hats, black riding jackets over white pristine shirts, buckskin breeches, and black riding boots.

Alicia stood out among the field of riders like a sapphire against black velvet wearing a navy blue riding habit that fit her to perfection. She and Charles each sat on one of the hunters her father wanted to show. Their horses stood side by side and though they were well-trained, they still high-stepped, anxious to be given their heads. Normally, Alicia would be just as excited as her mount to race, but this morning the presence of Mr. Jones took the joy out of the hunt. It must have shown for Charles leaned towards her from his seat to say, "Do not let him bother you, Alicia."

She turned to see of whom Charles spoke and saw Jones in the same coarse suit he had worn the day before raising his champagne glass in a toast to her. He stood on the manor's front portico steps, not part of the field but a spectator of them and of her. His particular attention made her uneasy and she quickly turned back around. She had no wish to further his acquaintance or give any suggestion she welcomed his particular attention. She thought she heard him chuckle but knew it was only a memory of yesterday's affront. He was too far away for her to hear him. She fretted knowing he watched her.

Her instincts told her he was a threat and she was smart enough not provoke an adder, much less, a villain. She quickly set her eyes on the field of men conversing with one another to take her mind away from her unease. The scene was jovial with men laughing and enjoying the champagne the servants offered while they waited for the hunt to begin. Most of the faces were familiar to her. Lord

Summers raised his tall hat in greeting when her eyes met his own. He had left his card a number of times when she was in London for the Little Season with an offer to take her up in his high perch phaeton for a drive in Hyde Park. Unfortunately for him, she was never "at home" to receive him. At the time, she did not want to encourage his attentions, but now looking at his warm and friendly face, she wondered if she missed an opportunity to know a good man. Beside him was Lord Castlebank talking to Lord Fieldmoore who were prompted by Summers' salutation to lift their hats in greeting to her. Alicia smiled and used her riding crop to salute and return their regard.

She continued her inspection of the field, recognizing the riders and their mounts and gasped in astonishment when she spied Maximilian. *"Oh,"* she softly exhaled looking at the man who sat him and thought, *"This is the gentleman who bought my horse."* His head was turned away speaking to Lord Felton, so it was not until he turned his head back around did she realize he was the same man who looked her over at Tattersall's. He must have also remembered the moment, though his reaction was different. She was cross, while he appeared delighted to see her.

She gaped at his audacity when he looked like he was about to steer Maximilian towards her as if to make her acquaintance. Of course, she would have met him at the morning meal except she waited until the hunt was about to begin, before joining the field of riders. She had sequestered herself and broken her fast in her room because she did not want to find herself in the company of Jones. Though she could not speak to the American without a proper introduction, nothing would have improved her spirits more than to deliver him a scathing comment for his underhandedness in acquiring Maximilian. He purchased the horse before auction. It was neither here nor there that she meant to do the same when it came to the disappointment she suffered from not acquiring the thoroughbred.

"Charles," she asked. "Is the man riding Maximilian, seated next to Lord Felton, the same man you ran into at The Albany?"

Charles searched the field of riders, found Lord Felton, Maximilian, and the man who sat him. His eyes widened before answering with annoyance, "Yes, and his damn riding crop. I am beginning to think he always keeps it with him."

Alicia saw Charles fidget on his horse and thought he was about to leave her to ride alone. She quickly offered up his earlier words of advice with a grin, "Do not let him bother you, Charles."

Charles shook his head in disbelief and then retorted with a smile, "Touché, Cousin. I guess if you can tolerate the scrutiny of that villain Jones, I can do no less than abide the presence of Mr. Donahue."

Kevin began to turn his horse to meet the termagant who had taken his fancy when Felton spoke, "We will start soon, Donahue. Most of Deneham's ostlers have reported back. They were out late last night stopping up the holes of the fox's known coverts with earth and other debris. These earth stoppers keep the fox from going underground when he returns from scavenging and forces him to lay underbrush where Quimley's hounds will flush him out this morning."

"Is that common, Felton?" asked Kevin.

"Quite. It is traditional; otherwise, the fox could wait us out. The sport has rules and ironically they protect the fox when it is not in season. Some farmers even plant gorse bush so they can make their dens."

"I thought they were considered vermin and the sport was designed to rid them of the land."

"Well, yes, originally, but the enclosures diminished the deer we hunted for sport, so now we hunt the fox. We also protect them during the off season to have them on hand when we need them."

"What should I know?"

"Just follow the field, unless you want a piece of the prize; such as, the fox's foot or his tail. Someone may even ask for its head. Be prepared. The hunt is fairly simple. The hounds flush him out from the brush and we chase him until he is cornered. The hounds are dispatched to do their grisly bit. I have no love for the kill, so I will probably return to the manor before then. You must see the hunt to its brutal end if you wish a piece of the fox. For most, the true sport of the hunt is the hard riding and jumping of barriers. I caution you to know your ability. Do not follow the path of the fox unless you are capable of maneuvering through it. More than one fool has broken his neck or worse injured his horse. There are gates and safer ways around the barriers the fox burrows through to evade the hounds which are less dangerous. There is no shame in using them."

"I will not jump any barrier I am unsure, Felton." replied Kevin. "Do not worry about me. I have been riding since before I could walk."

"That's good because I expect you will be hard-pressed to rein in your horse."

Kevin laughed. Maximilian was beginning to snort and prance. He was tired of holding still and was ready to run.

"Oh," added Felton. "Never outride the hounds. Quimley has been known to take them home at the affront."

"I will remember," chuckled Kevin.

The master of the hunt ordered his *whippers-in,* the men responsible for the pack, to give the signal to move them forward. The field of men and Alicia followed.

They trotted their horses to the first known covert and the hounds quickly flushed out a red-haired fox. A cacophony of barks and yipes exploded as the hounds pursued the animal in a frenzy. The wily fox raced away, changing direction multiple times to outrun his pursuers. He ran under a hedgerow and raced across some pastureland towards a creek near a copse where the foxes often found refuge in a hollowed tree trunk.

Kevin was about to give his horse free rein to run when he saw a smiling Alicia and Charles race past him.

Their horses' hooves kicked up divots as they thundered by him. They had trailed the group of riders, but now that the fox was flushed out of its hiding place and a "view halloa" shouted, the pair of them spurred their horses forward. Their diminishing figures sparked Kevin to chase after them. He liked the idea of capturing the lady more than the fox and gave his horse his heels. He was not the only one to follow their lead.

A hundred horses pursued the red-furred fox, pounding the dirt and earning whoops and hollers from those spectators who came to view the start of the hunt in their open carriages. They parked their conveyances on the outskirts of the pastures. Ladies sat erect holding parasols to protect them from the skin damaging elements of weather, while their escorts, some seated by their sides, others standing by their open vehicles, viewed the riders with their spy glasses, placing bets on who could outride whom.

Kevin closed the gap behind Alicia and Charles and watched them jump their first barrier. The low hedge offered little challenge. Kevin could tell they knew the land well and had ridden together often for they both took their leaps at the exact same moment. He, along with the field, followed their lead. Most flew over the hedge, but there were those with mounts who faltered from being pressed by other horses crowding them. Soon, the wide breadth of riders narrowed with the unskilled horsemen forming the tail.

The fox raced for its life and tried to outwit the hounds and riders on its heels by heading to another hedgerow to slip through; one of greater height and width. Again, the field took flight. Kevin saw Alicia and Charles jump without a hitch, never losing speed, for their mounts never faltered. They were showing their horses' skill to advantage and he was sure high bids would be made for their purchases. The chase continued, moving away from the spectators who could not follow in their conveyances, but even from their great distance, those watching in earnest exploded with cheers and hoopla at seeing the next barrier the riders faced.

Alicia and Charles took the four foot tall bullfinch in tandem without a pause in their approach. Alicia jumped first, clearing the massive hedge beautifully. She then reined in and steered her horse around to watch for Charles. The young man followed seconds behind her. They were about to continue their chase when the pounding hoofs of an advancing rider resonated. Most riders did not risk jumping a bullfinch. They either did not trust their ability to clear the enormous hedge, or their horses were not trained to jump it. The bullfinch, while solid at its base, grew like a bush with tall stems and leaves protruding out, making it look taller. Oftentimes, the rider is blind to what is on the other side of the tall bush, so he must rely on his skill and intrepidness to make the jump. Horses not used to feeling bushes or grass to their underbelly tend to be spooked, so rather than risk the jump, most horsemen make their way around to the pasture gate to proceed.

Kevin put his heels to Maximilian, leaning forward as his horse raised his front legs, stretched out his back, and skimmed the top of the tall hedge. He quickly shifted his weight back on his seat to ensure he did not fly over his horse's head and practically pulled up next to where Alicia and Charles sat on their horses watching.

Charles forgot his apprehension of Kevin and praised, "Well done, Donahue! Few take the leap."

Alicia was slow to offer her accolades and Kevin thought it was because he chuckled at her for having a gaping mouth.

Alicia begrudgingly offered her praise after she snapped her mouth shut, and then asked Kevin, "Have you jumped before?"

"Only our fences back home," he answered smugly, "nothing like your fox hunt."

The three of them could hear the riders swearing at one another as they tried to push through the bottleneck created when they all converged upon the gate. Kevin grinned at Alicia and Charles.

Quimley's horn, signaling the fox was sighted and away, reminded Alicia to rejoin the hunt. She turned her horse and pushed her heel into his side to start him and then pressed him into a gallop. The thundering hooves in her wake told her Charles and Kevin were close. Kevin's jump had surprised her and her gape bore evidence to her astonishment. She had been ready to follow Charles in his praise until Kevin laughed at her. The rogue knew he had impressed her, knew she found him utterly attractive as she sat on her horse all dreamy-eyed with her jaw dropped. Feelings she never experienced overcame her. Her heart beat faster. Her stomach turned over. Her face flushed. She actually had to stop herself from placing her hands on her heated cheeks to cool them down. *"Egad!"* she thought. *"I cannot possibly be attracted to an American!"*

Alicia lengthened her reins so her horse could race without restriction. She wanted to get away from the American and any thoughts of him. She did not push her hunter for long before bringing him to a canter. The sound of an approaching rider had her bringing her horse to a stop. She turned her head to greet Charles and was surprised to see Kevin and his toothy grin pass her with no Charles in sight. The man's arrogance to take the lead, ruffled her feathers and she used her riding stick to prod her horse into a full out gallop. Her horse did not disappoint her. She retook the lead and followed the pack. The field of riders followed. One by one, they crossed the stream and headed to the copse where the hounds led. A number of yips told Alicia the fox found some shelter. Most likely, the fox ran into a hollowed tree trunk whose prickly bark poked at the hounds' noses when they tried to follow.

Then, a disharmonious sound of vicious growls and barks caused Alicia to bring her horse to an abrupt stop. The field of riders passed her and she could hear them shouting in earnest with exclamations and a few unguarded expletives as they joined the pack and waited for Quimley to give his signal. She had no wish to witness the brutal end of the hunt and quickly turned her horse away from the gruesome scene. She pushed her horse into another gallop and raced until she came upon the river filling the creek she jumped earlier. Charles would know where to find her if he wished for it was her favorite spot to rest. The area's lawn was plush and a nearby oak tree offered protection from a radiating sun when present, but there was no need for cover. It was past one o'clock and the sky was still overcast and the air cool.

She slid from her sidesaddle and tied off her horse's reins on one of the fallen logs nearby. She was settling herself down on the carpeted grass when a rider appeared. Alicia was not surprised to see Kevin. The man seemed determined to outride her and most likely chased after her for sport. She did not think he followed her with evil intent for he did not leer at her like Jones, nor did she fear him as she did the moneylender. He was a friend of Lord Felton's and she knew the earl would never bring someone into her home he did not trust. "No," she thought. "I do not fear him." Upon further reflection, she summed up what she knew about him. He was a skilled rider. He sat his horse proficiently and managed Maximilian which was no easy skill. He held an assurance of himself which admittedly provoked her and he had an easy manner. He was bold, but did not seem arrogant like many of the gentlemen she knew. She did not think an

American would consider himself above someone else. *"Or would they?"* Even so, she did not think this man would condescend to anyone. He was disturbingly handsome, disturbing to her peace of mind and owned a rugged appeal she did not notice before his jump. No doubt, he had his choice of women who admired his thick blond hair, clear blue eyes, square jaw, and fine physique. *"Egad! When did I ever refer to a man's body as fine?"* She must have mused over him longer than she thought for she did not notice his descent from his horse or his movement until he plopped himself next to her on the grass.

"Great form; well-bred?"

"What?!" she thought. *"Is this his manner of courting a lady? Egad! Courting? From where did that idea emerge? No doubt, from my papa wanting me to wed."*

"Has the cat caught the lady's tongue? I know you are not mute. Tattersall, himself, can attest to it?"

"What nonsense are you speaking?" asked Alicia in a raised voice.

"Your horse, is he well-bred?"

"Oh," she answered, realizing how her wandering thoughts discombobulated her. He must think her witless. She quickly rallied in defense and said, "Yes. He is well-bred, trained to run, jump and heel; especially with a bunch of yapping hounds at his feet and wild grass poking his belly. I named him Thor because he is lightning fast."

Alicia could not believe the man smiled at her or how his smile made her go all girly. She opened her eyes wide to make sure she didn't flutter her lashes at him. She knew she was going to be in serious trouble unless she got her wits together and what better way to keep from acting like a debutante than to go on the attack.

"You stole my horse."

Kevin's light-hearted relaxed demeanor quickly hardened. His face scowled as he queried for further explanation. "Excuse me? I beg to inform you I have signed authenticated papers proving Maximilian is rightfully mine through purchase."

Alicia could tell she angered him. He looked ferocious and still, she did not fear him. "I did not mean literally," she explained.

"Then, what did you mean?" asked Kevin with raised brows.

"Well, I was there to purchase Maximilian the day we saw each other at Tattersall's, except Mr. Tattersall would not extend my offer because I am a woman. Charles was to meet me there, but was held up by you, as a matter of fact, and that is how you beat me to the sale."

"Well," retorted Kevin. "I do remember Charles and his unfortunate mishap, but the blame and resultant tardiness to Tattersall's rests squarely on his shoulders. I must say I changed my opinion of the lad after what I witnessed today. He is quite a proficient rider. As for my purchase of Maximilian, that was just luck, not thievery. Besides, by what I've seen you have a slew of horses and should not begrudge me one."

"They belong to my father, not me," said Alicia.

"Does it matter? I expect you have access to them."

"Not anymore."

"Why not?" asked Kevin.

Alicia was not about to reveal her family's troubles to this stranger, but she would share her dream. His answer would weigh heavily on whether she would like him or not. "I wanted Maximilian to breed with my own thoroughbred mare."

"You have a thoroughbred?"

Alicia saw the excitement in his eyes and wanted to laugh. She answered, "Yes and so do you or did you not know."

"Of course, I knew. What is your horse's name?"

"Cleopatra, Cleo for short."

"Named after the Egyptian ruler I suppose," grinned Kevin.

"Exactly," replied Alicia. "My Cleo, like the queen is strong and powerful, plus I liked how the Greek translation of Cleo means pride and glory. She is that to me."

"Do you still want to breed her?"

"You would allow it?"

"For a fee."

Alicia's sadness drew Kevin to ask, "What's wrong? Isn't it what you want?"

"Yes. It is just my situation has changed."

"How?"

Alicia ignored his question. She could not reveal her circumstances and dismissed the open query by rising.

She was glad when Kevin jumped to his feet to assist her, instead of pushing her to answer.

"It was not my intent to intrude into your personal affairs, Honorable Alicia," explained Kevin. "Maximilian is available whenever you wish to breed."

"I just remembered we have not been formally introduced and you, my man, are *beyond the pale* for addressing me, even more so for speaking to me."

"I beg your pardon and hope you will not hold it against me as I am still learning your English ways."

Alicia walked to her horse and said, "Be sure and rectify it this evening or I shall not be able to converse with you."

"I shall see it done," replied a grinning Kevin. He took in Alicia's diminished size next to her horse and asked, "How did you plan to mount your horse if I did not come along?"

She answered him by demonstration. Untying her horse's reins, she stepped up onto the log and then using the single stirrup, leveraged and pulled herself onto her sidesaddle. She almost laughed when she realized she circumvented his gentlemanly attempt to put her on her seat. She waited for him to mount his own horse before she took off. It did not take long for him to follow her in pursuit. She leaned into her horse and spurred Thor on to put some distance between them.

They raced across the pastureland and jumped a couple of hedges before they drew aside one another. He told her how much he enjoyed their ride and hoped they would be able to repeat the experience before he left. Alicia grinned and galloped forward forcing Kevin to once again pursue her.

They entered the manor's gravel drive and stopped short of the stable where a number of ostlers waited to be of service. Kevin dismounted and then helped Alicia down from her seat, leaving the horses to the ostlers' care. She blushed when Kevin placed his hands on her waist and quickly disengaged them from her person. She headed for the manor, choosing not to wait to walk with him. She was not sure if she liked how he made her feel. She had never felt so many emotions from the touch of another human being and the new feelings confused and excited her all at once. She was so distracted she did not notice Jones waiting for her at the top of the steps.

"My dear Alicia, I wish it was I who put that blush to your face."

Alicia balked and felt cornered like the fox they just chased. She quickly stepped back in fear and found herself pressed against a body. She was about to shriek when she heard Kevin's soft voice ask, "Has this man offended you?"

"No," Alicia whispered while trying to stop her trembles.

She could tell Kevin did not believe her, but would have accepted her answer had Jones not opened his mouth and snickered, "There is no affront here, sir. I saw how much she enjoyed being handled and simply relayed my regrets in not being the one to make her blush."

Jones barely finished his last word when Kevin's fist shot forward and nicked Jones' jaw. It would have knocked him clean, but the vile man agilely moved aside. Jones' swiftness astonished Alicia, as did the arm that pushed her aside. A crowd gathered and before an all out war could break out, Jones, like a chameleon, stepped back into the house and disappeared into its surroundings.

Chapter Six

Kevin followed Alicia into the house and then watched her ascend the staircase to ensure she made it safely to the landing. He did not think Jones would lay in wait for her, but he felt better seeing her beyond the villain's reach. He made his way to the baron's study. He did not know Jones' connection to Deneham, but felt duty-bound to inform the man of Jones' affront to his daughter. He did not even reach the study's door when Jones' scream exploded from it, "I want my money and I want it now!"

Kevin froze in his tracks when he heard the argument resounding from Deneham's study. He was embarrassed how he looked like an eavesdropper to any passerby.

"You needn't be so hostile, Jones," rebutted Deneham. "If you could just give me another week I will have the penalty fee. It was wrong of me to overlook the fine print in our agreement and wrong of you not mention it until the time lapsed."

"Bah!" Jones shouted.

Kevin began to retreat not wanting to be found listening to the baron's personal business, but was stayed by a hand. Mortified to be caught listening, he hesitantly turned to discover who had come upon him and then relaxed when he saw it was Felton. The earl placed his index finger to his lips to keep Kevin from speaking. It was clear Felton heard everything blaring from Deneham's study, but instead of taking his leave with Kevin, he walked into the highly intense room.

"Deneham," Felton greeted. "Good, I see you invited Jones as I asked."

"Who is this?" inquired Jones angrily.

Felton's statement astounded Deneham. The baron looked at Felton and then back to Jones and when no introduction was forthcoming the earl broke the silence.

"Well, man," demanded Felton in a raised and brusque voice to Jones. "I want the full accounting of the debt. Did Deneham not tell you?"

"What mischief is this?" sneered Jones.

"No mischief," replied Felton.

Jones squinted at the earl.

In response, Felton pushed him to answer. "What will it take to settle Deneham's debt, Jones, or perhaps, you forgave the loan?"

Jones laughed, "Hardly."

Deneham interjected, "I had the complete funds, Felton and was prepared to pay him the seventy-five thousand pounds due, but now he demands an additional twenty-five thousand penalty fee."

Felton raised his brows at the enormous thirty-three percent penalty, but before he could say anything, Deneham added, "I cannot deny it is in the contract I signed, though in such fine print I never even noticed it. You can see for yourself." Deneham directed Felton's attention to the contract on his desk and explained, "I needed the magnifying glass to confirm he told the truth."

Jones smirked again knowing the baron could not pay the full amount due and he could continue to extort more penalty fees from him.

Felton asked, "You have seventy-five thousand in cash, Deneham?"

Deneham dropped his head, embarrassed, but answered truthfully knowing the whole world would soon discover he was beggared. "A loan from my brother, horse stock, house goods, personal items, and some cash I have will meet the debt without penalty."

Felton responded with sympathy to the baron, "We will settle among ourselves later, Deneham." Then, he turned his attention to Jones and dismissed the man as the insignificant and vile creature he found him to be. "Mr. Jones, you may take your leave and return to London. There you may collect your hundred thousand pounds from my solicitor. He will receive you in two days' time." Felton handed Jones a business card.

Astounded, Jones' jaw dropped. He stood transfixed. He was not pleased he had lost control of the situation and in retribution was determined to take it out on somebody's hide. He would not be taken for a fool, nor would these gentlemen who thought themselves superior, ever take him lightly again.

"Well man, have you lost your wits?" disparaged Felton.

Jones shut his mouth and squinted at the lord who stood tall and arrogant. "No," he refuted, grabbing the card the earl held out to him. He was furious and before he stomped off, threatened dire consequence to the both of them if he didn't get his money.

Felton asked Deneham, "Whatever made you do business with him?"

"Not me," answered the baron, shaking his head from side to side. "Squire Bigsby gave him my IOUs as partial payment for his son's debt. The squire and I had a partnership of sorts. His money helped me buy my stock, build my fences and stables when I decided to go into breeding horses. It paid well for us both, but I kept reinvesting my profits instead of setting it aside for the loan's principal. I was not prepared when Jones came to collect, nor did I anticipate his villainy."

After a silent pause, Deneham added, "I don't know when I can repay you, Felton. You can take anything of value I have to settle a portion of the debt."

Alarmed, Felton clarified, "Deneham, I am sorry this trouble found you, but know I have no desire to add to your suffering. If you will allow, I will have my solicitor review your accounts and determine a payment plan that will not beggar you."

"You are too magnanimous, Felton."

"Not at all, I simply enjoy your hunts and your horses, too much, to have them denied to me."

Deneham smiled and extended his hand to Felton. The earl took it firmly in hand and said, "We must stand together against these villains who prey on our innocent."

Kevin never suspected danger until the burlap sack was placed over his head. His instinct was to try and remove the sack instead of lash out blindly at his attackers. He didn't remember anything other than waking up and finding himself in the bed he was given at Deneham's and the excruciating pains ripping through his head and body.

He felt as if a horse kicked and then ran over him. It was something he unfortunately knew about. As a young boy, he foolishly entered a corral to calm a wild stallion running aimlessly. He was ill-prepared when the horse ran straight at him, knocked him down and ran over him. Thankfully, only one hoof grazed his thigh and he survived the incident with only bruises to show for his naivety.

He tried to sit up to see what ailed him, wondering what in the world happened, but was quickly brought down by so much pain his head swoon and his vision blackened.

"Don't move!"

Kevin couldn't even open his eyes from the nausea overwhelming him. He concentrated on his breathing and then felt a damp compress placed on his forehead. He smelled lilac and blessed the person tending him. The floral fragrance and cool swab soothed his throbbing head. "Don't move," a woman said, and like a dog brought to heel, he kept still. Her voice broke into his thoughts, now crowded with silent commands to keep his body relaxed and his breathing easy. The nauseating pain eased on her authority and now that he wasn't overwhelmed by it, he tried to listen past his pounding head to her incessant soliloquy.

"Oh, I do hope you do not pass out again. Everyone is worried. Whatever happened to you? Mrs. Roberts, our cook wrapped up your ribs. You would not believe the colorful bruises sprouting up on you like a bed full of flowers. Lord Felton sent for his own doctor. I think he is afraid our country man will bleed you, but he is not the sort. Regardless, a rider on our fastest horse was sent to bring Felton's good doctor back with him. The day has been long gone since he left and we found you. Mrs. Roberts says your body is dealing with the pain by sleeping, but I wish you would open your eyes and tell me you are well. I am afraid that vile man Jones did this to you for taking a shot at him. He left without a *by your leave* and seems the sort to do such a thing. Oh, please be well. You have a knot on your head that must hurt dreadfully."

Kevin could take no more of the non-stop chatter and offered a rebuke that lost its power when the reprimand whispered from his mouth, "My head hurts like the dickens and you are not helping. Can you be quiet for a moment?"

Alicia's eyes widened and her jaw dropped at his raspy scold, but then her eyes crinkled and her lips pressed into a smile. She exclaimed, "Oh good! You are awake! And if you are well enough to reproach me, then I know you will be fine. I will go tell Lord Felton. He was here, you know. My Aunt Alexandra shooed him out to get some rest and that is when I snuck in."

"Please be quiet," he moaned.

At that moment, the door opened and Alexandra walked in. She looked surprised to see her niece talking to Mr. Donahue.

"Alicia, what do you think you are doing?"

"I am nursing our guest."

"You should not be here and you know it," chastised her aunt.

"Why shan't I? Am I not mistress of the house and are not papa's guests my responsibility?"

"Alicia you are a maiden and should not be in the company of a man without benefit of a chaperone, much less, one undressed."

"I did not even take notice he is so wrapped up like a gift."

"Do not play at words with me, Alicia. You know what the gossipmongers would say to learn of this intimacy."

"Intimacy!" roared Alicia. "Why I have not even touched the man." Alicia looked at the linen in her hand, the one she used to swab his head and shrugged her shoulders. She revised, "Well, I haven't touched him with any wicked intentions. He has been asleep most of the time I was here. Just ask him."

They both looked down to see Kevin's eyes and mouth wide open. He looked stunned as if a spirit from the beyond came into the room and frightened him witless. Both ladies asked in unison, "Are you well?"

Kevin groaned and closed his eyes. He wished he could turn away from them and cover his ears with his hands, but every move overwhelmingly made his head and body ache. He expected the ladies to continue their arguing, but to his relief the door opened and he heard Felton say, "The doctor is here, I need you ladies to take your leave so he can examine Mr. Donahue."

Alicia followed her aunt out of the room, but not before taking a look at Mr. Donahue before she left. She lied when she said she had not noticed the man's state of undress. His bruised form had initially distressed her, but then something else overcame her. Something wicked indeed! She took her full look of him and appreciated his stellar form. She thought him handsome, but seeing his muscular arms and broad chest made her appreciate him in a way she never thought about a man. She wondered what it would feel like to be held by those strong arms against his hard chest. The idea was foreign for she never met a man who inspired such thoughts in her.

Men were riding companions, excellent sources of information on animal husbandry and downright good company when you didn't have to worry about courting. Never had she wanted to be held by a man or heaven forbid, kissed by him. These were dangerous thoughts and she could easily see how this man could cause havoc in her life. She had to be careful or else she might grow *tendre* feelings for him. She had no wish to fall in love. She knew firsthand the grief suffered when someone you love is taken from you.

The doctor finished his examination and asked Lord Felton, "Do you know what happened to him?"

"No, he just woke when you arrived. I haven't had a chance to ask him, but I would guess he was attacked and pummeled considering his wounds are centered on his abdomen, arms, and head."

"I agree. It is his head wound causing him to slumber. His eyes look good and he was coherent enough to complain when I poked and prodded, so I expect he will recover. I recommend you wake him on the hour to ensure he does not fall into too deep a sleep from which he cannot awake. As for his other cuts and bruises, I did not feel any broken bones but that doesn't rule out a cracked rib. I would keep him bound for a week and no riding or anything else to jostle those bruised ribs and prove me wrong."

Felton looked at his lifeless-looking friend and asked, "Is he sleeping?"

"Well, my lord," replied the doctor, "If he wasn't, I would not be jabbering with you, I would be calling for the undertaker."

Felton scowled at the doctor and was ready to offer his own glib reply when Kevin's sorrowful moan turned his attention to him. Felton asked the doctor, "Can you give him anything?"

"No laudanum. I want you to be able to wake him, but you may give him some willow bark tea when needed. Your good cook will know how to prepare it."

Kevin woke again to the cool swab of perfumed linen against his forehead, but his throbbing head kept him from immediately opening his eyes. The smell of lilac reminded him of his mother and how she also used to soothe him as a boy with a lilac drenched cloth whenever he was sick. He tried to speak but his mouth was parched dry. He swallowed and tried multiple times to ask for what he desperately craved, until his raspy voice finally exhaled the word "water."

He relaxed in that manner of relief when one reaches a goal until he feared his request had gone unheard. He was about to ask for water again, but stopped when a small and slender hand carefully slid behind his throbbing head to raise it. A cup of water was pressed to his dry lips and the refreshing liquid soothed his parched mouth and throat. The anxiousness that had overcome him when he could not speak settled under the care of the person cradling and holding his throbbing head.

His head was returned gently to his pillow and began to pound dreadfully every time he moved it. Even so, he felt calmer knowing a caregiver was close at hand and wanted to tell the person not to leave when their departing footsteps echoed, but his words dried up on his tongue.

He was about to try to call out again when the person returned to his bed and began to speak to him quietly. He recognized Alicia's voice even though she did not speak in the rapid succession as she had done before. She spoke calmly and with authority. Kevin wondered if she nursed before, maybe Charlie. Her small hand slid behind his head again and the expectation of more water made him feel giddy. He was so thirsty it took him a moment to taste and gag on the water's bitterness which he was about to spit out until Alicia commanded, "No! You must swallow. It will ease your pain."

Kevin now recognized the vile brew and finished the willow bark tea. When the bitterness stayed on his tongue, he urgently rasped, "Water, more." Alicia responded quickly and raised his head while bringing a cup to his mouth. He gulped until he drank his fill and then his head was again lowered with great care back down on his pillow. Once his equilibrium returned, he opened his eyes.

The light from the fireplace illuminated Alicia's features and he would have returned her smile if his stomach had not just suddenly churned in the way a storm whips up the sea. To his horror, the water he just drank was quickly making its way back up his throat. He instinctively bolted up into a sitting position, heedless of the dizziness and pain he suffered, looking for a chamber pot he was in no position to use.

Alicia's alarmed features strengthened him to keep his lips tightly sealed until she left the room. She guessed his predicament and quickly stepped away. His body convulsed. He tried to hold back his expulsion until she left, but to his mortification his little termagant did not make her exit. Instead, she worked quickly to place a bowl before him in time to catch the void spewing from his mouth.

Kevin closed his eyes and fell back on his bed. He was acutely embarrassed at being ill in front of her and hoped she pitied him enough to make her exit. The sound of her departing footsteps overwhelmingly relieved him and he prayed this time she would leave him to face his indignity alone. Unfortunately, she not only returned to his bedside but leaned over him.

He was so embarrassed of his less than pristine sight he pretended to be unconscious. He kept his eyes shut, kept his breathing slow, and tried to relax his whole body. He expected his ploy to work and Alicia would leave, but with each silent pause passing, his heart began to beat faster. *"Dang!"* he silently exclaimed, *"Is the lady looking at me? Do I have spittle on my face? Why won't she leave?"* And then he heard her voice and felt the cool swab of the linen cloth on his forehead. He almost sighed until he remembered he was supposed to be passed out.

"You needn't be embarrassed, Mr. Donahue," she said. "The fault is mine. I should not have let you gulp so much water. I knew better, but did not have the heart to take the cup away seeing how you drank in earnest. Next time, I will."

Kevin opened his eyes and let out the sigh he held before saying, "There won't be a next time. I will be up and around by tomorrow. These injuries are no worse than being bucked off a horse."

"I doubt that," responded Alicia. "Do you know what happened to you?"

Kevin swallowed. His mouth was no longer dry, so his words were delivered succinctly, though softly so as not to annoy his aches and pains, "Only that I was attacked. Never saw them coming or who they were."

Kevin paused and then continued slowly as he remembered the details, "I know there was more than one because I felt two bodies holding me, while a third man either hit me on the head or I fell against something. I can't think of any other reason for the lump."

Alicia dunked the square of linen warmed by his head into a bowl of lilac water cooled with ice chips and then wrung the cloth out before placing it back on Mr. Donahue's head.

Kevin's grin was barely distinguishable when he looked up at her and remarked, "That feels really good."

Alicia returned his grin and then her soft expression froze. The sound of footsteps approaching his door made her eyes widen. She quickly pressed her fingers on his lips ordering him to be silent. When he made no sound, she raced and climbed out the opened window before Kevin understood what was happing.

Seconds later, the door opened and Felton came in. "Ah," he remarked. "You are awake. Can I get you some water?"

Kevin shook his head and moaned as the motion made him dizzy. Felton strode forward, began to pick up the linen on Kevin's head as if to refresh the cloth with cold water, but when he felt its coolness he left it alone. Felton raised his eyebrows and Kevin saw the question in the quirk. "What?" he asked.

"What, indeed!" replied Felton.

Chapter Seven

Kevin sat gingerly in an angel bed propped against the mahogany headboard carved with Acanthus leaves. A servant placed a warm tray of food on his lap and took his leave. The half tester bed having only two support pillars at the head of the bed reminded him of the British cabriolet where the canopy does not cover the whole conveyance. He had a clear view of his guest suit since the two bottom bed pillars and drapes of a full tester bed were not there to obstruct his inspection. Only the worsted dark blue side drapes made of the same material as the canopy could have blocked his sight, but they were pulled and tied back.

His room was sparsely appointed painted in a robin's egg blue versus silk-papered. A fireplace burned hot after being tended by the servant who brought his meal. His furniture consisted of a small mahogany bed table, a chest of drawers, and a chair all owning features of the Queen Anne style with pedestal legs and claw and ball feet. Aside from the small pedestal table by his bed, the other furnishings were placed at various spots against the walls where a number of thoroughbred prints hung. The room did not equate to the luxury he enjoyed at Beaumont Manor, or to the distinction of a valued or titled guest. There were no brocaded satin covers or drapes, nor any other accoutrements to add to his comfort. He was sure Felton's room was better appointed.

He had wanted to break his fast with Deneham's other guests in the dining room, but Felton squashed the idea under the premise of doctor's orders. The earl in recompense offered to keep him company while he ate, but Kevin insisted his friend take his meal with their host. He did not want his attack being conjectured about considering the argument he overheard between Deneham and Jones. The baron did not need speculation abounding about one of his guests and the last thing Kevin wanted was to cause Alicia's father further distress. The man had enough to worry about. Besides, Kevin doubted he would even be missed or discussed, since he had yet to make a friend of anyone. Even so, he felt better knowing Felton was there among Deneham's company to scoff any ridiculous notions regarding his injury.

He inspected the plate piled with food deciding what, if anything, he would eat. One half of the large plate was filled with eggs; the other half was stacked with various meats and breads. A kipper looking as if it had been trampled and then put aflame was immediately disregarded. The toast seemed like a safe choice for his stomach and he was just about to pick it up when the door opened and Alicia's head peeked around it. His spirits rose, then his curiosity when she hustled into his room and shut the door behind her.

Her singular presence reminded him of her aunt's scold and he teasingly inquired, "Didn't your aunt forbid you from being in my room with me?"

"Not exactly," she rebutted, adding with a mischievous grin, "My aunt took exception I did not have a chaperone, thereby making myself vulnerable to gossip insinuating we were intimate."

Alicia started to chuckle when he blushed. He never blushed. Damsels blushed, not manly men, but then this lady was not your ordinary lady. Recovered from her surprisingly and blatant remark, he smiled at her.

Alicia returned his smile and inquired, "I see your morning meal is untouched. Do you not like it?"

"I was just about to nibble. Would you like anything from my plate?"

Alicia pranced forward, grabbed a piece of ham and biscuit before thanking him. Kevin watched her break open the biscuit, insert the ham between the two slices and then take a bite out of it. She devoured the small meal with gusto and her enjoyment of it kept him attentive. He marveled over how her lips seemed to pucker after each morsel she chewed. His particular notice of her lips caused Alicia to suddenly swallow and timidly say, "Well, I see you are well. I shall leave you to your meal."

She started to make her exit when Kevin shouted, "Wait!"

Alicia stiffened her spine and turned around. Her expression was severe, showing her extreme dislike for his commanding tone.

Kevin regretted his scream the minute he released it. He did not mean to yell at her, but not knowing when he might see her again made him act precipitously. He quickly tried to ameliorate the situation by softening his tone, "Where are you going in such a rush?"

Alicia replied brusquely, "We have a house full of guests, Mr. Donahue. Plus, we have another day to hunt. Papa will want me to show another of his hunters. Thor was purchased."

Kevin offered his congratulations on Thor's sale and felt like an idiot for asking his question. Her obvious attire gave evidence to where she was going. She looked so pretty in her fitted riding habit he wanted to jump out of bed and join her in the hunt, but his bruised body retaliated at just the thought of it. He needed another day to recuperate before he could even try to leave his room. He settled for asking her, "Will you come back and tell me how the hunt went? Felton said I must stay abed and I will go stir crazy without something to do."

"And what precisely could we do, Mr. Donahue?"

Kevin laughed when Alicia realized her *entendré*. Embarrassed, she quickly left the room. He would kick himself for teasing her, if he wasn't already suffering from what was surely the result of several kicks. He forgot he was talking to a lady. A British lady governed by a score of rules while in the company of a man.

Alicia hustled down the hallway not wanting her aunt or heaven forbid her father to determine where she had been. She knew of gentlemen who were forced to marry a lady simply for being found alone with them. While she did not think the American subscribed to the edict, she knew her father would definitely press Mr. Donahue to follow a gentleman's code of conduct if he believed she was compromised. She knew you didn't have to do the deed to be ruined, only had to be found in circumstances where the deed might have been done. Her aunt was right. In the future, she would be careful to not be seen in his room.

She was determined if she had to marry, then hers would be a marriage of convenience; unlike her cousin Meg who fell deeply in love with Viscount Atwood. As Meg tells it, her heart raced and an overwhelming sensation embodied her the first time she met her future husband. Alicia thought Meg had eaten something gone bad when she heard her cousin's confession, but ever since she nursed Kevin she understood how Meg felt. Something changed while she watched over him. Now, like the stories Meg told, her own stomach fluttered at the mere thought of him.

She admonished herself for being a ninny. She knew nothing about him, and then as if lightning struck and illuminated her muddled brain, she realized it was not reason but emotion which drew her to him. The epiphany made her search her mind for answers. *Am I attracted to him? How is that possible? Is he attracted to me? How could such simple things like talking and eating cause so much tension between us?*

She recalled how her heart raced under his intense inspection of her lips while she chewed. He looked like he wanted to kiss her which now seemed absurd since she had been eating. No man would want to kiss a lady whose mouth was full of food. Besides, in retrospect, she doubted he could have left the bed to accomplish it. First, he would have needed to move the breakfast tray and then find the strength to stand. By then, she would have known what he was about and would have taken her leave before he could take a step towards her. *Or would I?*

The man was trouble and she should stay away from him, and she would, if she wasn't having so much fun being in his company.

Kevin watched the door close as Felton bid good evening after his visit of recalling the antics of the baron's other guests and left to find sleep in his own quarters. Kevin felt much improved since the first day of his injuries. He was bruised and sore but his head no longer throbbed. His thoughts quickly returned to Alicia without Felton's company to distract him. He had spent the day thinking of her and now with the sun set and everyone settled in their rooms, he realized how much he missed seeing her. Which seemed absurd since he barely knew her, other than she was feisty, funny, and rode like she was born in the saddle. He gave his pillow a good whack out of frustration and settled into his down mattress to await slumber.

He had just fallen asleep when a loud thump prodded his heavy eyelids open to see what woke him. Even drowsy, illuminated by moonlight, he recognized Alicia. He couldn't help but grin to see her plopped on the floor with her derriere pointing to the ceiling. His heart quickened and his lips broadened into a full smile.

"Are you awake?" Alicia whispered as she quickly scrambled from her knees to stand where she clumsily tumbled from the window.

"Just barely, Honorable Alicia. Don't you think it an odd entrance and time to make a visit?"

Moving to the side of his bed, she answered, "Well, yes, I guess it is, but I am being cautious."

Kevin scrunched his brows in confusion and asked, "About what?"

"Us," she replied. "I do not want to marry you."

Astounded, Kevin blurted a bit curtly, "I don't believe I asked you."

Offended, Alicia was about to reply in kind with a terse remark, then realized the absurdity of their conversation and laughed. She quickly explained why she snuck into his room to visit him and how consequences were dire for a maiden found without a chaperone in the company of a man; especially a man unclothed in his own room. She admitted she did not consider the ramifications when she first came to visit. After all, he was unconscious and her only thoughts were to see to his care. Not until her aunt arrived did she realize the wrongness of her actions or what her father would demand if her visits came to his attention.

She confessed, "My aunt was right to scold me."

Kevin grinned and replied, "Well, I am not such a bad catch, so in this case your situation is not so dire."

"I know no such thing," Alicia grumbled. "In fact, I know nothing about you; aside Lord Felton calls you friend and must care a great deal for you to send for his own physician. How long have you known him?"

"Not long."

"Be more specific," Alicia scowled.

Kevin laughed. "I met Felton through Atwood. You should know the story. You are Meg's cousin."

"I know nothing other than she wanted me to meet an American friend of Viscount Atwood's. Are you his friend?"

"Yes."

"To what story are you referring?"

"I am sorry I mentioned anything. Of course, Meg would not be privy to Atwood's and my first meeting for it was before I knew her."

"You are speaking in riddles and I expect you do not wish to tell me how you met. Was it so bad?"

"Not at all, but it could cause embarrassment to another young man to which I do not want to do. Will you leave be the questions if I tell you it is of no matter?"

"I suppose I must since you will not answer them."

"Tell me about the hunt?" he asked. "Did Charles ride with you?"

"No, he stayed to keep young Lord Harry company. The fool tried to push his horse through a bullfinch instead of taking the gate and injured his thigh when a branch poked and scored him. He was lucky he did not injure his horse. His father, the Earl of Belcrave, would have set the birch rod to his backside if he lost one of his best hunters."

Kevin asked, "What of Harry's injuries? Are they serious?"

"No, but his wound required some stitches that brought the man down before the needle even touched his skin," laughed Alicia.

Kevin shook his head at her. "Not compassionate of you to laugh, Honorable Alicia."

Alicia grinned, "True, but I was remembering the tale as told by Charles and his description was most amusing. You may rest your mind. Harry did not suffer. They stitched him up while he was passed out. Charles likes him enough to keep his company, so he did not ride today. He had no need since Belcrave already purchased the stallion Charles was assigned to show. Harry and Charles are of the same age and Charles can use a friend."

"Why so?"

"Charles is in that awkward position of having prospects but no wealth. Since those prospects are contingent on my papa and uncle not producing an heir, even his expectations are tenuous. It is hard for him to find his proper niche."

"So," asked Kevin, "if not Charles, with whom did you ride?"

"Lord Summers has been trying to ride with me since the Little Season."

Kevin's hackles rose as a tinge of jealousy overcame him. He asked rather brusquely, "What do you mean 'trying to ride' with you?'"

Alicia chuckled at the man's display of temper. *Why is he angry? Does he know Summers?* It was obvious by the scowl on his face Kevin did not like her laughing at him. To soothe his temper she quickly explained, "I attended the Little Season at my papa's insistence, Mr. Donahue. He wants to see me marry and apparently since I have been so disinclined to wed, there was a wager placed in White's betting book on whether or not I could bring a gentleman up to scratch."

Kevin opened his mouth to say he already knew about the wager, but changed his mind not wanting to interrupt her disclosure. He quickly shut his mouth when Alicia raised her eyebrows at him and shook his head, prompting her with a wave of his hand to continue.

"My salver was full of invites, but unfortunately for those men who only wanted to win a bet, I was 'not at home' to receive them. Summers was one of the gentlemen who sought to keep me company."

"Felton told me about the bet," he confessed, feeling honor-bound to do so. "I told him I could not believe any cousin of Meg's would have difficulty finding a man to wed."

Alicia pressed her lips together and responded sharply at his unintended affront, "I am not having difficulty finding a man to wed. You misunderstand. At the time, I did not wish to wed."

"And now you do?"

Alicia sobered and responded sadly, "I have no choice. I shall attend the *marriage mart* this coming Season and hopefully negotiate a marriage of convenience to suit me." Alicia's eyes lit up as the idea occurred to her, "Maybe Summers will wish to further our acquaintance. He likes horses and took no issue to my outriding him!"

Kevin's mouth gaped again and she asked him, "What is wrong?"

"Do you not want to marry for love?"

"No, I have no time for such foolishness."

"If no time for hearth and home, then what do you have time?" asked Kevin.

Alicia grinned and enthusiastically explained, "I love horses. Our horse breeding farm has been my papa's and my saving grace since my mama died."

"Can't you find a man to love who also loves horse breeding?"

"Oh, no! That would be horrendous!"

Astonished at her ardent reply, Kevin asked, "Why horrendous? My parents and grandparents before them were in love and led very fruitful lives."

"Oh, I am not saying it cannot be done. I just don't want to risk the grief."

Again, Kevin's jaw dropped. He quickly recovered from her revelation and asked, "What grief?"

"The grief when that loved one is taken away from you. Have you not been paying attention? I told you my mama died."

Kevin's downturned mouth made Alicia almost choke on her emotions. When it looked like Kevin was going to press her to open up, she quickly changed the subject by asking, "How are you feeling?"

Sympathetic to her sadness and understanding her need to change the subject, he replied he was improved and then offered his counsel, "I know you don't want to speak of this further so I won't press you, but do not marry just to breed horses. I have similar aspirations and will enter into a partnership with you to build a horse breeding farm if you like. We can call it the Double D for Deneham and Donahue. Our own two thoroughbreds can beget our first foal."

Kevin could not believe he suggested a partnership. For heaven's sake, he barely knew the lady, but he genuinely liked her and he could not deny he found her beautiful and funny which might be what attracted him the most to her. She did not put on airs like most of the aristocracy, nor did she prim and pout. She was forthright, intrepid, for how else could she ride and jump as she did? He felt comfortable in her presence, aside from his heartbeat speeding up every time she came into his company; otherwise he felt like he could tell her anything without having to offer an apology. She was not the sort to act differently towards a man versus a woman. She was rather American in that way. At least where he lived, a wife was a helpmeet not a trophy to display, nor a bank of money. He did not think Alicia would hesitate to stand by her man and work hard for the betterment of her family's welfare. He almost choked when the revelation hit him. *Could this woman be my helpmeet? And if so, why can't I offer her the marriage of convenience she covets?* His thoughts stopped as quickly as if he pulled the reins on a fast moving horse. *"Whoa! I don't want to marry for convenience. I want to marry for love!"*

Alicia grinned and said with regret, "The Double D sounds like one of your Western novels. I am not sure our English gentlemen will associate prime thoroughbreds with such a name, and as much as I would like to accept your offer, Mr. Donahue, I must decline it. I could not shame my family."

Kevin scrunched his forehead and asked, "How so?"

"I am a maid, Mr. Donahue," she answered. "I cannot engage in a partnership with a man; especially in a horse breeding business. My virtue would be questioned and then shredded as innuendo and scenarios would be created to feed the rumors. Truth would be overlooked for entertaining speculation. Thank you, but I cannot accept."

"Then, you shall marry?" he asked.

"I am to live with my aunt and uncle after the hunt. My papa is closing up the house while he tours our country visiting friends. He will join me in London after the New Year for the Season. You will wish me luck, Mr. Donahue, in making a suitable match?"

Alicia looked at him beseechingly and he felt his answer was important to her so he profoundly said, "You have my heartiest wishes for a fruitful marriage, Honorable Alicia." After a moment, he asked, "Tell me, would your reputation suffer if your horse bred with mine. We do not have to be business partners for us to benefit from combining resources."

Alicia voiced her thoughts, "Where? Deneham Manor will be closed."

"I might have property by spring," replied Kevin.

"I would not want to be away from Cleo," replied Alicia. "She is too important to me, plus I would want to oversee her care."

"Of course, she is a magnificent thoroughbred. The day I rode up to your manor with Felton I saw you and Charles take the field. Your riding proficiency is extraordinary. There wasn't a hitch between you or Charles when you flew over the hedgerow. You both ride exceptionally."

Alicia laughed. "Thank you. Cleo does make me look good. My good fortune is based on the fact I let her do all the work. I just hang on for the ride, trusting her to know what she is doing. "

"I am the same way with Maximilian. I do not hesitate once I commit to a jump. You see, we are of like mind and would make excellent partners. Maximilian and Cleo should breed. Felton would let you keep her at Beaumont Manor. It is but an hour out of London and since you will be in Town for the Season it is the perfect solution."

Alicia beamed and said, "It is perfect!" Sobering, she looked at him with squinted eyes as if the act could determine his truthfulness and asked, "Who will own the foal?"

Kevin grinned and said, "We both will."

"My future husband may take exception," she remarked.

"Let us deal with him when there is one. For now, shall we shake on a deal well-done?"

Kevin offered his hand and felt the warmth of her small one when she placed it in his palm. He wanted to pull her forward and seal their agreement with a kiss, but settled on a gentle squeeze. The act proved as precious as cuddling a new puppy. He felt Alicia tug her hand away when he failed to release it and reluctantly let her hand go. To keep her with him, he asked, "Do you hunt tomorrow?"

Chapter Eight

"What in the world are you doing?" asked Felton. Embarrassed, Kevin turned to look at his friend who interrupted his watch and awaited an answer to his question. He had been spying on the field of mounted gentlemen fashioned in their black riding coats and tall black beaver hats waiting for the hunt to begin. He grimaced. He could hardly admit he left his room to search for an unoccupied room with a window's view of the manor's front.

Last night, Alicia spoke so much of Summers' riding proficiency and the man's amiable personality that he took an immediate dislike to the seemingly incomparable man. Her enthusiastic praise of Summers lingered on his mind like a bad hangover and kept him from a sound sleep. He woke irritable and determined to see for himself if this specimen of perfection was indeed all Alicia vouchsafed.

He had listened at each bedroom door until he found a vacant room overlooking the front drive. For an injured man he moved with remarkable speed to carry a heavily carved and giltwood chair to the side of the window where he was hidden from view, yet still had a clear view to spy on the hunting party. He searched for Alicia and spotted her immediately. The ostrich feather in her fashionable hat signaled her position like a beacon. He thought he would always be able to recognize her trim figure and form, with or without a feather, no matter where she stood in a crowd. Why he thought so, he wasn't too sure other than he just knew.

The feather in her hat began to bob up and down like a seesaw and Kevin surmised she was agreeing with what the gentleman mounted on his horse next to hers said. No doubt the man was Summers. He acknowledged his lordship sat his horse well, but little else could be discerned by viewing his straight and broad back. The one thing Kevin knew for sure was he did not like the way the two of them were thoroughly engaged in each other's conversation. Nor did he like the way Summers tended to lean closer to Alicia whenever she spoke. At least, he could discern no other reason for the man tilting his body towards her. Kevin thought it all a ruse since every time Summers did lean, Alicia moved her horse closer to the gentleman's mount.

His instinct or perhaps it was his rising temper at seeing them so cozy in company made him want to march down to where they sat on their horses and interrupt their tête á tête with a slap to Summers' horse. The vision of the man's hunter galloping away with him gave Kevin great satisfaction until Felton's arrival made it disappear.

"Well?" pressed Felton when Kevin failed to answer him.

Kevin barked, "Why aren't you down on the field with the others?" His snappish response surprised even himself. He was embarrassed and peaked to be caught playing a child's game of stealth. He had no wish to confess his sin and hoped his terse question diverted his friend from probing further.

Unfortunately for him, Felton only grinned at his ill manner and answered with aplomb, "I surmised the walls might be closing in on you and thought to distract you with a game of chess. Now, will you explain what you are doing out of your room and spying?"

"Who said I was spying?"

Felton walked over to the window and looked out upon the field of riders waiting for the signal to begin the hunt. He found Alicia sitting tall in her saddle and remarked, "She is a lovely lady and lucky for you she also likes to breed horses."

"Who?"

Felton laughed and guided his friend back to his room and to the table where he set up a chessboard with pieces. He motioned Kevin to sit, took the chair opposite him, and then made a gesture for Kevin to make the first move. He casually asked, "How are you feeling?"

"I am fine, Felton," replied Kevin with frustration. "I am too good to be in bed as you probably know since I expect you spoke with the doctor."

"Yes. He said the ruffians who beat you did not injure your organs nor crack your ribs; otherwise you would not be up and snarly at being confined. If you like, you could travel back to London tomorrow in my carriage. I had my traveling coach brought when I collected the doctor. "

"I would not cut short your pleasure, Felton," said Kevin.

"I came mostly for your benefit, Donahue. The trip seems pointless since you are not able to meet your fellow guests. You will need to become acquainted with them and others of their ilk to prosper. Profiting from breeding horses depend highly on whom you know and your relationship with them.

Kevin rolled his eyes. Of course he knew he had to meet the people who would buy his horses. He was no man's fool. A lady's fool perhaps, because at this moment the only person he was interested in befriending was the Honorable Alicia. She was a conundrum of sorts. She was fearless and bold but also vulnerable and wary. Two sides of a different coin calling forth both his competitive and protective instincts.

Kevin looked up from the rook he held in his hand and said, "I would not mind staying a few more days, Felton."

"Deneham's hunt concludes tomorrow," informed Felton. "Most will follow the pack, but I am sure it is common for the baron to host some of his guests for a couple of days after his hunt ends. Shall I inquire if you may extend your visit?"

Kevin smiled and placed his rook on the board, while Felton laughed at his friend's obvious ploy to spend time with the Honorable Alicia Deneham.

Alicia entered the drawing room. The rectangle shaped room was well appointed with rich wood paneling contrasting against a white plaster ceiling decorated with a bead of crisscrossing arches. A gold-toned Aubusson carpet covered the breadth of the floor and several brass wall sconces illuminated the room. There were a number of leather wing chairs and a marble-topped side bar full of tumblers and liquor decanters on one end of the room. The other end was furnished with a number of embroidered satin upholstered and giltwood chairs, sofas, and small mahogany pedestal tables. A beautifully wood-carved Norman arch with an inset mirror, hung over the burning marble fireplace dividing the two areas distinctly catering to ladies on one end and gentlemen on the other.

For a number of years, ever since her mother died, Alicia and her aunt acted as hostess for the baron's annual hunting parties. Most of her father's guests attended faithfully and were familiar with the dictate that kept

Alicia from making an appearance until the second night of their arrival. By the time Alicia joined the party, the gentlemen were well-mannered and effusive in making their bow to her. They made a great production of their salutations and offered compliments intended to make any maiden blush. They would have made a similar show to Aunt Alexandra except the lady told them she would not stand for such foolishness. Alicia, on the other hand, accepted each gentleman's outrageous flirtation as the *flummery* it was intended to be.

Alicia did not often dress to impress, but she knew the high-waist evening gown she wore, fashioned in pink gauze over a white satin slip was the height of fashion with its low cut bodice and embellishments. She adored the blushing color and all the lace and rosette trimmings that decorated her puffed sleeves and the falls of her two skirts. Her aunt's nod of approval upon seeing her removed any doubt she might have had regarding her appearance. She almost proffered a curtsey in response.

She turned her eyes upon the room and searched for Lord Summers. After the hunt, he said he looked forward to seeing her at dinner and she believed he meant it genuinely. She found him standing amongst her father's other guests near the marble fireplace and when he spied her, he began to walk towards her with a look of admiration that made Alicia blush.

She was about to walk up to meet him when a hand cupped her elbow and escorted her in the opposite direction towards the drawing room's draped windows.

She was surprised at the audacity of being manhandled and was about to admonish the offender, but the sight of a remarkably handsome and fit Kevin in black evening attire made her speechless.

The notion he was healthy enough to join her papa's company quickly diminished the sting of his affront, until she saw him beam a smile as if he thought he just bested her. Instinctively, she jabbed his side with her elbow and found herself immediately freed from his grasp. She enjoyed her small victory until he moaned and grabbed the side she just punished. She immediately remembered his injuries and regretted her attack on him. "I beg your pardon, Mr. Donahue," she apologized sincerely, "but what do you think you are doing?"

"I thought I was rescuing you from the attentions of Lord Summers," he groaned. "I figured the man a tedious bore after your characterization of him last night."

Alicia's jaw dropped in astonishment at Kevin's absurd remark and then she laughed realizing he was being facetious. She saw him hold back his own chuckles, most likely to keep the jostling from hurting his ribs. She was about to ask him what prompted him to tell such a *faradiddle*, when he said, "I have not forgotten your British protocol, Honorable Alicia. I asked your aunt to introduce you to me this evening and she said the request was absurd considering our recent time together."

Alicia grinned at her aunt's reply. She did not suffer fools gladly.

The butler entered and announced dinner was served ending any further discourse between them. Everyone began to pair up and Alicia turned her attention away from Kevin to look around the room. She saw her papa escort her aunt into the dining parlour with Uncle Marcus following behind them, chatting away as if he hadn't seen them in forever. Then, every gentleman knowing their precedence placed themselves in proper order. She and her escort would precede the men and she waited for her designated escort to collect her. Aunt Alexandra would have asked a gentleman to walk her in, so she was not surprised when Lord Summers joined her and Kevin.

He informed, "Your aunt, Honorable Alicia, gave me the privilege of walking you to your chair."

Kevin queried in what she thought a very supercilious voice, "You cannot manage on your own?"

Before placing her hand on Summers' arm and walking away, she stuck her nose up at him and rebuked, "Indeed not!"

Alicia heard him chuckle and then moan. The pain his bruised ribs suffered from laughing at her was a just reward for suggesting she was too weak to seat herself. Obviously, he knew nothing of British protocol, but then the idea of him injuring himself made her want to turn around to have a look at how severe he was hurt. She balked when she caught Summers watching her. Alicia had no wish to start tongues wagging about her and the American, so she kept her face forward and let Summers lead her to her chair. She would know soon enough whether Kevin was well enough to sit for dinner.

She sat down and waited for Summers to take the empty seat next to her, but to her amazement he left. He looked like he was about to sit down and then stopped, straightened his body and walked away without any explanation. She was sure her aunt would have placed her escort by her side. Her eyes searched for the place card, but Kevin took the chair before she found it.

"And how," she queried, "did you manage to sit next to me?"

Kevin picked up the card bearing his name and said, "I am sitting where I was placed, Honorable Alicia."

Alicia knew better; especially when she saw Lord Summers direct a steely-eye at Kevin. His lordship was clearly vexed and Kevin looked like he just stole someone's portion of *blancmange*. Peaked at his underhandedness to have his way she gave Summers her cheeriest smile. His lordship was a handsome and amiable man, aside from the scowl he currently wore. He was not difficult to look at with his thick brown hair and light tawny eyes which always beheld a gleam of amusement. He was of the Corinthian set and most likely spent his idle days pursuing those activities testing his strength and ability. He was good company during the hunt and knew how to keep a lively conversation.

She would have been perfectly happy to sit next to him during dinner and since she did not want him to think she had anything to do with him being ousted from his seat, she offered him her brightest smile. In return, she saw his features gladden and his lips break into a broader smile. His unwarranted joy prompted Alicia to see what Kevin did to amuse Summers, but Kevin's frown turned her eyes back to Summers. His lordship was biting his bottom lip, fighting to contain his laughter from exploding into chuckles, so as not to draw attention.

Alicia's temper immediately rose. She did not like being the center of their ungentlemanly sport, nor did she like being fought over like a *piece of muslin*. She almost blushed at the thought, knowing no lady should have any knowledge of the *demimonde*. She decided to just ignore both men and their antics. She quickly turned to her left to give Lord Castlebank her singular attention and without meaning to, asked rather tartly, "Did you enjoy the hunt, my lord?"

Castlebank was too excited to notice her cutting tone. His mind was on the day's hunt and enthusiastically pulled the fox's paw he received. He shook the paw pad from its chain to show her and explained "Was the first to follow behind the hounds! Quimley let me have a prize. Figured the paw might give me luck like a rabbit's foot. I will need it when I follow the Quorn pack."

Alicia kept her stomach from purging by taking her eyes off the fox's foot which still had dried blood on it. The recollection of hearing the hound's vicious barks earlier in the day upon finding their mark, made her forget she was upset with Kevin. After offering Castlebank a quick smile and nod, she turned her attention away from him and the sad remnant making her queasy. She sat with her hands against her stomach trying to settle the turbulence brewing inside her. She concentrated on her breathing, while silently begging her stomach to calm. She was so deep in her thoughts she did not notice Kevin lean in towards her until his warm breath brushed her face. His concern was evident in his voice, "Are you unwell? Is there anything I can do?"

Alicia groaned and answered carefully, fearful more than words might escape her mouth, "I will come about in a minute, thank you." After the lightheadedness began to fade, she added, "I just turned a bit green at seeing Castlebank's prize. The man is delighted with it, but I have no stomach for seeing or thinking about the end to that poor fox. As many years as I have ridden in the hunt, I only rode to the end once to be initiated and regretted it ever since. Just hearing the hounds barking as they corner their prey turns my stomach."

"I understand, but according to Fieldmoore, Quimley trained his hounds well and unless given leave, the kill is made by a nip to the varmint's neck."

"Perhaps, but dead is dead, Mr. Donahue."

Alicia opened her eyes wide when she heard Kevin choke. Her temper rose when she saw he was holding back a laugh. *The rogue! Does he think me childish for being squeamish?*

Kevin had a hard time holding his laugh at Alicia's witty remark, especially when her facial coloring went from sickly pale to flushed crimson. It seemed her sudden rise to temper cured her queasiness. *'Dead is dead,' she said* and so he thought was this conversation if he did not change the topic. He rallied his mind, struggling for something clever to say until she took the burden of saving the conversation on herself.

"You are lucky I distracted you the first day of the hunt," Alicia remarked arrogantly.

"What do you mean?"

"It is tradition for the fox's blood to be rubbed on the face of first time hunters," she explained.

"Really?" queried Kevin raising his eyebrows.

"Indeed, it could be you and not me ready to suffer the indignity of voiding my innards."

Kevin saw Alicia's face blanch from mortification. It was coarse for a lady to mention body parts, much less any mechanics of them, so to distract her from her distress, he reminded her, "I already had the honor, Honorable Alicia, which you well know and to which I hope you never share."

Alicia's apologetic eyes told Kevin she remembered the night when he overindulged with water and disgraced himself in front of her. Her clear regret for teasing him made him bellow a laugh over how quickly her expressions crossed her face. First her facial features scowled in anger, then her jaw dropped in mortification and finally, her lips softened into a pout of pity. His loud outburst drew the attention of Deneham's other guests and since, he was too American to prevaricate, he pointed to Alicia to explain his amusement. The good lady had the sense to check what she was about to say; no doubt an expletive meant for his ears alone.

He restrained himself from laughing out loud again when Alicia pressed her lips together in frustration. She must have sensed his near chuckle for she squinted her eyes at him as if to say, "don't you dare." Kevin did not and waited for what she was about to say to their attentive audience.

"Mr. Donahue," she explained to the table at large, "took exception to our hunters' initiation rite."

"What initiation rite?" called out Lord Harry before Deneham's guests could offer their own opinions on the tradition.

Charles, sitting by Harry's side, explained how the Master of the Hunt initiates first time hunters by smearing the fox's blood on their face.

"Egad! That could have happened to me!" exclaimed Harry.

"It is not so bad, Harry," consoled Charles. "It is not like they wipe the carcass against you. Quimley only dips his fingers in some of the fox's warm blood and then smears it on your face. It is over in a minute."

Harry's eyes rolled back in his head and Charles caught him when he fell to his side. Before Charles could ask for help, a footman took Harry from his arms, hoisted him over his shoulder like a sack of grain and carried the young lord to his room. Unsurprised by the boy's weak constitution, Harry's father, the Earl of Belcrave, picked up his goblet to sip his wine and explained how his son's sensitive nature was due to his lady wife's coddling.

Alexandra remarked there was nothing wrong indulging one's child and her opinion sent every man to turn and speak with their neighbor on any topic other than the rearing of one's child. The chatter about horses and hounds resounded and the embarrassment caused by Kevin's outburst was forgotten. Kevin grinned at Alicia and his heart skipped a beat when the lady returned his smile in earnest.

Chapter Nine

Alicia stood on the manor's front steps along with her father, uncle and aunt. They were bidding their guests good hunting as they left to join the Quorn and Pytchley packs. The courtyard resonated with the cacophony of horses snorting, harnesses jiggling and carriage wheels grinding the driveway's gravel as guests mounted their horses or entered their carriages. The ruckus proclaimed the end of the Deneham Hunt.

The gentlemen sat tall in their saddles and wore the customary multi-caped tan greatcoat, tall black beaver hat and Hessian boots for travel. Each gentleman held his high stepping horse in place to tip his hat to his hosts, before starting down the long tree-lined avenue to depart.

Lord Summers conspicuously lagged behind his peers to say his goodbye. "I am sorry to leave your company, Honorable Alicia," he confessed while taking her hand in his, bending over to kiss it.

Alexandra raised an eyebrow at her niece when she saw the intimate gesture and Alicia blushed afraid her aunt would think she favored Summers above all others as a suitor. She quickly jerked her hand back before Summers' lips made contact and her response surprised him. He immediately straightened looking nonplussed. It was no wonder he was confused after the way she had outrageously flirted with him the evening before.

Last night, after Harry fainted at the table and the attention was no longer focused on her and Kevin, she fell into easy conversation with him. They spoke as if they were life-long friends, with no artifice or need to engage in parlour talk to fill a quiet void. Of course they spoke of the niceties, asking each other on their health, but when they both confessed they were well, their conversation turned to more poignant topics, especially after she asked, "Who taught you about horses, Mr. Donahue?"

His immediate smile to her question must have sparked a fond memory because Kevin responded affectionately, "My grand-da. He hailed from Ireland and his voice could soothe the most ornery horse on earth. He used to talk to them the same way he pacified a child, speaking calmly and compassionately. He always said it was the horse's troubles and fears which made it anxious and if I wanted to learn to tame one, then I best understand what troubled it. He had such a harmonious relationship with horses he didn't even need to bribe them with sugar or carrot. They responded to his voice. My grand-ma said it was his Irish lilt that first drew her to him and that same spellbinding and lyrical rhythm brought every horse within hearing distance to his side. I remember falling into slumber listening to his Irish lullabies."

Charmed by his recollection, Alicia pressed him with another question, "Did your grand-da teach you to ride, also?"

"Yep. He said I have a gift and only need to hone it to reap its rewards."

"My papa said the same of me," she revealed. "I think it is why he let me trail him when I was a girl and taught me all he knows about breeding horses. Many criticized him for it, but he said it would be a sin not to nurture a God-granted gift."

"I agree," replied Kevin smiling.

Puzzled, Alicia inquired, "I thought your family grew tobacco. Did they breed horses, too?"

"No, the tobacco farm was inherited and the living for my family over the years, but grand-da always had a hand in taming horses or caring for an injured one. He loved the magnificent beasts and could never see one afraid or hurt. Men from miles away came for his expertise, especially when they had a troubled horse."

"He sounds like an amazing man. I would like to meet him. Are your grandparents living?"

"No, but they left this earth content. My grand-da would have liked you. He could always recognize a fellow guardian."

"Guardian?"

"Yep, that is what my grand-da called anyone having a special talent with animals. He said we have a greater responsibility to care for the creatures, more so than those who are unable to relate to them as we do."

"I never thought about it in that way," she said. "I just thought I had a soft spot for horses."

Kevin laughed, "As do I. Did all the hunters you show sell?"

Alicia beamed with pride. "Yes. Thank goodness," she replied. "My papa counts on his yearly hunt to show and sell his best hunters. Tell me, aside from your injury, did you enjoy the hunt?"

"I very much enjoyed the one day I participated," he confessed. "I love to ride and the idea of racing across a grassy meadow with obstacles to test my skill is a lot of fun. However, I admit even more than the riding, I enjoyed your company the best."

Alicia blushed at his compliment, extraordinarily pleased at being liked by him, especially since she liked him, too. She responded in kind, "I also enjoyed your company. It is a shame we did not get to ride together again. Do you depart with the others tomorrow?"

"Your father has allowed me to stay a couple more days to heal before I make my way back to London. While Felton's carriage springs and amenities are more than adequate to make my trip comfortable, I still have no wish to be stuck in it. Perhaps, you will do me the honor of keeping me company and riding with me before I take my leave."

The idea of spending time with him cheered her, until her inner voice squelched her enthusiasm by reminding her she was headed for heartbreak if she wasn't careful. Her cheery disposition quickly diminished and she could tell Kevin noticed. He opened his mouth to speak, but her aunt's rising from her seat stopped him. It was time for the ladies to leave the men to their port, tobacco, and conversation. Alicia felt a profound relief, until she realized Kevin would press her later for answers to what had saddened her.

Her pulse quickened, each beat pounding faster than the last, as she followed her aunt out of the dining room into the drawing room like a sleepwalker, moving without notice of her surroundings. Without thought, she took the seat across from her aunt at the low set mahogany tea table and fixed her sight on the Sévres teapot resting on the silver tray the maid was placing on the table before her aunt. Her worries over the interest she had not only promoted, but invited between her and Kevin caused her heart to accelerate.

He had confessed he enjoyed her company the best. The compliment should not have distressed her. Many men had delivered similar remarks, but never had she reciprocated the feeling. No man had ever intrigued her, charmed her, or sparked her emotions as Kevin.

Her self-absorption had her aunt raising her voice to get her attention, "My dear girl, are you well?"

Alicia looked from staring at the porcelain teapot into her aunt's eyes and in a slow swooshing breath, lied, "Yes, aunt."

She felt the benefit of her long exhalation as her racing heart slowed and released another slow breath, before explaining to her aunt how she was simply caught woolgathering.

The excuse satisfied Alexandra and her aunt continued, "Well, it was obvious you were not paying attention. I complimented your gown. You look lovely and I dare say you had every gentleman's admiration, especially Lord Summers. The man looks smitten. Do you like him?"

"I do not dislike him, aunt," replied Alicia contrarily, feeling better now that her heart beat normally. She had no wish to be pushed towards Summers even if she considered him a good candidate for marriage.

Aunt Alexandra pressed her lips together in frustration when Alicia did not give her a direct response. She tried to get her niece into revealing more by remarking, "You rode out with him twice during the hunt, Alicia."

"Indeed, but only because he is an accomplished rider and can keep up with me."

Alexandra gave up trying to draw out any declaration from her niece and neatly changed the subject, "We will have to see to purchasing a new wardrobe when we get to London."

"It is not necessary, aunt," Alicia replied.

"I disagree," rebutted Alexandra.

"You cannot," argued Alicia. "Papa has already burdened you and uncle with my living expenses, you need not add to your cost."

Alexandra put her cup and saucer on the tea table and glared at her niece. Alicia could tell she had provoked her aunt, especially when her aunt ranted, "Do not tell me what I can and cannot do, Alicia. You are like a daughter to me and it gives your uncle and me great pleasure to sponsor you this Season. Your papa gave his consent, so it is settled. Do not begrudge me."

The drawing room doors opened before Alicia could respond. The gentlemen entered, some shoulder to shoulder in conversation, others striding forward to greet her and her aunt whose vexation was now replaced with a cheerful expression to greet the baron's guests. The gentlemen carried the pungent smell of tobacco on their clothes and the sweet aroma of port on their breaths. They were in a fine fettle, smiling and conversing with one another. Alicia saw Kevin pull away from the circle of gentlemen heavy in discourse to make his way toward her.

She panicked and out of self-preservation quickly made a bee line to Lord Summers. Kevin scowled at her for walking away from him and Summers stretched his back to stand tall like a proud peacock when she came upon him. Summers thought she had singled him out and rightfully, since Alicia asked him and no other if he would like a cup of tea. Her bold move suggested to the rest of the party she had a personal interest in him. Even her aunt was surprised when Alicia returned to the tea table, poured Summers a cup and returned the filled cup and saucer to him as if she was his to command.

Throughout the rest of the evening, Alicia stayed close to Summers to keep Kevin at bay. She showed Summers particular attention, pointedly rebuffing every effort Kevin made to speak to her. She trembled knowing she was provoking him, but found comfort in knowing the end justified the means. He would take her in dislike and leave the manor immediately. She felt bad causing him grief, but it was the right thing to do. Kevin already made her feel things she never felt before. She liked him, liked to talk to him, liked to tease him, laugh with him, and even spar with him. She felt his equal which was important to her for she had no wish to be subservient to any man, which was a problem since wives were the property of their husbands and owed them their obedience.

It would be easy to fall in love with Kevin since he was everything she dreamed a man should be. She was probably half-way there if the emotions bubbling inside her were any indication, but she was determined not to suffer as her father did when her mother died. Besides, among the aristocracy, marriages were not arranged for love. They were negotiated for benefit and she would ensure her marriage contract included a degree of independence for herself. Maybe, she should consider Summers.

The man she just affronted by pulling back her hand before he could kiss it. *Good heavens! How long was I woolgathering? Should I apologize?* As she thought it over, she realized Summers did not look angry for either affront.

Never the less, they stood looking at one another in silence. The quiet unsettled her and she toyed with a suitable expression of regret to assuage the situation, but before she could utter a word, Summers eyes widened as if he had an epiphany. His grin broadened into a smile.

He said, "I hope you will be home to receive me when I call upon you, Honorable Alicia."

Surprised her contrary manner did not offend him, she replied, "Of course, my lord," and watched as he placed his foot in his horse's stirrup and heaved himself up onto his horse.

He cantered off, stopping at the pillar gates to turn his horse around before he entered the long avenue. He made a striking sight, sitting tall in his saddle and with much fanfare, brought his hand to tip his beaver hat to Alicia in farewell. She knew he would not depart without a send-off, so she gave him a less than enthusiastic wave and then it dawned on her how Summers must have taken her reluctance to have her hand kissed as shyness, or perhaps worse than that, he thought she was behaving as a demure debutante should.

Summers was indeed a viable suitor since he did not seem to mind her independent nature or her riding acumen. He appeared to be a decent man and if she could present herself honestly to him and not as the adoring debutant she misled him last night to believe, then maybe he might still like her enough to court her. He would be a perfect candidate for marriage since he did not put her out of sorts the way Kevin did. There was definitely no anticipation to see him, nor were there any thoughts about what it would be like to be kissed or held by him. Only Kevin stirred her mind to amorous notions and that, while tempting, would absolutely lead to heartbreak.

She never thought herself to be contrary, but what else could she be. Instead of being happy Summers, a man who fit her needs was interested in her, she was worrying over the scowl Kevin gave her when Summers tried to kiss her hand. She should turn around, enter the manor and leave the results of last night's foolishness alone, but her heart and mind were not in accord.

Kevin deserved an apology for her behavior, even though last night she believed she was acting in their best interests. She did not want him to think badly of her and so she went to the stables to speak to him.

She passed through the stable doors and immediately saw him saddling his horse. Without thought, she exclaimed, "You are not leaving without saying goodbye?!"

Her outcry surprised him into looking up at her and then his anger marked his features. If possible, he looked angrier than last night when he replied, "And what would it matter to you if I did?"

Alicia hung her head in shame over her ill treatment of him and knew he had every right to be angry with her. Still, she didn't want him to leave disliking her, even if it had been her plan. Last night she was scared, but today she was more sure-footed and she realized she overreacted to the attraction she held for him.

After all, Kevin simply asked to keep her company while he rehabilitated, not marry him. While he did offer her a business partnership, he did not offer marriage and why should he? They had only known each other for a couple of days. Of course, that was neither here nor there. Aristocrats were known for arranging marriages for their children even before the lady and gentleman had a chance to meet. Some betrothals were arranged at birth, joining families and estates for future generations, while others were negotiated when a lady came of age to a man in need of an heir. There were other reasons for the noble to marry, but among the peerage only few married for love, though she heard the Americans were known for it. Kevin said love was the reason why his own parents and grandparents married.

Her own parents had been in love, but Alicia believed it was serendipitous for they were betrothed before ever meeting one another. She probably would have looked for a man to love in marriage if her mother had not died, but the grief suffered by her and her father diminished any romantic ideas she held about a marriage.

By the time she reached her majority, she was determined to live independently of any man's care, but her dream was now impossible without any means of support. She accepted she needed to marry to secure her livelihood and to help her papa. She would choose a man who respected her as a person, who would not need to control her, and who would support her aspirations to breed horses.

She realized this morning if she had not panicked over her attraction to Kevin, she could have spent her last days at Deneham Manor with him, a man she found both charming and companionable. Instead, she rejected him and now he was leaving. She offered an earnest apology, "I behaved terribly towards you last night and I am very sorry."

She could tell by the widening of his eyes how she surprised him and how she was forgiven by the grin broadening into a smile. He had a way of dazzling her with his smile. He was a strikingly handsome and physically fit man, with a ruggedness which made him look strong and capable. He walked towards her and as he neared, she took a step back. Her retreating steps were in response to each forward step he took, leading her backwards as if in a dance. The anticipation of what he planned had her heart pounding in her chest. She knew they were in a battle of wills and she girded herself to stand her ground. She would have been scared out of her life if any other man advanced upon her with such intent, but she didn't fear Kevin. When her back hit the wall, she gasped, "What do you think you are doing?"

In response, he leaned into her, coming so close she felt the warmth of his breath on her face. Her heart pounded harder making it difficult to think and breathe. *Merciful heavens! He is going to kiss me!* Instinctively, she closed her eyes and waited for the brush of his lips against her own. She could smell a trace of Bergamot in his cologne and her nostrils flared to breathe in more of his citrus and musky scent. She waited in anticipation until the jingle of a bridle caused her to open her eyes. Discombobulated, it took her a moment to realize Kevin had moved away from her. In his hand was a horse's leather headgear and bit. His eyes held amusement and while she continued to stare at him in confusion, he asked her pardon for reaching over her. It was then she realized, not only did Kevin not kiss her, but he misled her to think he would. She crimsoned in anger. In retaliation, she pushed him with both her hands to move him out of her way and stomped out of the stables.

Chapter Ten

Kevin heard Alicia bluster "good riddance" when she left. She was fired up mad and he thought she looked adorable all flummoxed. She had read him right. He was going to kiss her when he drew close and he would have, except he remembered how she did not want to marry for love. It took a lot of will power not to press his lips to hers, but he was not going to give her a reason to evade him as she had done last night.

He was darn right angry at her for avoiding him and giving Summers all her attention. Summers wasn't intolerable. He seemed personable and he showed a respect for Alicia he could not fault, but he didn't like the idea of her belonging to him. Whether he wanted to admit it or not, he staked her out for himself and no bloody marriage of convenience was going to interfere with him having her. The problem was he wasn't sure how to go about it.

It was obvious to him he and Alicia were attracted to one another and how those feelings could grow into something deeper. She said she wanted a marriage of convenience and the way he was starting to feel was far from convenient. He thought it would be easy to build on the feelings burgeoning between them, but it was those feelings that were making the lady reluctant and caused him concern. The last thing he wanted to do was force her into Summers' hands. It seemed every time he and Alicia connected, she scurried away or acted foolishly like she did last night.

At first, her blatant disregard for him and her particular attention for Summers angered him. He almost choked when she batted her eyelashes at the man and had to turn a chuckle into a cough when her father asked if she had something in her eye. Even Summers raised his eyebrows at her coquette manner and the fool took it all in believing she admired him above all others.

Kevin knew better. He immediately noticed after his temper cooled how she was performing for his benefit. She only became effusive and fawned over Summers when he came close to her. After a while for his own amusement, he plagued her by drawing close just to get her to act contrary to her true nature. Unfortunately, because of his antics, Summers now believed Alicia would favor his suit.

This morning's sentimental goodbye between them confirmed Kevin's belief Summers was a problem in more ways than one. The man was a credible threat because he was Alicia's viable marriage of convenience.

Kevin had his work cut out for him if he was going to win his lady. First and foremost, he needed to break through Alicia's reserves. Second, he needed to establish himself among the nobility to compete with Summers at his own level. Third, he needed to sabotage any efforts Summers put forward and fourth, the most important element of all, he needed Alicia to let go of her fear of falling in love with him. He never expected to have to work so hard to win a lady's hand.

Back home, he would never put so much effort to gain a lady's admiration. If the lady wasn't interested neither was he, but Alicia was different. He felt a connection with her he never felt before. He saw her in his future by his side. The idea of her not being there seemed incomprehensible. He was going to have to battle the lady herself to win her and approach her like an ornery horse that was more likely to bite his hand than take the carrot he offered. Kevin laughed. He would never share the notion with anyone; especially Alicia, but maybe that was why he was attracted to her. She was far from domesticated. She was full of spirit and if there was one thing Kevin admired was spirit.

Alicia left the stables furious and stomped her way to the manor. She almost ran into the Earl of Felton when she strode into her home without care to where she was walking. "Oh, I do beg your pardon, my lord," she quickly apologized.

"Not necessary," he replied, smiling.

Alicia took note of Felton's greatcoat and the tall black beaver hat held under his arm. She queried, "I see you are leaving. You have seen Papa?"

"Yes. I just finished extending my gratitude to him for his hospitality and especially for his care of Mr. Donahue. I asked him to extend that same gratitude to your aunt."

"I wish you and Mr. Donahue good travel. I was surprised him capable of riding."

"Well, he is not one to be idle. He assured me he will take care and not ride long."

"Long? He does not return with you to London?"

"Ah, I see you are unaware Mr. Donahue has accepted your father's hospitality for a few more days."

Alicia scowled. "No, my lord, I thought he was saddling Maximilian to leave."

Alicia left a bemused Felton and practically raced up the stairs. She ran into her room and called for her maid to help her change from her sprig muslin day dress into her crimson riding habit. She was mad and her red Merino wool ensemble suited her temperament. She wanted Kevin to see her coming and if he knew what was good for him, he would dig in his heels and get Maximilian to run like the wind.

Kevin missed riding Maximilian. After last night's fiasco, he was ready for a good gallop and was glad he taped his ribs when his horse broke into a run and his seat hit his saddle hard. He had been bucked a number of times to recognize a bruised body versus a broken one and knew he only risked feeling sore by racing. He quickly became one with Maximilian's powerful gait and reveled in the fresh cool air passing over him.

He steered his horse towards the place near the river where during the first day of the hunt he had followed Alicia. It was pure sentiment driving him to visit the spot where they had their first tête á tête and he would have fallen into reflection, if the sound of hoofs hitting the ground at a fast clip did not have him pulling up on his reins to look over his shoulder.

He saw an avenging angel and smiled. Alicia was bent low over Cleo pushing her horse to reach him. Divots of grass flew from the beast's fast moving hooves, Cleo's nostrils flaring to fill her lungs. The wind and Alicia's grueling pace dislodged pins from her coif, freeing several strands to flutter like a shimmering flame.

She looked magnificent.

Kevin fought to keep Maximilian in place as he waited for Alicia to join him. His horse was ready to run; especially with the sound of Cleo advancing upon them. At first, Kevin thought Alicia followed him because she was angry, but he soon saw her delight when she passed him.

The vixen had not come out to rant at him as he first thought, but to best him. He quickly pushed his heels into Maximilian's flanks and gave his horse his head to race. Like Alicia, he bent low over his horse's neck and soon Maximilian was nearly head to head with Cleo. He saw Alicia laugh and they both pressed their horses to win. They arrived at the place Alicia called her favorite spot and though they arrived together, Alicia exuberantly called herself the winner.

Kevin checked his chuckles at Alicia's boast and quickly brought his horse to a halt. He dismounted and dropped his horse's reins on the grass to keep him from running off. Before Alicia even realized what he was going to do, he pulled her down from her saddle and kissed her.

At first, Kevin meant to give her a hasty kiss so as not to alarm her, but her soft and pliable lips encouraged him to indulge, especially when she did not stiffen up to his embrace or bite his lips in rage. If anything, he felt her sway into him. His heart began to beat faster when she returned his kiss or maybe it was just trying to keep pace with hers. He could feel her pulse beating as fast as his own. He reluctantly ended the kiss, pulled away and waited for Alicia's reaction. He never knew how his termagant would respond to his advances, so he waited and watched.

Alicia slowly opened her dazed eyes and through a dreamy sigh, asked, "What was that?"

"That," he uttered with a brimming smile, "was your prize."

His response broke the spell she was under and in a confused tone, said, "My what?"

"Your prize, did you not declare yourself the winner?" He wondered how long it would take her to realize she was no longer the victor. He felt rather triumphant on turning her win into his victory. *"Ah, not long,"* he silently said to himself when she scowled.

What just happened? She was feeling so good beating him to the finish line and now he was the one acting as though he had won the race. She was confused and a bit wobbly after that amazing kiss and it was amazing. She never liked kisses. The few she experienced were awkward and downright disgusting. One gentleman pressed against her lips so hard she was afraid he was going to crack her tooth. Another man practically slobbered her and if that wasn't enough to turn her away from the affectation then being pressed against a man was pure horror. She kept away from the sentimentality, except it appeared with Kevin. *Why didn't I shove the arrogant man away?* She feared she knew why.

"You cannot kiss me!"

"Just me?"

"What do you mean?"

"Well, I was just wondering if any man could kiss you or if it was my kiss you took exception. I thought you rather liked it."

Alicia was dumbfounded and while she was confused Kevin brought her closer and kissed her again, but this time his audacity provoked her. She pushed at his broad shoulders and when he didn't move away from her, she swung back her leg and kicked him in the shin. She was wearing riding boots, not the soft slippers of a debutante so he felt the impact immediately. He quickly released her to comfort his bruising shin. "Ow!" He groaned, "Why ever did you do that?"

"I told you not to kiss me!"

"Actually, you told me I could not kiss you and I was only proving you were wrong and I am more than capable of kissing you."

Alicia's mouth formed an "o" in astonishment before opening up to release a bubble of laughter. Kevin grinned and joined her in chorus with his own chuckles.

"You are ridiculous," she announced when her laughter faded.

"Perhaps," he said. "but I enjoy being ridiculous with you."

"Men," she grumbled. "I thought I explained my position to you."

"And what position is that?" asked Kevin.

"I told you I was going to marry for convenience sake!"

"And I am not convenient?" he asked.

"Mr. Donahue," she started.

"Kevin," he interrupted. I believe we are on a first name basis. You have snuck into my room, kept me company while I was déshabillé and now kissed me. Call me Kevin."

"You must not speak of those things."

"I won't. Now call me Kevin."

"Kevin," she started again.

"Alicia," he said.

"Honorable Alicia," she corrected.

"Of course," he replied.

"What do you mean 'of course?'"

"Of course, you are a lady."

Alicia's eyes widened and her face flushed. She asked, "Did you think I wasn't a lady and that is why you kissed me?"

"No. I wanted to kiss you as I expect others have tried."

Alicia stuck up her nose at him and said, 'That is not of your concern."

"I agree. Just as it is of no concern to you of whom I have kissed."

Alicia's face drained of all color and Kevin looked like he regretted his rejoinder; especially when she walked away. She sat on the log she used to mount her horse. Kevin followed and sat down next to her.

"Tell me," he said.

Alicia felt wretched. The idea of him kissing another crawled at her skin. Usually a kiss was a prelude to marriage or other things she should not know about, so the vision of someone kissing her man made her down right angry and that was the problem. Kevin was not her man and if she was smart she would never see him again. Her emotions were in turmoil and she didn't even love him. She knew she liked him, a lot, and that he made her heart skip a beat or two. Her mind was filled with thoughts of him and she wanted to spend as much time with him as possible. He made her laugh, but most of all she liked the way she felt when he was near: protected, cherished and adored. He looked at her in a way that made her insides mushy and when he kissed her nothing had ever felt so perfect, which was why she had to stop this flirtatious game they were playing. How would she ever survive if she let herself love him and then like her mama, found him gone? She heard him say, "Tell me" and so she did.

"I know we barely know one another, but you are a threat to my happiness. You must desist in your flirting and amorous attention. I am not like those debutantes who are masters of artifice and innuendo. I speak my mind and take what is given at face value. You are only flirting with me and yet I take everything you say to heart. Your kiss is more than a kiss to me."

"I want it to be more," he confessed.

"But I don't. I have tried to explain myself, but still you persist in your amorous attentions."

He grumbled, "You prefer the attentions of Summers."

"Not necessarily."

"What is that suppose to mean?"

"It means I am not averse to him. He is very eligible. According to my aunt, he has expectations to inherit a piece of property from a maternal grandmother. We get along fine and he comes from a good family. More importantly, I don't feel all discombobulated when I am around him, nor do I care where he is when he is not in my company. I think we would suit very well."

"You mean you would not be grief-stricken if something happened to him."

"Ah," Alicia thought. *"He has been paying attention."*

Chapter Eleven

Kevin could tell by Alicia's open-mouthed expression to his intuitive retort she believed he would now concede his pursuit of her. She was wrong. If anything, he was more determined than ever to win her, but at least he now knew what he was up against. Her idea that love in marriage coincided with devastation had been concocted when she was a young girl grieving and while he sympathized, the notion was still unfounded. He cared too much for her to let her settle for less than a love match and he was too confident not to believe he was part of that equation.

He had a heavy task set before him and would need more than words to break through her resolve. A notion to tackle the problem from a different direction came to mind and following his instincts, he announced, "I am leaving tomorrow."

Alicia's mouth turned down at his news.

Kevin wanted to give her a good shake. This woman would be the death of him with her contrariness. He would gladly keep her company for a few more days if he wasn't concerned Summers would call on her once he took his leave. Since he couldn't remove her fear of falling in love with him, then his only option was to shadow Summers and intercede when possible to his advantage.

He planned to ingratiate himself with the man. As Summers' friend he could learn of the man's plans and with luck, disrupt them to his favor. *"Ha!"* He wanted to laugh. He could just see Alicia's face when Summers came to call with his dear friend Mr. Donahue by his side.

A plethora of comedic scenes began to take shape in his mind of how he could outmaneuver his rival. He was rather enjoying himself until Alicia's query interrupted his musings, "Felton said you were to stay for a few days. Are you mad at me for rebuffing you?"

Sobered by her downcast mien, he teased to lift her spirits, "Did you? Rebuff me, I mean? I thought you said you liked me."

"Oh! You know what I mean. I do like you. It is just I am afraid of liking you too much and then where will I be?"

"I expect with a man you love," replied Kevin seriously.

"Oh, stop. Now you are simply provoking me. Do you depart for London?"

"No, I have decided to follow the pack. I am going to take up your father's offer and travel with him to the next hunt so he can do the honors of introducing me. He feels responsible for my injury and wants to make amends for it."

"Do you blame him?"

"No, he is not the one who tried to smash Jones' face for affronting you."

Alicia grinned and extolled, "You were quite magnificent. I never thanked you for coming to my aid. The man frightened me."

"He is wicked, Alicia. You were right to be wary and no thanks are necessary. It was my pleasure to come to your aid. Anytime, you need me, simply send me word and I will come."

Kevin almost fell over when Alicia pivoted in her seat on the log to embrace him in a tight hug. "Thank you," she said.

"May I write you?" he asked.

"A maiden cannot receive correspondence from a man who is neither father nor brother."

"Oh," he said with a frown.

"However, if you are so inclined," she added, "you could include a postscript to Atwood. I know Meg would forward your words to me in a letter and perhaps I could send a message to Meg that Atwood could include in his letter to you."

Kevin grinned at her ingenuity and liked the way she was bold enough to speak her mind. He knew he would never have to guess what she wanted for he was sure she was forthright enough to tell him. He stood, helped her to rise from her log seat and then walked her over to her horse. Before he could help her mount she reached up and wrapped her arms around his neck and kissed him. He felt the jolt through to his toes. When she released him and stepped back, she said, "A proper thank you for defending me from Mr. Jones and a proper goodbye, Mr. Donahue. I wish you well and hope you will think of me on occasion. I will remember you."

The Shires
November

My Lord Atwood and Friend,

Well, my good friend, I was happy to hear you and Meg tied the knot. I hope to see the both of you soon to give you my heartiest wishes in person. You may have heard I met Meg's cousin, the Honorable Alicia Deneham. She and I both have a keen interest in horses. She told me I could communicate to her through you since your British protocol forbids me to write her directly. Please give her my regards and tell her I was initiated by the master of the Quorn himself and did not faint. It is a private joke, Atwood. Do not think me so green as to let a little blood disturb me, so you shall not refer to my glib remark to anyone, Meg aside. I lived in the country, after all, and have seen more of the crimson stuff than I care to explain.

Donahue

Mayfair, London
November

Dear Kevin,

I should direct this to you as Mr. Donahue, but my pen hesitated to put the formal name to paper remembering how insistent you were I call you Kevin. Meg wrote me she would enclose my sealed letter to you, so you may do the same in the future for any correspondence you send me through Atwood. Meg says it is easier than trying to transcribe your message in a letter. I know she is trying to grant us some privacy. You would think we are writing billet-douxs to one another, but we know better. Be assured I clarified our relationship to Meg, so you shall not be teased by Atwood.

My aunt and uncle are most generous in letting me stay with them in London though I miss my home and grassy pastures. I take Cleo out daily to compensate for my homesickness and often find myself thinking of our time together. Among other things, I mostly enjoy remembering how I bested you in our last race.

I am glad you survived our "bloody" initiation rite and may now call yourself a true English hunter. My aunt informs me Lord Summers is among your company for he wrote to my uncle.

I am not averse to receiving your correspondence.
Alicia

The Shires
November

Dear Alicia,

Your Lord Summers is indeed following the pack with me. I hate to tell you he is well-liked and calls me a friend as well. He is a good man and you may be assured he will treat you well should you choose him to marry. Shall I congratulate you now? I doubt you will have trouble bringing him up to scratch, as you British say, for he speaks fondly of your time together. He asked me if I had anything to do with changing the table cards at the dinner where we sat next to each other. I denied any knowledge of the incident for I shall not wish for any servant to be reprimanded. However, since we have been honest with one another, I shall confess to you and you alone, I am guilty. It was well worth the trickery to enjoy your company.

Kevin

Mayfair, London
November

Dear Kevin,

I am glad you and Lord Summers are friends. I know him to be good company and an excellent horseman. Perhaps I may marry him, especially now you seem all keen for us to do so. As to your switching out the table cards, I *cannot take offense any longer since I now recall dinner that evening with delight.*

Will you return to London before Christmas or do you head directly to Beaumont Manor? Meg, on behalf of the marquis, invited me and her parents to spend the holiday with them. Will I see you there?

Alicia

The Shires
December

Dear Alicia

I am not keen on you marrying Summers. Yes, I will be at Beaumont Manor for Christmas. I would have returned to have Thanksgiving with you; however, I discovered you British do not celebrate the holiday.

Kevin

Beaumont Manor
December

"You are pacing, my friend," remarked Atwood.

Kevin who indeed was striding to and fro on the drawing room carpet stopped in his tracks and rebutted, "Am I?"

"Leave him be," said Meg. "He is no doubt anxious to see Alicia. She is expected today."

His friends greeted him earnestly when he arrived at the manor and did not harass him to answer questions to which they had many. They encouraged him to see to his own comfort, so Kevin took the stairs to the spacious, beautifully appointed room he once called his own when he was Felton's houseguest. He quickly saw to his ablutions, fed his hunger with the small tray of food Meg sent up to him, and after a short rest went looking for his friends.

He went to the drawing room where he thought to find them and as he entered was struck again by the room's improvements. Felton's lady wife Anne made redecorating the manor's drawing room her first priority after marrying her earl and moving into the manor. The walls were covered in sky blue striped silk with crowned mouldings to frame the ornate white plaster ceiling which was quartered off with distinction and decorated in each center with a medallion motif. The white paned windows of the multiple double doors were draped with light blue velveteen curtains and tied back to let the day's light in. Matching tasseled swags festooned across them and added to their elegance.

Anne reupholstered the original French-styled cabriole chairs with blue striped satin to match the wall coverings. She added two giltwood carved sofas, upholstered in green velveteen and bolstered at each end. She placed them at opposite sides of the drawing room to provide a respite for guests who truly needed to lounge. She also purchased a number of ornately-carved gilded pier mirrors to hang above equally ornamental side tables. A few mahogany tables were added for her guests to gather around. Miniature portraits, vases filled with greenery and other personal items were on display throughout the room.

A beautiful crystal chandelier hung from the center of the ceiling. Gilt wall sconces and other candelabras were present on tables to offer additional light when needed. A floral Aubusson carpet covered the breadth of the floor and a number of beautiful English landscapes framed in ornate gilt frames hung on the walls bringing cohesiveness to the welcoming, airy, and ostentatious room. No guest could ever doubt the Earl of Felton was a very wealthy man.

As soon as Kevin entered the drawing room, Meg immediately rose from her seat and assaulted Kevin with the questions weighing heavily on her mind. She wanted to know exactly what transpired between him and her cousin. One question rapidly followed another before Kevin could give answer. He looked to Meg's husband, Viscount Atwood, for assistance and breathed a sigh of relief when his friend intervened, saying, "Meg, desist. Give the man a chance to oblige you."

Meg closed her mouth and glared at her husband. She returned to her seat on the sofa and showed her patience by gently clasping her hands on her lap.

Lawrence moved to stand by her side and then they both looked to Kevin for answers.

Kevin opened his mouth to speak and then shut it in frustration. He did not know what to say. He was too embarrassed to admit Alicia did not want his addresses, but he owned a forthright nature and saw no other course but to tell the truth. He took a seat on one of the cabriole chairs facing the sofa where Meg sat and soberly confessed to his friends how he admired Alicia, but unfortunately for him the lady had no wish to reciprocate his tender feelings. When asked why, he told them of her fear of losing another person she loved. Meg offered a "tsk" and shook her head in sympathy. She explained how Alicia never entered the *marriage mart* after being presented at court. At the time she thought it was because Alicia was actively involved in her father's horse breeding business and her cousin knew a husband would never allow her to engage in those activities the *ton* considered scandalous for a lady.

Kevin rose and began to pace. When his stride brought him back to his friends, he asked, "Why is her situation different now? Everyone knows she is active in her father's business. Why is Deneham not badgered about Alicia and why isn't Alicia the center of your gossipmongers?"

Meg answered, "Who says she is not? My uncle does not care his peers think him light of touch with Alicia. He is rather proud of her independent nature and strong will; and since Alicia never attended any of the balls and events making up the Season, she was not affected by any speculation made of her. Of course that will change this Season, especially since she is favored by many gentlemen. The marriage mart mamas will use her manly passion to disgrace her in the eyes of the *ton*. I do not think uncle or my cousin have prepared themselves for the malicious innuendo which might occur if Alicia's popularity threatens the prospects of other debutantes. She has made many friends through her papa's hunts and it would not surprise me if there are those like you, Mr. Donahue, who would be happy to win her hand."

"Well, I know Summers would be ecstatic to win Alicia," he offered. "It is unfair he has the advantage."

"What advantage is that?" asked Atwood.

"She doesn't love him," Kevin replied.

"She loves you?" asked Meg, surprised at the man's perceptiveness.

Kevin grinned and said, "I believe she cares for me enough to make her want to keep her distance."

Meg revealed, "I believe my cousin more than cares for you, Mr. Donahue, and just has not accepted it yet. She writes to you, as you know; but what you do not know is how she writes of you to me. I don't even think she realizes how often she inserts your name into her letters to me. In one letter where I described a scrumptious dessert I enjoyed, she wrote back and informed me how much you would have liked it, too. Apparently, you have a sweet tooth, Mr. Donahue."

Kevin laughed and confirmed he did.

"In another letter," Meg continued. "I expressed my sympathy for one of our tenants who was kicked by a horse and would be abed for a week." She wrote back to tell me how a horse would never keep you down for a week and then went on to tell us about your villain Mr. Jones and the injuries you sustained at his hands."

"There is no proof it was him," offered Kevin, "though he is most likely the culprit."

"You must tell me more of this villain later," interjected Atwood.

Meg concluded, "There are too many variations of how Alicia mentions you in her letters for me to describe; but enough to know you are in her thoughts."

"As she is in mine, though to what purpose if the lady refuses my ardor."

Kevin took off on another stroll of the room. His friends watched him until Atwood brought his pacing to a stop by remarking upon it.

Kevin heard the sympathy in Meg's voice when she chastised her husband. Kevin did not want sympathy. The idea made him frown. What he wanted was an intervention. He would not settle for defeat. He was determined to win Alicia's hand in marriage and just needed someone to tell him how to get it done.

Atwood laughed. "It seems the table has turned and instead of Meg trying to secure the hand of a reluctant viscount, you are the one trying to win a very reluctant lady. What will you do?"

"What did Meg do to help you let go of your fears?"

"She did nothing," replied Atwood. "I realized how much I cared for Meg when that cad Spencer pursued her. I guess I just couldn't accept Meg belonging to anyone but me."

"I also feel Summers helped me realize the feelings I have for Alicia," confessed Kevin, "but he is far from a cad."

"His lordship," informed Meg, "has written to papa to request permission to call on Alicia."

"Should he not have asked permission from the baron?" asked Kevin.

"Of course, but since my uncle is traveling, my papa stands in his stead so he has told me."

"I expect Alicia will marry him if I cannot overcome her fear," stated Kevin with regret.

"Perhaps," said Meg. "You need not overcome her fear but replace it."

"What do you mean?" asked Kevin.

Interested to hear her idea, Atwood also prompted her. "Yes, my lady wife, what do you mean?"

Meg laughed and said, "You, my lord husband, are the one who gave me the idea."

"Well, by all means enlighten us," retorted Atwood. "We are all ears."

She sobered and said, "Instead of Alicia worrying about the grief endured when a loved one dies, she should consider the sorrow sustained when a beloved is lost to a rival. You see, her fear resides from her mama's death. There was nothing she could do to prevent her suffering or dying. I remember Alicia confessing how she had no control over her mama's death and that, more than anything grieved her. However, there IS something one can do from losing a beloved to a rival."

"By jolly, Meg!" exclaimed Atwood. "You may have something there."

Kevin clarified, "Perhaps in theory, Meg, but may I remind you Alicia does not have a rival for my affections."

"She will," laughed Meg, and before he could ask any more questions, she practically skipped out of the room.

"Where is she going?" asked Kevin.

"Probably recruiting reinforcements?" replied Atwood.

"What do you mean?"

"You would not know how Anne earned a living as a debutante chaperone when she met Felton. The lady's lineage is impeccable, but her father left her nothing but a townhome when he died. She survived by employing herself to those ladies with no time to watch over their daughters during the Season."

"What does that have to do with anything?" asked Kevin.

"Everything," answered Atwood. "Meg probably went to ask Anne who would be the best candidate to make Alicia jealous."

"Alicia is not the sort to be jealous," replied Kevin.

Atwood laughed and said, "My dear friend, everyone is the type when they are unsure of the affections of the one they love."

Chapter Twelve

The Marquis of Beaumont had no qualms leaving his nephew and heir, Edward Brentwood, the Earl of Felton and his countess, Lady Anne, to greet their newly arriving guests, especially when the Christmas party was of Anne's making. Beaumont was in his sunset years and having already handed over all his business affairs, estate management, and host responsibilities to Edward, he saw no reason to suffer through polite chatter, parlour games, and whatever else a Christmas party entailed. He told Edward and Anne he would keep to his private quarters while they entertained, so he was not informed when an advanced rider heralded the arriving Deneham carriage.

Instead, the earl and his countess asked Lawrence, Meg, and Kevin to join them on the manor's front steps to welcome their guests. They stood in a line anticipating the first glimpse of the traveling coach. Meg was excited to see her family and rose on her tiptoes to spy a better view of her parent's carriage, while Kevin shuffled his feet which caused Felton to remonstrate, "Do not fidget, Donahue."

"I am doing no such thing," Kevin rebutted even though he looked like he stepped on an ant hill and a number of the insects were moving up his leg.

Felton raised an eyebrow at his friend, but let his obvious lie pass when his butler proffered a silver salver where a folded note lay. Felton waited for his servant to explain the note and after a moment's silence the man quickly informed, "The rider who just arrived said it was from Sir Marcus, my lord. He is breaking his fast in the kitchen if you have need of him."

Felton quickly read the missive and then dismissed his servant.

"Problem?" asked an attentive Kevin.

Felton waved the note to his wife and guests, a gesture to indicate he was imparting the contents of the letter. "Sir Marcus informs me he is bringing a guest."

"Who?" asked Kevin.

"He did not say. Only the gentleman was in route to his grandmother's estate and would stay but two nights with us."

Kevin shook his head in disbelief. It would be his horrid luck to have Summers accompany Alicia to Beaumont Manor. Summers said he was spending the Christmas holiday with his grandmother and it was easy to conjecture he contrived an invitation to join the Deneham party. The man was as determined as himself to marrying the Honorable Alicia and he knew because as planned, he could now call the man "friend."

He had followed the pack with Summers and during each hunt maneuvered to ride by his side. In the evenings he joined Summers' circle of peers and made himself amiable by offering flatteries, telling jokes, and recalling some of his American vignettes to amuse. Before long, Summers was signaling him out in jest or just to keep his company. They came to admire each other's horsemanship and through the antics played during the hunt, discovered they shared a similar sense of humor. Their camaraderie even diminished the anger Summers held against Kevin for stealing his dinner seat next to Alicia. Kevin's plan had been to befriend Summers. He never guessed they would actually come to like each other.

It was not long before Summers confided to Kevin about his future inheritance and the requirements of marriage he had to meet to gain it. He confessed he was "bloody lucky" to discover the Honorable Alicia Deneham favored his attentions for he needed to marry expediently. His grandmother wanted to approve the lady he chose for wife and was pressing him to wed with haste. Summers confessed the Season's marriage mart did not appeal to him for he did not want to marry a young lady out of the schoolroom. He wanted a mature lady, one still capable of breeding, and who could manage on her own. He had no wish to coddle a wife.

Kevin remembered Summers saying, "Alicia has managed Deneham's home and guests for years. I know she will manage my home excellently and not harass me about my sporting pursuits. If anything, she might follow the hounds with me and any other excursions appropriate for a lady. I hear she is not one for balls and such, so she should be happy minding hearth and home. I could not have found a better candidate who fits my needs to wed."

It bothered Kevin how Summers did not mention Alicia's needs, nor any modicum of affection for her. All he cared about was how the lady suited his needs. She was just a means to an end and while he did not doubt Summers would respect and provide for Alicia, he was sure the lord was clueless to what made her happy. Kevin had no qualms upsetting Summers' courtship of Alicia and he began by dropping snippets of courtly advice.

"Felton once told me the Honorable Alicia would choose no one to wed. She sounds like a nervous filly. I would not rush your attentions. She might balk and refuse your suit."

Kevin almost laughed at the truth of his remark for that is what happened to him. Regardless of how helpful his counsel might be, he needed time to win Alicia. Unfortunately, he might now have to share that time with his rival.

Sir Marcus' traveling carriage pulled up the gravel drive crunching its way to a stop at Beaumont's front steps. The coachman locked the break and then held tight to his reins while one of Beaumont's grooms rushed to hold the lead horses' headgear. A footman quickly placed a step stool in front of the carriage door and then opened it.

Sir Marcus exited first from his carriage and then to Kevin's regret, Lord Summers followed him. They both waited to assist the ladies. Lady Alexandra's hands found purchase on the door frame and she pushed her way out, much like a butterfly escaping its cocoon. She took her husband's helping hand to step down from the carriage. Then, like the Greek goddess Persephone rising from the underground, Alicia's gloved and small hand emerged, followed by her slender arm from the darkness of the carriage. Summers took her hand and Kevin wished it was he who was helping her to alight into the sunlit day.

Alicia stepped down to the foot stool and onto the ground, releasing Summers' hand the moment she was steady. She looked weary until she saw Kevin and then her features cheered. At least, he wanted to believe he was behind her changed expression. *Is she happy to see me? Should I rush to meet her?*

While he contemplated what to do, Meg raced down the steps to greet her parents and cousin. Felton, Anne, and Atwood followed her example and welcomed Meg's family with appropriate hugs and handshakes. All the while, Kevin remained fixed at the top of the stairs like a sturdy oak firmly rooted in the ground.

A shout from Summers finally released him from the anxiety holding him where he stood. Coming to his senses, he looked at Summers and grimaced. The man's expression was too happy and he worried he was too late to court Alicia. *Did she accept his suit?*

The idea made him angry. He felt as though a thief absconded with his most prized possession, so he was far from cordial when Summers ran up to him, slapped him on his back and greeted, "Donahue! Honorable Alicia said you would be here. It is good to see you though it was not that long ago we bid each other adieu."

"Not long at all," replied a stone-faced Kevin. He took Summers' hand in his when the man offered it to him and was quickly pacified by Summers' earnest and friendly salutation. He was hard-pressed to stay angry at a man he now called his friend. Especially since that man had no idea how much grief he was causing him.

Kevin returned Summers' smile and hearty handshake, silently admitting, *I cannot fault him for wanting to marry Alicia? She is amazing and in all fairness, it wasn't Summers' fault Alicia did not want me for her husband. Besides, Summers does not even know I hold a tendre for the lady or I am his rival.*

He asked Summers, "I am told your stay is for only two days. Why so short a visit? And how did you come to be part of Sir Marcus' party?"

"Serendipity," he replied. "I went to call on Honorable Alicia at her uncle's house before I left town. I found their coach being packed for departure. Lady Alexandra offered me a ride and good company when she heard I was headed in the same direction as them."

"You are indeed fortunate, Summers," Kevin replied. "I can think of no better company than Honorable Alicia."

Lord Summers grinned and turned to look at Alicia whom Kevin had already set his eyes upon.

"Yes, Donahue, I am fortunate, indeed."

Alicia wanted to stomp her foot at the two fools looking at her like a prized mare. She was taken unawares to find Lord Summers a traveling companion and even more uncomfortable when it looked like her aunt was promoting a match between them. She could not fault her. Summers was a highly eligible gentleman with exceptional lineage, expectations of a piece of property and income to sustain her in a style she was used to living. Her aunt knew she was not looking forward to entering the Season and probably thought finding a husband before then would make her happy. Plus, she could not fault her aunt for thinking she might be enamored with the man after her foolish behavior towards him during her papa's hunt. She worried she might now be obligated to marry him, if she could not rectify the misconception she was ready to receive his addresses.

The moment Summers entered her uncle's carriage she had decided to thwart his advances by ignoring him. She held her back straight and stretched her spine to its limit, while holding her head at an angle that tilted her nose to the coach's ceiling. She projected the epitome of hauteur and snubbed him by keeping her eyes directed to the view outside her window. Anytime Summers made a query to her, she deflected it to her aunt and uncle to answer. Either he was ignorant of her rebuffs or just too stubborn to care. It was obvious he meant to win her over and Alicia could not resist his amiable nature for long. The man was too charming and witty to ignore. He had them all laughing at his fox hunting tales. He mentioned Donahue a time or two which made her engage him more in conversation.

She discovered the two of them rode together during the hunts and dared each other into jumping feats which was common among the aristocracy who loved to wager. The story of them coming upon the fox and carrying him to safety made her laugh. Summers said he would never have done such a thing had Donahue not argued a fox with an injured leg was unsporting. The tale became even more amusing when the hounds trailed the scent to their horses and sent them racing across field to outrun them.

The recollection made her grin again which she quickly turned into a smile when the Earl and Countess of Felton approached to welcome her. She thanked them for their invitation to spend the holiday with them and then, after they turned their attention to her aunt and uncle, delivered a scathing glare to Kevin and Summers for their blatant appraisal of her. Usually, a young lady would enjoy the regard of two eligible gentlemen looking handsome and broad shouldered in their finely woven tailcoat jackets and tightly fitted buff riding pants, but Alicia did not like to be gazed upon as if she was some type of prize to be won. Even Meg's exuberant hug did little to appease her.

"You look angry. What's wrong, Alicia?" asked Meg.

"What do you think they are talking about?" returned Alicia.

"Who?"

"Mr. Donahue and Lord Summers."

"Oh, don't mind them," Meg counseled. "Come on, let's go inside and have a cup of tea. Then, I'll take you to your room and you can tell me how Lord Summers came to be of your party."

Felton beckoned everyone to retire to the drawing room where refreshments were waiting for them. Once inside, he directed them all to take a seat and then helped his countess to one of the gilded chairs around a low mahogany table inlaid with rosewood. A silver server waited with a number of Sévres porcelain cups, saucers, and a teapot. Anne immediately began to pour the brewing, aromatic tea into the cups and hand them to the ladies seated at the table. She waved her arm to a console table where a silver tray of sandwiches were placed asking her guests to help themselves. Felton inquired if the men preferred something stronger and within minutes, everyone had a cup or tumbler in hand and was engaged in the niceties of social discourse.

Once Anne saw her guests' thirsts and hunger were sated, she rose and offered to escort Alexandra and Alicia to their rooms. She announced to the whole of their party before leaving how they would take an early dinner as was done in the country. Meg quickly took Alicia in hand and all the ladies left the men to their own company.

Kevin had no chance to have a private word with Alicia and could only watch as she left the room with Meg. He looked out the double door paned windows at the sleeping knot garden where he had hoped to stroll with Alicia before she made her way to her room. Before he could repine on his regret, Summers joined him and began to talk about his prospects, "I am on my way to my grandmother's property, Donahue. I have not visited the estate for a decade since she moved in with my parents. The estate is under her trusty steward's care and it seems to profit. There are tenants who farm the land. I do not think there is any stock: horses, cattle, or sheep, but once I inherit, I can decide what is best for the land."

"Have you considered breeding horses?" Kevin asked, thinking of how important it was for Alicia.

Summers exclaimed, "Heavens, no! I am a proficient rider but have no love for the maintenance of them, much less, breeding them."

Kevin grinned. Perhaps, all was not lost. He knew more than anyone, a man with no passion for horses, would not make a good match for his termagant. *"Now,"* he thought, *"How do I inform her?"*

"You are early for dinner," Kevin said to Alicia surprised to find her alone in the drawing room.

"As are you?" she rebuffed.

With raised eyebrows, he inquired, "Did I make it sound like a reprimand or is the anger directed at me misplaced?"

Alicia laughed. "I am sorry, but yes, I guess you did raise my ire. I would have hoped to see pleasure in your eyes to find me alone, instead of the disconcerted look you gave me. In all honesty I was expecting the welcome you did not give me when I first arrived."

"I beg your pardon." Kevin strode to where she stood, wrapped her in his arms and kissed her without a thought to the consequences of so doing. He knew he surprised her for her body went rigid before she relaxed into his embrace. He grinned when she kissed him back; unfortunately, his grin quickly brought back her temper. She pushed at his shoulders until he released her and then remonstrated, "You are not supposed to kiss me!"

"Now you are being fickle," he answered. "You chastise me for not being pleased to see you and for not welcoming you properly. I quickly ameliorate the affront and the moment you notice my joy you scold me for it."

"I am not scolding you, only reminding you how we cannot risk falling in love with one another."

"Are we at risk, then?" he asked.

Alicia opened her eyes wide in alarm and asked, "Is it only me, then?"

Kevin wrapped her up in his arms and kissed her again, before asking, "What do you think?"

At that moment, voices were heard and they quickly separated to an acceptable distance that would not be remarked upon when the rest of Beaumont's party arrived. Kevin saw Alicia touch her hair to ensure it was still in place and no pins were popping out from his amorous attention.

Meg entered first and was not at all deceived. She went directly to Alicia and placed herself in front of her cousin to protect her from the view of the other guests entering. She quickly smoothed Alicia's hair and tugged her cousin's dress into place. Kevin had not even noticed how his embrace twisted her gown so it was off kilter and silently thanked Meg for coming to Alicia's aid.

Everyone fell into proper precedence when the butler announced dinner was served. Felton escorted his lady wife, Anne, to Lawrence who under him was the highest ranking peer among them. He then offered his arm to Lawrence's viscountess. Sir Marcus took his wife Alexandra and his niece in hand since Summers only held a courtesy title. Sir Marcus had no wish to single out the American to walk alone, so settled any possible affront by leaving Summers and Kevin to walk into the dining room together.

The dining table which could easily seat thirty guests with all its extensions was shortened for their small party and looked like an island in the middle of a vast ocean with so much open space surrounding it. The table was elegantly covered in pristine white linen and set with crystal goblets, china and sterling silver service. The only feature suggesting dinner was an informal affair was the lack of place cards and the ostentatious epergne centerpiece which prevented guests from speaking to anyone aside from their neighbor. Felton, acting on behalf of the absent Beaumont, assured his guests they need not stand on ceremony, could sit where they liked and converse across the table at will if they so choose.

Anne was first to speak and inquired of Summers, "I was informed Lord Summers your stay with us will be short?"

"Yes, my lady. I am on my way to my grandmother's estate. She granted it to me on the terms I marry." At this remark he smiled at Alicia who quickly blushed.

Lady Alexandra beamed at his obvious admiration of her niece and said, "I do hope your business will not keep you long from our company."

Summers eyes widened as if lightning just streaked the sky. He exclaimed, "Say!" All eyes were upon him as he suggested, "Why not come with me? It would be advantageous for Alicia to inspect the property and give her opinion on the estate."

Kevin saw Alicia's hands fall from the table to her lap. Her face went pale. Summers' suggestion was as much of a surprise to her as it was to him. The man practically declared himself and he worried how she would respond. *Will she say yes, before I can even inform her of Summers' disinterest in horse breeding?*

Kevin's head swiveled to Sir Marcus believing it was upon his authority to accept or refuse the invitation, but the man's eyes were on his lady wife Alexandra. Kevin did not even have time to offer up a prayer.

"I think that is a marvelous idea, my lord," the lady replied.

"Mama," asked Meg, "you would spend the holiday without me?"

"Of course I won't, Meg," Alexandra clarified. "We would not stay with Lord Summers for Christmas. I am sure he has other plans."

Summers offered, "You are welcome to journey and spend Christmas with my family, but I would not be so inconsiderate as to hijack Beaumont's party."

Kevin could not believe his ears when Felton said, "Not at all, Summers. Sir Marcus and his family will not offend me or Beaumont should they accept your kind invitation."

"Well, I am not going," grumbled Meg.

Lady Anne offered a new topic for conversation and the meal continued with awkward pauses until news of Atwood's and Meg's wedding tour filled the void. Everyone asked a question of the newlyweds, aside from Kevin and Alicia who seemed occupied with their own thoughts.

Before long, Anne stood and led the ladies to the parlour so the men could enjoy their port. The moment they entered the room, Meg pulled Alicia aside and asked, "Are you going to go?"

"I suppose I shall," she answered.

"But, why?"

Alicia answered, "Father wrote me. He made an offer to the Countess of Heathmoore."

"The miner's daughter who married the earl?" asked Meg.

"The very rich miner's daughter who is now a widow," clarified Alicia.

"Good for uncle," replied Meg. "Now, you have no need to marry. Uncle settled everything by refilling his coffers and you can go back to being mildly independent."

"I cannot go home to live with my papa," confessed Alicia.

"I cannot believe uncle said so to you."

"He did not, but I am no longer mistress of the manor and I refuse to be looked upon as a spinster. No, I shall marry and start my own family."

"With anyone?" asked Meg.

"Summers is not anyone, Meg."

"But, is he the right one?"

Before Alicia could answer, the parlour doors opened and the gentlemen entered looking as if they swallowed something ghastly, aside from Summers who wore a radiant smile.

Chapter Thirteen

Alicia harrumphed at her inability to rise from bed. She looked down the length of her body and saw her legs were trussed up with her voluminous night shift much like a ship's sail to a yard. Her feet were also tangled with the bed sheets at the bottom of her mattress reminding her how she had kicked at them during the night as she searched for a comfortable repose.

She was exhausted and now after finally falling asleep, the dawn light had the nerve to pierce her eyelids and wake her up. She resigned herself momentarily to lay flat on her back. She stared at the green brocaded canopy above her and then pushed herself up on her elbows to let her eyes roam the room she was given for her visit.

Last night she had dropped onto the canopied bed without any appreciation for the beautifully appointed room. Her bed was ornately gilded and carved with the same circular neo-classical motifs that adorned the high plastered ceiling with crown moulding. A beautifully crafted and colorful Brussels tapestry depicting the countryside hung on one wall. Against another wall was a gleaming mahogany tallboy and clothespress with brass fixtures. A number of other pieces beautifully carved and embellished with gilt were placed around the room for a guest's comfort.

Alicia saw a toilette table that when closed served as a writing desk, a full-length cheval mirror, chairs, and at the foot of her bed, a small sofa upholstered in green brocaded satin. The bed and windows were draped in the same brocaded material and were topped with heavily fringed valances. The walls were covered with green Damask silk. The glowing embers in the marble-faced fireplace and an Aubusson floor carpet kept the room from growing chilly. Her suite was called The Green State Room for the obvious reason and previous guests, according to the countess, had always found the room as peaceful as nature itself.

However, Alicia was not at peace. Neither her room, nor her bed was the reason behind her restlessness. The fault lay with her contrary mind. On one hand, she worried she was misleading Summers to believe she would accept his addresses. *After all, why shouldn't he believe I want to wed him? Why else accept his invitation to visit his grandmother's property? He is a perfectly amiable and eligible gentleman, so why not negotiate a marriage of convenience with him?*

On the other hand, she was not sure she could marry Summers after Meg planted the seed on whether he was the right man for her and there lay the problem. She knew who was the right man. At least she knew who filled her thoughts and whose kisses she enjoyed. Kevin could easily make her want to forget her resolution to marry for convenience. Unfortunately, he could not dissuade her from the notion marrying for love only led to heartbreak. The memory of her father's inconsolable grief over her mother's death was a constant reminder why she should not marry for love.

Yet, the idea of a lifetime of heartbreak if she chose the wrong man to marry added to her insecurities. She did not know what to do and until she did, she would allow herself to be carried along even if it meant she had to marry Summers. After all, there was no reason not to want to marry him, except for the doubt Meg created. Besides, Aunt Alexandra liked him. She would not be the first daughter whose parent or guardian chose her husband and negotiated the terms of her marriage. She would not be the last.

Alicia dressed in her dark blue riding habit when she finally rose from bed and broke her fast with a tray of food one of the house maids brought her. Last night, she requested the loan of a horse from Felton. She did not bother to ask Meg to join her for an early morning ride because her cousin would not want to leave her husband, nor her warm bed. She was now glad she was to ride alone for she needed to think and clear her mind of all the burdens muddling it. She always rode when she was troubled and the only thing that could further placate her would be to have Cleo at Beaumont Manor to ride. She left her beloved mare in London because she did not want to burden Felton with the feeding and stabling of her. Sir Marcus assured her the earl owned enough horses to mount any guest, so Alicia was not surprised to have her request granted.

However, she did not expect the earl to insist a groom accompany her. Her nettled features revealed her umbrage and Felton quickly explained how he could not in good conscious let her ride alone. At this time of the year, the hard as ice wintry ground posed too much of a hazard, especially if she was unseated. Alicia opened her mouth to rebut, but was stayed by Felton's raised hand and acknowledgement, "I know you are a capable rider but these are my terms, Honorable Alicia."

With no other recourse, Alicia agreed to abide by the earl's wishes.

The majority of Felton's horses were stabled at the Home Farm. He offered to have a horse brought to the manor, but Alicia declined. She liked the idea of walking through the knot garden onto the dirt path meandering its way to the Home Farm. The day was cool, but there was not a cloud in the sky and Alicia looked forward to having the crisp wind brush across her face as she galloped.

She was surprised to see Kevin holding the reins of Maximilian and another magnificent bay horse when she entered the stables. She stopped and waited for him to explain.

"I am your groom, Alicia," he informed. "I hope you do not mind. I like to ride in the morning and when Felton saw me head for the stables, he asked if I would accompany you."

The idea Kevin could ride alone each morning while she was required to take a groom vexed her, until she realized how foolish she was to begrudge her situation, especially since she enjoyed Kevin's company. Who knew when she would see him again or if she would be allowed to stay his friend? She had no idea what Summers thought about wives having male friends or if she could subdue her feelings to only think of Kevin as her friend. Perhaps she might never see him again. The idea made her frown which caused Kevin to raise his brows at her when she did not answer him. She quickly walked forward bearing an apologetic smile and explained, "I beg your pardon, I was woolgathering. Of course, I do not mind."

"I must be lacking in charm if the sight of me causes you to think of other things," he jested.

"Not, at all. If you must know, I became quite vexed at hearing you are not required to ride with a groom for your daily jaunts. Does Felton think my horsemanship skills so inadequate? The idea boils my blood."

Kevin laughed and said, "Not at all, he is just being a good host. Most likely he thought you would prefer a guide, rather than suffer a solitary ride in the bleak of winter."

"There he is wrong. I often ride alone to clear my thoughts or to shake off the gloom that wearies me."

"Are you in need, now?"

Alicia frowned, released a sigh and said, "Must we talk? I prefer to ride."

"As you wish," replied Kevin.

Alicia allowed Kevin to lift and place her on her sidesaddle. She quickly settled her right leg over the pommel, situated herself onto her seat and then placed her left foot into its stirrup. She took her time to smooth out her skirt when she felt Kevin's eyes on her. He undoubtedly recalled she wore the same unadorned navy riding habit during her father's hunt. It was a sober ensemble that allowed her to blend in with the field of riders and thereby, not draw attention to herself. She almost blushed from his obvious inspection of her, embarrassed to be wearing less than fashionable attire by *ton* standards, until she realized it was her figure and not her fashion under his gaze. Then, her cheeks did turn rosy, which made Kevin chuckle. Peaked at being the brunt for his humor, she grabbed the reins out of his hand and cast her eyes forward.

Kevin grinned at her snub and quickly pulled himself into his saddle. After a cursory look at Alicia, he heeled Maximilian to step forward. Alicia started her horse and they walked their horses in tandem, until there was room for them to ride abreast.

Alicia's excitement to ride cast off her annoyance of Kevin. She rode up beside him when the path widened and asked, "Where shall we ride?"

"Do you have a preference?"

"No, I have been here only once before when I came to Beaumont's Ball earlier this year. It was when I met Lord Atwood. He was quite smitten with my cousin and asked me to help him win Meg's hand. I obliged him only because I discovered Meg loved him and was letting her pride stand in her way of them being happy."

Kevin's jaw dropped in surprise and Alicia explained before he opined on the wonderfulness of love matches. "Oh, do not look surprised. I am not against a love match; I just have no wish to engage in one. I believe I will be much happier in a marriage focused on mutual benefit instead of emotional duress. I cannot tell you how often your Atwood vexes Meg. I shall have none of that nonsense for I will live my life and my husband will live his." Alicia took a breath. She was rambling and gotten off track. She started again, "Anyway, the three of us went on a ride I mapped out after I talked to one of Beaumont's grooms." Alicia grinned at the memory, recalling, "We raced across the east lawns and Atwood had to press his horse to keep up. We jumped a fence separating Beaumont's property from the forest bordering it. There are pastures, farm land, and a creek on the other side of the woods; and a hill where we eventually stopped to picnic. The view was quite picturesque."

"Then, you lead, Alicia," remarked Kevin, "and I will follow."

Alicia liked he trusted her to lead. She gave him a big smile and taunted, "Try and keep up for I will not wait for you."

She pressed her heel into her horse's flank and jostled the reins with a flick of her wrist to start her horse into a gallop. She was not disappointed when she loosened the restrictive reins. The mare galloped as if she had wings and Alicia reveled having the crisp cool wind blow in her face. She didn't dare turn to see her lead on Kevin, but she knew he was gaining. She could hear his horse's thundering hoofs hitting the ground as he raced behind. She traveled the same path she mapped earlier in the year and galloped across the east lawn to fly over the three foot beech wood fence dividing Beaumont's property from the neighboring forest. She pulled up her horse as soon as she cleared the fence to watch Kevin make the leap. Maximilian stretched out his body and in one fluid movement, flew over the fence. Kevin pulled up by her side and gave her a huge smile. She offered a smile in kind and proceeded to guide him through the woods.

She remembered the reverence she felt the last time she visited. Like before, the sunlight filtered through the canopy of tall silver birch and oak trees. The beams of light illuminated the floating dust motes making them look like fairies fluttering about to bless their visitors. The bluebells were gone that once carpeted the floor, but in their place were golden and crimson leaves aplenty to announce the changing season.

They kept their horses to a walk being mindful to keep the quiet peace of the forest. As soon as they came through the trees onto the open grassland, they simultaneously heeled their mounts into a gallop again to race towards the meandering stream in the valley. Once across, Kevin called for Alicia to hold up, saying they should let their horses drink and take a rest. She came back to where he dismounted and let him take her horse's reins. He led both horses to the stream and then he helped Alicia to dismount so she wouldn't tumble off her horse when her mare bent her long neck to drink.

"That was fun!" she exclaimed. "Oh, how I miss my home, but being here amid all of this glorious land lifts my spirit."

Kevin frowned and asked, "You have been unhappy?"

"I did not say I was unhappy," Alicia grumbled.

"No, only your spirit needed lifting. You confessed earlier how you like to ride to shake off the gloom that wearies you. What gloom, Alicia?"

"My papa is to marry. There is no role for me to play at home aside from an unmarried daughter in need of a husband. I am no charity case for a new step-mama to manage."

"You may marry any time you wish, Alicia. Do not think I am blind to your admirers of which Summers is one. Will you accept his offer which is sure to come?"

"I expect so," she said as she dropped her head in almost shame.

Kevin grabbed her shoulders and said, "Look at me, Alicia." She did and he said, "Marry me."

"You know I cannot," she railed.

He wrapped his arms around her and kissed her. She kissed him back and he hugged her harder, whispering, "How can you marry Summers when you kiss me like that?"

"I have never kissed Summers. How do I know I won't feel the same?"

Angered, Kevin released her and walked away to contain his temper. No matter how he plotted and planned, he was not going to break through her stubborn resolve. He kept his eyes focused on the ground to concentrate on steadying his emotions. He was angrier than he ever experienced and it came from not being in control. He knew being vulnerable is what scared Alicia. The sad truth was she didn't even realize it was too late for them. They were already invested in one another and would be destined for unhappiness, unless he could change her resolute decision to marry a man she did not love.

He would just have to trust Meg and hope her scheme of producing a rival for his affections worked. He had no other options and prayed Alicia had a jealous bone or two in her body. If not jealousy, then Kevin hoped Alicia's competitive nature would spark her to engage in the courtship game where he was the prize.

His eyes spied a rock shaped by the elements into a heart. He sentimentally picked it up and walked back to offer it to Alicia.

She asked, "What is this?"

"A token of my love, my heart belongs to you even though you won't have me."

She sat down and whimpered. Kevin knelt in front of her and scolded, "Don't! If you are miserable, then change it. Be the bold lady I saw at Tattersall's. If you don't want to marry me, then fine, but don't marry Summers simply because you feel obligated. Go with him and see his property. Meet his family if you must, but be sure you suit, Alicia. You have dreams of breeding horses. Make sure the man you marry supports your dreams."

"What will you do?"

"I don't know why you care."

"You do know."

He shook his head in disbelief and revealed, "I will be finding a piece of property and growing my stock, taking steps to make my dream a reality. I will come to London for the Season. It seems Meg has someone she wishes me to meet."

"What?!" exclaimed Alicia.

"I have needs as equal to those of Summers. I want a helpmeet and a family. Since you are not so inclined, I shall look elsewhere. As you kindly informed me when you said you had not kissed Summers, well neither have I looked for another whom I might fancy."

Alicia listened with her mouth gaping open. She could not believe he would replace her in his affections.

Kevin tapped Alicia's jaw to close her mouth and said, "Let's head back. There is a chill in the air and I am sure Summers is searching for you. I would be."

Summers House
December

Dearest Meg,

Can you ever forgive me? I never thought Aunt and Uncle would accept Lord Summers invitation to spend Christmas with his family. I expected us to return to Beaumont Manor and spend the holiday with you, but your mama agreed with his lordship that the timing was advantageous. How could I argue against meeting his parents and grandmama without sounding impolite?

I have to tell you I was dumbstruck when Summers practically jumped for joy when I told him I held no romantic notion for him and wanted a marriage of convenience. He said he was far from ready to marry and only sought a wife because of the terms of his inheritance. He loves the idea of marrying a lady who will not fuss or clamor for his attention, as if I ever would even if I loved the man.

My lord! Meg, am I engaged to be married without an offer for my hand. Summers has not even spoken with my papa. Things are moving very quickly and though I cannot say I ever wished to enter the marriage mart, I did believe I would not have to wed till then.

I expect you are having a wonderful holiday. Is Mr. Donahue still there? If so, you have my leave to tell him I am not averse to hearing from him.

Your loving cousin,
Alicia

Beaumont Manor
December

Dear Alicia,

I was quite vexed when Mama wrote to say she would not be returning to spend Christmas with me. She is most contrite and said she will make it up by purchasing me a new bonnet when I come to London. I cannot fault her as her motivation was selfless. She believes you to regard Summers above all others and since she knows you hate the Season, she is trying to help you in your endeavor to wed the man.

You never had trouble speaking your mind, so I suggest you do so before you find yourself married to a man who has no intention of breeding horses. I heard from Mr. Donahue himself Summers has no love for the care of horses. Apparently, like many of our aristocrats, he leaves the caring and stabling of his mounts to his grooms. I know you do not wish for a love match, but what about your passion of animal husbandry?

Mr. Donahue is good company as always and takes daily rides with my lord husband and Lord Felton. I informed Mr. Donahue I would enclose a note from him to you if he liked. The man was at first surprised, quite discombobulated and then downright thunderous. What happened between the two of you? Enclosed is a note which he insists is far from a billet doux.

>*Your loving cousin,*
>
>*Meg*

Beaumont Manor
December

>*Dear Alicia,*
>
>*I was surprised you were not averse to hearing from me since last in your company you refused my addresses. You were quite clear Summers was the man for you, so asking me to write you seems contrary. I do not think you know your own mind.*
>
>*While Summers is a good man, he is not the right man for you. You know who is and that man would never abide his lady corresponding with another man.*
>
>*Enjoy your visit.*
>
>*Kevin*

Summers House
December

>*Dear Meg,*
>
>*I am to have a Season after all, thanks to Uncle. He informed Lord Summers Papa was adamant all offers be approved and negotiated by him. Papa has not forgotten*

about me as I admit I feared when he sent me away. Lord Summers must wait to see him in London where we will be headed shortly after Boxing Day.

I am all asunder. I want to marry and have my own home and family, yet I don't want to marry for fear of living a life where I am not my own person. Am I to become property and not a person with thoughts and desires? How do you do it, dear Meg?

I enclosed a note for Mr. Donahue who at present has my ill favor. Can you believe he said I did not know my own mind? Well, I informed him he has no right to chastise me. I will be anxious to see what he says to that!

Pray tell, when do you return? Does Mr. Donahue return with you?

Your loving cousin,

Alicia

Summers House
December

Dear Kevin,

You have no right to scold me. I am not a child in need of guidance and I do know my own mind. I have definitely and explicitly given you a piece of it and I will continue to do so should your letters prove vexing to me.

Summers IS a good man and he is perfectly amenable to a marriage of convenience. He told me specifically he has no romantic notions about marriage, so I expect you will see me wed in the near future.

Do not ask me why I want you to write me. You know why.

And I WILL enjoy my visit.

Alicia

Beaumont Manor
December

Dear Alicia,

Mr. Donahue is to rejoin the hunt. He is wise to make connections with those who would be his customers. In addition, he will be inspecting properties for sale. He has dreams I am sure he will realize for he is persistent if nothing else. He also has stalwart supporters in both Lord Felton and my husband who are actively championing him with letters of recommendation and other means available to them to establish him with our nobility.

We shall return to our home in the north before going to London. My viscount has duties to see to before he can comfortably attend the Season, but we shall be there in time to offer you our felicitations should you accept an offer, be it Summers or someone else. I have not forgotten your question regarding a wife being chattel. There is a difference between how the law defines a wife and how a husband treats her. I caution you to choose a man who defies the law to respect his wife as his equal. A rather American thought, don't you think?

Enclosed is a sealed letter from Mr. Donahue. I have no idea what he wrote, but I am witness to the smug smile he gave when he handed me his letter to mail to you.

Your loving cousin,

Meg

Beaumont Manor
December

Dear Alicia,

You are quite right. I should not have scolded you and I shall abide by your wishes. I will write to you until that day you accept Summers or any gentleman's marriage proposal.

The same applies to me. I shall gladly correspond with you until the day I decide to marry. I expect the lady I wed will not tolerate any exchange of letters between you and me. Unlike Summers, I am sure she will have a slew of romantic notions about marriage.

Kevin

Chapter Fourteen

Mayfair, London
May

Three crystal candelabras, holding a hundred candles each, hung from the ceiling to illuminate the Weathersfield's expansive ballroom. A plethora of flowers displayed in white clay urns atop white Corinthian pillars stood at intervals along the walls with swags of white gossamer hanging between them.

Ladies sparkled in gem and beaded encrusted flounced ball gowns, while lords of the realm, stood among them in their black and white formal attire. Some debutantes waved their fans to summon their suitors, while others dropped their chins demurely to attract them. All of them actively flirted with a tutored artistry.

Alicia stood among the crème of society looking the height of fashion in a high-waist white lace dress lined with a white satin slip. Her deep cut bodice and its sides were covered in pink satin, shaping and accentuating her femininely endowment. Her slender arms extended from short puffed sleeves; elegantly embroidered with flowers and finished with pink bows. From her bodice hung a deeply flounced skirt of white lace trimmed with three narrow rows of satin strip rounding the skirt. White satin floral wreaths decorated the top strip. White satin embroidered slippers, long white gloves, a pearl necklace, and flowers in her coifed hair finished her ensemble.

The scene before her was like every other ball she had attended and she almost cringed. While she enjoyed conversing with men and women alike, she never understood the silliness erupting whenever those two sexes were brought together for the Season. She was tired of the crowds and the pretensions, but the Season was far from over.

Invitations abounded and her aunt and uncle seemed to accept every one of them. The notion was impossible since many events were held on the same day at the same time. Never the less, her aunt was determined to introduce her to every eligible gentleman in England, regardless of the misconception, she favored Lord Summers above all others.

The Season had opened with Parliament. There were breakfasts, soirées, balls and other amusements, like the opera to attend. Alicia was plumb worn out. In addition to formal events, there were varied other appointments, from shopping to making house calls, that took up her time. She missed the country and the Deneham stables. She knew once her father remarried the stables would be filled again and his business prospering, but it saddened her to know she would not be a part of it.

She had thought a marriage of convenience would satisfy her. After all, those types of marriages were negotiated for mutual benefit and what could be more beneficial than giving herself as hostess, wife, and mother to an amiable man, in order to realize her own dream of breeding horses. It was the way of the *ton* to marry for title, property, and wealth. She might be low on the ranks of the aristocracy, but she was most assuredly blue blooded and dowered enough to contract for what she wanted in a marriage.

Unfortunately, the man she thought would help her realize her dream was quickly proving her wrong. Lord Summers had been all conciliatory and good company during her father's hunt and seemed to admire her horse riding and equine acumen. Never was there a hint he thought her inferior to him in mind or body, but ever since they came to Town, she found herself under his censure and protection. She was rarely asked for her opinion and when she asserted herself, she felt condescended. *A novel idea? When had anything she ever opined been anything but well-considered and voiced?* She was turning into someone she did not recognize. She constantly found herself refraining from offering insight or opinion when in the company of Lord Summers. He was far from a brute, but his patronizing manner made her want to slap him across the face. She could not even walk away from his self-righteousness without causing the gossipmongers to wag their tongues. The man acted as if he had authority over her and since she did nothing to disabuse him of the notion, others were beginning to accept he did.

The Season was far from anything she ever desired. She did not care for the scrutiny or the regulations governing debutantes. She always felt herself capable, equal to any lord or lady of the realm, but this past month her self-assurance dwindled. Presented as a debutante in the market for a husband was quite different from being introduced as her father's daughter, the mistress of his manor where she was in command of herself and household. As a debutante her behavior and movements were observed and any misstep remarked upon. She suffered more than once from a matron's reprimand regarding what befitted a lady and laughing out loud was far from acceptable. She wanted to go home where she felt safe and loved, but then she realized she no longer had a home.

"He's not here," remarked Meg.

Alicia shook off her homesickness and the thoughts clouding her mind into forgetting the ball where she stood with Meg. She gave her cousin a quizzical look even though she knew exactly to whom her cousin referred. As of late, the only person she frequently asked Meg about was Mr. Donahue. Even so, she had no interest to be teased or prodded by Meg about her feelings for the man who constantly occupied her thoughts. Speaking in a nonchalant manner, worthy of any actress who wished to portray herself indifferent, she asked, "Who is not here?"

Meg rolled her eyes to the ceiling.

Absence makes the heart grow fonder, indeed! Her admiration and affection for Kevin had grown leaps and bounds since she last saw him. She missed him enormously. She missed his company, his conversation, his wit, his competitiveness, and his kisses, which surprisingly, drove her to act counter to what her heart wanted.

Driven from fear of falling deeper in love with Kevin or out of sheer stupidity, she responded by flirting with Summers. Once again, she acted like a coy debutante wanting to bring a suitor up to scratch. She smiled adoringly at him and cooed compliments upon him. At first, Summers was skeptical of her ardent attention. After all, Alicia had confessed she did not love him, but when his peers began to compliment him on his good fortune, he believed her feelings towards him had changed. He liked how Alicia's attentions raised his cachet and so he began to treat her with all the authority he was due as the man she would someday wed. Confident he had won his prize he was determined to protect it.

In the beginning of their courtship, Alicia found no fault in Summers' manners. He was attentive and considerate. He offered his arm when she needed an escort and was quick to grant her any request. But now, instead of Summers being solicitous of her needs, she found herself being controlled by him. She was not asked if she was cold, but ordered to wear a wrap. She was not asked if she was tired, but told to take a chair. Then, to add to her annoyance were the approving nods directed at Summers by his peers whenever he pressed his authority over her. More than once she had to bite her bottom lip to keep from telling the overbearing man a thing or two. Instead, she kept her opinions to herself, behaving as society expected a debutante to act. She could blame no one but herself for the folly she was in. Blaming Summers for acting as someone who had the right to command her was no fault but her own.

"Mr. Donahue is not here, yet," stated Meg again when Alicia failed to respond.

It took Alicia a moment to comprehend Meg's "yet," but when she did, she demanded, "What do you mean 'yet?'"

"Lawrence has been in his company, Alicia, and my husband told me Mr. Donahue would be attending tonight's ball. Of course, he most likely would have informed me of his plans if I asked him at Lady Billingstone's soirée."

Alicia's eyes widened. "You saw him at Billingstone's soirée? Why did you not tell me?"

"You were not at home when I called the next day, and then I simply forgot. Was it important?"

Alicia steeled her eyes at Meg's innocent look. "Was he alone?"

Meg laughed. "Not for long. A handsome and charming man like himself is never alone for long."

"Who invited him?"

"The countess invited him, of course."

"Not on her own, surely. How did she even know of his existence?"

"Well, Anne might have encouraged the invitation, but you must not diminish his good character and charm. He made many friends among some of our highest sticklers during the hunts he attended. His horse acumen drew a number of our lords to his side and invitations to their dining tables. He is highly admired and many have come to call him a friend. Your own Lord Summers is one as you know. I expect this is hardly news considering all the letters you both wrote to one another."

Alicia grinned. It was true Kevin wrote to her faithfully, but his letters, aside from the one speaking of his dream, were all about the hunts, the horses, the properties he inspected. Not one romantic word was shared, unless you consider their love of horses. It was extraordinary, how the description of a horse or how well it performed, made her feel singularly connected with him.

She could easily admit she and Kevin were a perfect match. They both had the same aspirations and values. She never doubted he would respect her, value her, protect her, care for her, and love her as she would him, if she wasn't petrified to trust in a forever after.

She enjoyed every letter he wrote and felt as excited as him when he purchased a thoroughbred or gained the support of a peer. He was being asked to join all types of clubs and she knew before long, he would establish himself among the aristocracy as a man with integrity owning a superior knowledge of horses. She did not doubt he would realize his dream and while she wished it was still her own, she took great pleasure in sharing his successes. She admittedly fell in love with him the first time she gave her opinion and he wrote back with his gratitude. Never before had she felt of one mind with another person or so special. It became natural for her to continue to offer her insight and thoughts as he shared his plans. It was as if they were partners and she reveled in the notion, even if it was a false one.

"Anne plans to make a match with him and Lady Billingstone's daughter Priscilla," stated Meg.

"Why ever for?"

"He is looking for a wife? I thought you knew."

"*Yes. I knew,*" she thought, "*but the reality of him searching for one, while I am still single seems incomprehensible.*" Alicia felt her stomach tighten and was ready to excuse herself when Lady Priscilla entered the ballroom on the arm of Kevin. She looked stunningly beautiful in her white satin slip dress overlaid with a sheer net skirt deeply flounced with blond lace and satin bows at each peak. The high-waist gown was also trimmed with matching lace and ribbon around the deep neckline of her bodice and the border of her puffed sleeves. The lady looked like a fashion plate, especially as she took a pose when she entered the ballroom prompting her suitors to sigh in appreciation. However, Alicia only had eyes for

Kevin. He looked amazingly fit and handsome in his formal black tailcoat and trousers, a white linen shirt, a white waistcoat embroidered with silver thread and a crisp white elegantly tied cravat. His overall appearance distinguished him among his peers as beau monde.

He held her enthralled as she watched him escort Priscilla to a group of friends where the lady began to make introductions. Alicia might have continued gaping at her American friend if Meg did not jab her with her fan.

"What?!" Alicia almost shouted.

Meg rolled her eyes again and said, "Close your mouth, dear cousin, and be prepared to greet your Lord Summers."

"Oh," responded Alicia, blushing at her juvenile gawking. She barely had to time to collect herself, before Summers took his bow and offered his felicitations and compliments on her dress.

"Thank you, my lord." Alicia dipped a curtsey and rose. She opened her laced fan to cover the blush she knew she sported from gawking at Kevin. Summers grinned and Alicia surmised he attributed the blush to his compliment.

"You have saved the first dance for me I hope, Honorable Alicia?" asked Summers.

"Of course, my lord, it is your wish to always do so, is it not?"

"Always, shall we take the floor?"

Alicia looked at Meg and then returned her focus to Summers and said, "I would not leave Meg alone, my lord."

"Nonsense, Alicia," offered Meg. "Take your dance. I shall seek out mama and stay with her until my lord husband finds me."

Summers smiled at Meg and offered his arm to Alicia who took it obediently.

"Come join us," called Meg to Alicia and Summers. It was the supper hour. Card tables and other dining furniture were set up among a number of formal rooms to accommodate the guests who looked for a respite before the orchestra returned from its break and the dancing began again. Alicia entered the room with Summers and his friend Lord Marlabout. Before she could suggest they sit somewhere else, Summers pulled her towards the table where Meg and her husband, Lord Atwood, sat, along with Mr. Donahue and Lady Priscilla.

The last thing Alicia wanted to do was watch Kevin and Priscilla flirt with one another. She was hurt Kevin did not ask her to save him a dance, especially when she saw how he danced with Priscilla and all her friends, nor did he take the time to greet her. He remained part of Priscilla's court, never leaving her side unless to dance with one of her friends, and now it seemed he won the honor of taking Priscilla to supper. Alicia did not want to dine with them even though Meg sat at their table, so to discourage Summers from accepting their invitation, she whispered, "There is no room for Lord Marlabout, my lord."

"Nonsense, we will squeeze the fellow in," he replied and turned to look at Marlabout before adding with a chuckle, "You shall manage, Marlabout. You are not too thick, yet."

Introductions were made and then an awkward pause lingered causing everyone to look at each other. Meg did not falter to break the silence by asking Priscilla in jest, "Did you find you needed your muff today, Lady Priscilla?"

Priscilla grinned at the outrageous query made to make her laugh and to bring some humor to their sober group. She replied in kind to the impromptu farce and said, "Dear me, no. I did not even chance being caught outdoors where a gale might ruin by best hat, much less my favored fur muff."

Alicia grinned. She knew Priscilla since they were children. She was no simpering miss and would see a gale as an adventure. Priscilla was teasing and Alicia was about to laugh at her friend's effort to lighten the mood until she saw Summers nod in agreement.

"You were right to stay indoors this morning, my lady," agreed Summers. "The winds were quite forceful. Luckily, they diminished or I would have sent our regrets for tonight's ball. I would not put Honorable Alicia in danger."

Alicia saw Kevin raise his eyebrows at her and felt everyone else's disbelief. They knew her too well to believe a little thing like inclement weather would ever keep her indoors. For heaven's sake, Summers knew she rode with the hounds and could ride and jump better than most. Perhaps that was the problem. Everyone knew the Honorable Alicia spoke her mind and was a jolly good horsewoman. For a lady, both traits were frowned upon by the *ton's* highest sticklers and she wondered, *Is Summers regretting his courtship of me? Does he think he can change me with his censure?*

Kevin quickly interrupted her thoughts when he said, "I found the windy weather delightful this morning when I took Maximilian out for a ride. It was quite refreshing. I plan to go for a morning gallop tomorrow in Hyde Park. Perhaps, I could entice one of you to join me."

"You will not find Honorable Alicia galloping in Hyde Park," reproved Summers.

Alicia felt her face crimson from embarrassment, especially when she saw Lord Marlabout nod in agreement to Summers' dictate. Of course, Summers was right. Ladies did not gallop. His outburst was his gentlemanly way of protecting her, but she did not feel protected. She felt smothered and controlled. She did not like the feeling and desperately needed a breath of fresh air. She did not want to draw attention to herself, but she was more than ready to take her leave. She pushed her chair back to rise, but was stayed by Meg's hand on her arm.

"Of course, Lord Summers," remarked Meg. "No lady at this ball would consider an early gallop tomorrow. Dear me, I expect none of us to seek our beds till three or four o'clock this morning. Besides, you gentlemen should be making house calls tomorrow and paying your respects to all the ladies you danced with this evening." Meg looked pointedly at Summers while she said, "It is another of society's dictates, my lord, which I am sure you do not need reminded. I suggest the day after and Richmond Park as our destination. It is less crowded there and we can give our horses free rein. Now, who will join my little party?"

"I am afraid I am already engaged Lady Atwood. Perhaps, another time," replied Summers grimly.

"Well, I am not engaged and would love a good gallop in Richmond Park," said Alicia.

"Count me in," added Priscilla.

"What about you Donahue? Marlabout?" asked Lawrence.

"Oh, I am definitely coming," stated Kevin with a gleam in his eyes.

Everyone turned to Marlabout. Lawrence spoke directly to him when he failed to give his answer and said, "We will be an odd numbered party without you, Marlabout."

Marlabout flattened his lips when he saw a grim-faced Summers. He was the sort who would easily accept a jaunt to Richmond Park, but he had no wish to offend his friend, so with regret he turned down the invitation. His response earned him a smile from Summers whose mood immediately improved upon Marlabout's reply.

Summers turned his attention from his friend to Alicia. He showered her with an affable countenance and offered in recompense, "I would not wish you to be unaccompanied Honorable Alicia. Perhaps, I may call on you after I finish my business. I would be happy to take you up in my phaeton to Hyde Park during the social hour."

"You are most considerate, my lord," stated Alicia, quickly adding to disabuse Summers she was accepting when he began to smile, "but it is unnecessary. I am sure my cousin Charles will accompany me to complete our party."

"As you wish," replied Summers whose soft features turned hard when he frowned.

Chapter Fifteen

Richmond Park, London
May

Viscount Atwood and his countess led their small party through the brick pillared Richmond Park Gate. They rode two across in tandem following proper precedence and made quite an imperious display sitting on their horses with their backs straight, their shoulders back, and their chins slightly lifted. They walked their horses forward on the dirt path worn down and rutted from frequent traffic and would have drawn approval by the highest sticklers if they were riding along Rotten Row in Hyde Park. The men looked distinguished in their tall black beaver hats and multi-caped greatcoats pushed back at their thighs to reveal muscular legs encased in fitted buckskin breeches and glossy black riding boots.

The ladies sparkled like rare gems in their bright tailored riding habits. Meg's rich dark hair gleamed against the stunning pea green finely woven Merino jacket she wore. The collar and cuffs were trimmed in mink and black braided frog fastenings ran down the front of her coat, a testament to her wealth and position. Priscilla matched Meg in couture. She wore a crimson tailored Merino riding coat. The rich red color brightened her golden locks and the design owned all the pomp and circumstance of a French Hussar Guard. Gold tasseled epaulets decorated her shoulders, fancy gold braiding adorned her cuffs, and gold frog fastenings closed her coat. Alicia, not to be outdone by her betters in style if not in expense, displayed her trim figure to advantage in her favorite cobalt blue riding habit. Also made of Merino wool, the jacket's lapels and cuffs were decorated with silver embroidery. Sterling silver buttons adorned the front of her coat with small silver buttons on her cuffs.

A hussar-style hat decorated with a tall peacock plume topped off Priscilla's and Meg's ensemble, while Alicia sported a crowned hat adorned with a spray of feathers on her luxuriant soft brown coils.

Lady Priscilla outranked the Honorable Alicia and Charles, so she and Kevin followed second in line with Alicia and Charles taking up the rear. Alicia did not mind being cast to the tail of their group for she did not desire to be under Kevin's scrutiny; though by the likes of his tête-á-tête with Priscilla, she doubted he gave her any thought.

Today's disregard of her was contrary to yesterday's visit where he had showed her remarkable attention. It was a gentleman's code of conduct to call or send flowers the day after a ball to any lady of which a gentleman danced or paid particular notice. Many men, unless they feared a parson's noose, brought the flowers themselves and paid the requisite fifteen minute call; especially if they wanted to further the lady's acquaintance, so Kevin's day-after visit had surprised her.

After all, he had not danced with her or paid her any particular attention at the Weatherfield's ball, aside from the judgmental raising of his brows during supper. She could argue he had intentionally ignored her, but instead of being angry at him, her curiosity moved her to rise from her seat and welcome him. She thanked him for the flowers he held out to her and offered him a seat near her aunt.

Kevin made his bow to Alexandra and received a wide grin for his gesture. He took the seat offered by Alicia and began on a hearty discourse, speaking much like a long-lost relative who needed to update his family expediently on all the news, most of which Alicia already knew about from the letters he had written to her. After his disclosure, he asked Alicia of her Season, what engagements she had accepted, and about her beaus, remarking, "I am surprised Summers is not here to pay court to you."

"He was reminded of a boxing bout he scheduled with his friend," explained Alicia. "I am sure he will call on me later."

Kevin grinned, partly because he was responsible for the boxing bout keeping Summers from Alicia's side and partly because he liked to ruffle her fine feathers. She was easy to rile and he liked her fighting spirit versus the submissive nature she displayed at the ball. He was working hard to interrupt Summers' courtship of her and it was costing him some of his hard-earned cash. He was amazed how easy it was to pay an acquaintance to keep Summers engaged with a myriad of activities.

"I would have sent my regrets to my friend rather than disappoint you," remarked Kevin. He did not mean to reveal his displeasure, but the honest response came out of his mouth before he could stop himself. While he was glad his machinations to thwart Summers' courtship with Alicia were working, it also riled him the man could set aside the woman he meant to marry so easily.

The slur on Summers made Alicia quickly come to his defense. She rebutted rather vehemently, "I am not disappointed!"

Kevin grinned and said, "Good. I am glad Summers absence does not bother you, for neither will he be present at tomorrow's ride to Richmond. Be assured, I shall not disappoint you for I will be there."

His response had puzzled her until his lips turned up in a grin. The confounded man had cleverly reminded her how she favored his company over Summer's. However, she was quickly realizing, as she spied Kevin and Priscilla riding before her, it was Kevin's singular company and not him with Priscilla that she preferred.

Alicia nudged her mare to catch up to Charles when Cleo shook her head and blew out from her nose.

Her thoughts had distracted her into falling behind her party and her wise horse had remarked upon it, since no one from her group had noticed.

Ugh! Alicia rolled her eyes at the flagrant courting before her. *Priscilla is so obvious.* She could not believe Kevin kept falling for Priscilla's flirtatious ploy of leaning her body towards him whenever their horses drew apart. Priscilla's action had Kevin steering Maximilian back to her side where they practically brushed legs while they rode. Alicia knew it was all a ruse because she could hold a conversation with Charles and he rode more than a foot away from her.

Hearing Priscilla giggle again to another of Kevin's comments caused Alicia to silently rant, *No man is that witty.* The constant amorous scene was too much for Alicia to bear and the next time Priscilla leaned over, Alicia let her mind imagine Priscilla falling from her saddle to unseat not only herself, but Kevin. The notion of them smarting on the ground made Alicia smile until Priscilla giggled again.

Alicia knew Priscilla was expert in the art of flirtation and had honed her laughter to sound light and airy. The lyrical sound was dainty and pleasing. She wondered if Charles was also delighted by Priscilla's melodic giggles. While she could do nothing to erase the stupid grin she spied Kevin wearing, she most definitely could banish Charles' mooncalf expression with a severe look if he had one. She turned ready to admonish him with her eyes until she saw his somber expression. Her ill humor was immediately replaced with concern and she asked, "Are you well, Charles?"

Charles abruptly turned and gave Alicia a look as if she insulted him. He retaliated by saying, "Are you, Cousin?"

She would have laughed at his glowering face except she knew it would not help. He was distraught and she was determined to learn the reason for it. She replied, "I am, but you look as though you lost your best friend. Do you still call Lord Harry your friend?"

"Not exactly," confessed Charles, his downtrodden expression returning.

"Spill, Cousin. It will do you good to vent your spleen."

"Well, you know how we got along famously while he convalesced from his hunting injury at Deneham Manor, but now he is back on his feet and has returned to his life as a gentleman, a lifestyle far above my touch. He spends his time at his clubs with peers who have deep pockets. He did invite me to be his guest, but these fellows bet on every frivolous thing you can think. I am smart enough not to join in, but it makes me a dull sort in their eyes and not good company."

"I am sorry, Charles. What of your dandies?"

"Well, they are no better. They have all been called home to rusticate once their fathers learned of their gambling debts. I doubt I will see them this Season."

"Then you are feeling at sea. Why have you not come to keep me company?"

"You would have been hard-pressed to find time for me with all your social events."

"True, but like you, I am also at sea. Besides, I would rather spend time with you where I can be myself than attend another *ton* event."

"You are not yourself?"

"No, Charles. I am a debutante which is far from being me than anything. I don't remember ever having to watch my tongue or manner as I now do. I would rather be with family by my side, than without in the marriage mart."

"I would be happy to keep you company, Alicia."

"Thank you, Charles. Tell me, have you heard from my papa?"

"Not really, he has been good to send my allowance, but no other word. And you?"

"Nothing, so it seems I have a short reprieve before I must marry Summers."

"You have no wish to do so?"

"I am beginning to fear we do not suit, but I do not think I can back out without ruin. I would be marked a tease or worse, a man-hater, that female who relishes in breaking a man's heart. I cannot deny I have given Summers every reason to believe I will accept his suit."

"Nonsense, no offer was made. You are not betrothed."

"We shall see." Alicia saw an open field. She was tired of watching Priscilla and Kevin. Her mean-spirited thoughts no longer amused her and she was ready to break free of the group's tiring walk. She asked Charles, "Want to race me to the other end of the green?"

Charles grinned and with lightning speed, they broke from their group and gave their mounts a heel and a shout.

Kevin took a peripheral glance at Alicia whenever he turned to look at Priscilla. He hated being on stage to perform the ruse of courting Priscilla, but by the likes of Alicia's scowls the scheme was working. He couldn't help but grin and find amusement in how his happy expression vexed his termagant.

He felt Alicia's glares like darts poking his backside every time Priscilla leaned towards him to coax him closer to her side. He never would have thought Alicia had a jealous bone in her body, but he was very glad she did.

Priscilla was a born actress or just an experienced flirt. He would have worried of playing the lady false if he was not assured she was in on the scheme to make Alicia jealous. The lively debutante was full of topics or tales to keep up a healthy discourse and while she looked quite happy to play her role, he was growing weary of the nonsensical banter. He wished for the ordeal to end. Then in answer to his silent prayer, Alicia and Charles broke from their line and spurred their mounts into a gallop.

He did not even need to ask Priscilla if she wished to follow. The lady was one step ahead of him. Kevin quickly pulled his reins to turn Maximilian and then spurred his horse to chase after the rebels. He heard Lawrence and Meg laugh when they brought their own mounts to chase after their truant party.

Alicia and Charles were the first to rein in their horses to a walk after galloping across the open range. Richmond Park was far from cultivated. Aside from the trees planted to line the Queen's Ride, (the avenue leading to White Lodge from Richmond Lodge and once Queen Caroline's private road), and a number of other trees to border the other manors within the park wall, everything in the park grew naturally and wild. The park's expansive landscape consisted of wide open green pastures, groves of thick trees, and ponds fed by natural springs. The feral land offered a number of stunning views for artists to capture on canvas and plenty of room for the avid horseman to gallop at leisure without censure from the *ton's* highest sticklers.

They rode in earnest. Their horses' nostrils were flaring and their bellies heaving by the time they pulled their mounts up to a stop. Alicia, a keen observer to a horse's distraught, asked her group, "Shall we rest here?"

"Keep your seat, Honorable Alicia," commanded Viscount Atwood. "We will keep our mounts to a sedate walk as to not distress them, but I have a better spot for us to take our rest."

Lawrence led the way but suffered numerous taunts when he would not tell them their destination. Priscilla remarked they were going in circles, while Kevin glibly commented how Lawrence was leading them all in a merry dance. Lawrence ignored them for his reward soon came when they saw he arranged a picnic for them.

Lord Atwood's servants followed the map he made with instructions to arrive before him with a cart full of rugs and pillows. They were commanded to set up a cozy repast near a grove of trees which offered shade and a picturesque view for his party.

His servants brought a number of baskets filled with apples, cheeses, breads, nuts, and a number of tarts, both of the meat and fruit variety, to set upon the rugs before retreating to the cart that brought them. They watched over their master's and guests' horses until it was time for them to retrieve the items they brought and return to the viscount's town home.

"Oh, well done, my lord," laughed Priscilla when she spied the picnic. "I beg your pardon for ever doubting you knew where you were going."

"As you should, Priscilla, my lord husband always knows what he is about," chastised Meg.

"I still think you led us on a merry dance, Atwood," commented Kevin. "I am sure there was a faster way to get here."

Lawrence grinned. "Well, I was not the one who led us off into a gallop in the opposite direction."

Everyone laughed, except Alicia who gave Lawrence a stern eye for making her the brunt of his remark.

Lawrence played the common host and invited everyone to take a seat on the rug and to use the pillows placed haphazardly. He tried to preserve the rustic manner of a picnic, but his blue and white liveried servants, standing in the background waiting to serve, contradicted him. He offered wine and lemonade to each of his guests and then opened the baskets to display what was brought for them to eat. Kevin suggested Meg do the serving honors, but quickly changed his mind when Meg scolded him for insinuating her lord husband was incapable of the job. Her chastise caused Kevin to laugh and raise his hands in defeat. Lawrence grinned at having his lady wife play knight to protect his honor.

They all watched and remarked on the portions Lawrence arranged on each plate. Priscilla tittered she was incapable of eating the gigantic serving, no doubt meant for two, and suggested she share the plate with Kevin. Alicia bit her bottom lip to keep from suggesting Priscilla ask for a smaller serving.

Chapter Sixteen

Meg grinned at Alicia and then gave a nod towards the interplay between Kevin and Priscilla. It was an *I told you so* kind of gesture and Alicia did not like it. She did not like Meg promoting a match between Kevin and Priscilla, even if she had refused Kevin's offer of marriage.

The couple's ardent overtures provoked Alicia into mocking Priscilla's voice in her head. *You must simply try this cheese, Mr. Donahue.* Alicia could not believe Kevin could be enticed by such overt coquetry and almost gagged when Priscilla took a bite of her pasty and boldly licked her lips, letting loose a sigh of delight as she savored the morsel. She wanted to knock Kevin on the side of his head when his jaw dropped in wonder. He must have read her mind for he quickly shut his mouth and gave her a big grin. *The cad!*

Alicia watched them with the same anxiousness she often experienced when reading one of Ann Radcliffe's gothic novels. Her nerves were strung tight and her heartbeat quickened. She almost snapped when Priscilla reached across to wipe the berry juice dribbling from the side of Kevin's mouth. *The sheer audacity of her!* Alicia could not believe Priscilla blatantly ignored the manners that behooved a lady.

Affronted, Alicia turned to look at Meg. She expected her cousin to reproach Priscilla. After all, as the matron of the party, Meg was the group's chaperone. Unfortunately, Meg was consulting with her own husband and had not witnessed Priscilla's scandalous display. Alicia returned her watch upon the couple. Her eyes widened at seeing Priscilla beam at Kevin. *What did I miss? Why is she so happy?* Her heart pounded, keeping all her emotions pent-up. She was not sure how much longer she could watch the intricacies of Priscilla's and Kevin's burgeoning romance without venting her temper, so she was relieved when the remnants of their meal were put into the baskets from which they came and Lawrence called forth his servants to retrieve them.

She thought they would now return to London, but to her annoyance, it seemed the men were in no state to ride. Vociferously, they informed, almost as if they had a previous agreement, how they needed repose after their feast and before any lady could object, they removed their tall hats to stretch out onto the blankets cleared of litter. Alicia wished she could follow suit, but since Priscilla kept a proper seat she had no choice but to stay seated with her back straight and her legs discreetly bent and covered to her side.

Lawrence stretched out his body on the rug and placed his head in his wife's lap for her to run her fingers through his hair. Kevin reclined on his side near Priscilla and held his head on the pedestal made from his bent arm and hand in order to give his full attention to the lady he wooed. Charles lay flat on his stomach with his head turned to his side to rest on his bent arm, almost in slumber. The sight of her cousin at rest reminded Alicia of their many rides to the creek near her home and how they often fell asleep on the grassy bank after finishing the food they brought with them.

Alicia put her head back to look up at the swaying branches to reason out the faux sound of rushing water made by the rustling leaves. She saw sunlight dance from one spot to another as a slight breeze swayed the full branches to and fro to redirect the sunlight. The rushing sound and light show lulled her. She closed her eyes to the warmth penetrating the tree branches and began to fall into slumber, until the pillow supporting her back moved and caused her to tumble.

Embarrassed by her clumsiness, she quickly resettled herself on the rug and looked upon the open range. She did not want to see if anyone saw her mishap, nor did she wish to see if Kevin and Priscilla were enjoying more amorous play. A number of sheep and cattle grazed on the wild green grass and showed their content with an occasional baa and moo. She knew the stock came from the ranger's farm and were allowed to wander unrestricted to feed. Beyond them grazed a group of red deer. Some of the fawns had their legs folded beneath them to nestle in the tall blades of green grass. The scene reminded Alicia of a lovely painting she once viewed and she heard her own thoughts voiced by Kevin, "This is a lovely park."

She was not alone admiring the landscape and upon his remark, she turned to look at the man who seemed to match her in thought and heart more than any man she knew. It pleased her to see he was now sitting up from his lounge and seated a respectable distance from Priscilla. He must have read her thoughts or maybe he was simply returning the grin she unconsciously wore at seeing him apart from Priscilla. The idea he thought her jealous made Alicia immediately frown. The man had enough female affirmation to know he was handsome and charming. He did not need to think she was another admirer. Yet, she could not deny she missed spending time with him, and aside from her father and Charles, she knew no other man she could say that about, not even Summers.

"It is pleasingly rustic," Priscilla added. "Most of our peers like the park because it is private, unlike Hyde Park where every action is noted, discussed, and placed in the rumor mill to become the *ton's* latest *on dit*. We could not have indulged in our comfortable repose without censure there. Does America have similar parks, Mr. Donahue?"

"America itself is a wilderness, my lady. There is much uncharted land and much of what is inhabited is untamed." Kevin grinned and added, "It must be the reason why the park feels like home."

Alicia watched Priscilla ask Kevin about his family and where he lived. She was amazed to learn the Donahue farm came from a royal land grant given in 1670 through his maternal side of his family. She was also a little angry he had not confided the information to her first. Ridiculously, she felt injured and a pang of sorrow overwhelmed her at not being the person with whom he shared the revelation.

"Osborne, you say, Mr. Donahue?" asked Priscilla.

"Yes," he replied. "That is my grandmother's maiden name."

"You may be connected to one of our noblest families," she remarked. "George Osborne is the Duke of Leeds."

"I hardly think I am any relation to him. I am sure my grandmother would have told me."

"She might not have known. Most of us nobles are related one way or another to each other. What a lark if you have a title and a piece of property waiting for you to claim. The *marriage mart mamas* will quickly wish to ensnare you for their daughters."

Lawrence laughed and said, "It happened to me, so it is not as impossible as it sounds."

"I hope you will not spread any speculation regarding such a notion, Lady Priscilla," stated Kevin firmly. "I would only disappoint anyone believing it to be true."

Kevin's response made Priscilla laugh, while Alicia bellowed an "Ow!" Her alarming shout caused Meg and

Priscilla to reflexively shiver and scream. The men jumped to their feet and assumed a defensive stand looking for the prevailing threat.

"Damn!" cursed Alicia in anger drawing everyone's attention to her again. She removed her hat and grimaced when she saw one of her feathers broken. Her eyes immediately sought out the cause. Up in the tree branch stood a wide-eyed squirrel chattering away and shaking his fists at her as if she was at fault for the acorn pelting and ruining her hat. She shook her fist back at the squirrel and yelled, "You wretched varmint!"

Her outburst brought a number of chuckles from her company, but before she could utter a word of rebuke, Meg screamed when an acorn hit her. Priscilla was the squirrel's next victim, her screech prompting everyone to run. The men laughed while ushering their ladies away from the rodent's throwing range.

Gathered at a safe distance, Priscilla severely remonstrated Alicia, "He would not have reacted so violently if you had not shouted at him!"

Alicia glared at Priscilla. Kevin laughed again. Before Alicia could utter a scathing remark to Priscilla, Kevin tucked her hand into the joint of his arm. He kept her hand securely pressed against his side, and escorted her to a distance where their conversation could not be overheard or their features discerned.

"The wretched varmint deserved nothing less," remarked Kevin with a grin.

Alicia glared at him and then laughed.

"That is better," Kevin said. "I was starting to worry over your silence. I have not known you to be so reserved. I am glad the squirrel woke you from your reticence."

Alicia bristled and responded curtly, "I had no wish to interrupt your intimate interplay with Lady Priscilla. You both seemed enthralled with each other."

Kevin laughed and asked, "Enthralled? I think there is a burr under your saddle. Tell me, what have I done to deserve your anger?"

Alicia pouted her lower lip and then bit it when she realized she was about to whine her response. She took a cleansing breath and asked in a higher octave than she wished, "Why did you never tell me your mama's family came from England?"

Kevin's brows raised in surprise. He answered, "I guess it never came up. It is not a secret, nor is it of significance to which I feel the need to profess it to everyone I meet. Is it important to you? Are you hoping I am a lost heir? I assure you I am not."

"It is not your connections that are important to me, Mr. Donahue," stated Alicia with fervor, "It is your character."

"Ah," he released in a breath and then his lips pressed into almost a grin when he asked, "And does my character meet with your approval, Honorable Alicia?"

Alicia wanted to cry. *When did my life become so complicated?* She had no wish to tell Kevin she liked him, more than liked him, but she knew she could not lie. Before he could prod her to answer to whether his character met with her approval, her temper flared again when she saw the corners of his pressed lips turn up in a smile. "You very well know it does," she replied curtly, *and therein lies the problem,* she thought while turning and making her way back to the rest of the party.

She was annoyed she had to accept Kevin's assistance to mount her horse since everyone was already seated. She worried her tattered emotions were there for all to see, especially Kevin. It bothered her he knew she liked him more than a friend. Over the years, she had formed many male friendships, but she never cared who they admired or loved and she certainly never worried of their opinion of her. She had been quite content in her life, but now it seemed she was destined for heartbreak no matter how hard she worked to evade it.

Mounted, everyone quickly moved their horses to fall into the line of proper rank. She had to keep herself from galloping off when she realized she once again rode behind Kevin and Priscilla and would have to endure watching their flirtatious play. She was angry, especially at the notion she was jealous of Priscilla. Unconsciously, she tightened her grip on her reins and Cleo whinnied at having the bit pull her mouth. Cleo's distress drew Kevin's and Meg's attention to Alicia. They knew it was unlike her to cause her horse distress and she was mortified they might ask her what was wrong. Thankfully, Priscilla's announcement distracted them.

"Well, Honorable Alicia and Mr. Donahue, while you were away, we agreed to an early morning ride in

Hyde Park tomorrow and then to attend Lady Hummingsburgh's musicale in the evening. My mama volunteered me to play a sonata. I hope I may persuade the both of you to attend, as well. Perhaps, Mr. Donahue will agree to turn my music pages and the rest of you will offer me some undeserving applause when I am done." Priscilla laughed. Alicia knew Priscilla was a superior pianist, so the lady's request was made in jest.

"So, what do you say?" inquired Priscilla. "Will you both join us for tomorrow's ride and attend the musicale? And of course, Honorable Alicia, you must extend the invitation to Lord Summers."

Unable to refuse without looking churlish, they both agreed. Kevin even promised to turn the lady's music pages much to Alicia's displeasure.

Kevin regretted seeing Alicia sad. Unless he misread the signs, his termagant did not like him admiring Priscilla, much less, courting her. He only hoped it was because she wanted him for herself and not because she thought him too common for her friend. Now, that was an idea he never considered. *Am I too common for Alicia?*

He grinned when he realized he didn't care. If Alicia wanted nobility she could marry Summers. Kevin instinctively knew his bloodline was unimportant to Alicia. What mattered to her was what they shared, a love of family and of horses. They were matched in heart and soul and if he ever doubted they belonged together, all he had to do was look at her. He knew her and her thoughts, even when she didn't want him to know. The anger she kept a tight rein on during the picnic made his grin grow into a smile. She thought she had kept her musings to herself, but Kevin saw her lips move when she silently rebuked him. He was sure she called him a "cad" when he gaped at Priscilla savoring her beef pasty. Even he was surprised by the lady's bold display which spurred Alicia's jealousy. The recollection made him chuckle. He had not lost his termagant and if he had his way, she would be his before long.

"Something funny, Mr. Donahue?" inquired Priscilla riding by his side.

"Not funny, but definitely something to make me happy," replied a grinning Kevin. His grin grew into a full-faced smile when his back felt the dart of Alicia's glare.

Chapter Seventeen

Mayfair, London
May

"Alicia," insisted Meg, "you cannot be mad at me for missing this morning's ride in Hyde Park. Trust me, I would have sent you a message to my mama's home, rather than have Lawrence tell you if I knew you were to be the only lady present."

"I am not mad at you," responded Alicia abruptly. Her ill humor had more to do with the scolding she received from Lord Summers after he learned of her popularity in Hyde Park. However, she could not explain that to her cousin with Lawrence present. She was sitting on a plush red leather squab opposite Meg in Atwood's luxuriant carriage. The well-appointed vehicle had a brass lamp on each side wall which lit up the chamber for Meg to clearly see her somber expression. Lawrence offered to take the back facing seat, but Alicia demurred, insisting he sit with his wife which was why Meg thought she was mad at her. They were on their way to the musicale they all promised to attend. Alicia thought it unfair she still had to go to the affair since Priscilla failed to ride with her this morning. Unfortunately, she had sent her acceptance to Lady Hummingsburgh and manners dictated she attends. Meg's raised brows told Alicia her cousin awaited an explanation for her bad mood.

"You may speak plainly in front of Lawrence," announced Meg who seemed to read Alicia's thoughts. "He will learn of your discontent by your mouth or mine. You know we do not keep secrets from one another."

Alicia grumbled in response, "Lawrence said you were ill."

"I wasn't exactly sick," replied Meg.

"But Lawrence distinctly said you were not well and could not get out of bed this morning," argued Alicia.

"You do not have to be ill to be sick in the morning," replied Meg with a grin.

It took Alicia a moment to puzzle out her cousin's clue, but when she did, her eyes lit up with excitement. She quickly offered Lawrence and Meg her congratulations, "How splendid, do aunt and uncle know?"

"Yes, we spoke to them while we waited for you to come downstairs. I would have included you in our familial announcement, but you took so long to arrive I feared we would be late to the musicale and thereby draw attention to ourselves. Lady Hummingsburgh would expect an extraordinary reason for our tardiness and I, for one, have no wish to announce I am with child. I want to enjoy the next few months without anyone putting their nose into my business. Besides, I want to take a seat at the musicale. Of late, I prefer to sit and believe this baby is the reason. I expect he is going to be a trial. I am already dancing or should I say sitting to his tune."

Lawrence grinned and Meg added, "My lord husband needs his heir, so I am already calling my baby a 'he' to nudge fate in the right direction."

"Not at all," responded Lawrence. "I happen to think it is going to be a girl. You practically affirmed my guess when you said the baby is going to be a trial."

Meg swatted her husband's arm and said, "Not funny, my lord husband."

Alicia laughed.

"That is better," remarked Meg. "Now tell me what troubles you and don't try to change the subject!"

Alicia looked down at her hands.

Lawrence counseled, "You did nothing wrong, Alicia. Summers overreacted. Aside from Kevin, the men in your party were family and more than adequate chaperonage for you to ride without a maid in Hyde Park."

"The bounder," exclaimed Meg. "Did he make a scene?"

Alicia blushed and said, "You are not being forthcoming, my lord."

Lawrence grinned. Meg rebuked, "I thought we did not keep secrets from one another, my lord husband!"

Lawrence raised his hands like a thief giving up any pretense to innocence. He explained to his wife,

"There is no secret, Meg." Before his wife could take offense, he collected her hand into his own and placed it on his thigh to keep her from shifting away from him in anger. He further explained to her, "Your cousin had a following. There were a few gentlemen who greeted her and asked after her father and then began to talk of horses. Donahue, Charles, and I fell back to make way for her greeters. Without intending to do so, we created a tail. Gentlemen continued to fall back to allow newcomers to greet Alicia and then they just fell into conversation with the chap next to them. I found it highly amusing, Kevin, not so. I could tell he wanted to herd them all away in another direction, but I managed to dissuade him. The sight of Alicia on parade reached the ears of Summers. Kevin told me Summers confessed he upbraided Alicia for her unseemly behavior."

Embarrassed, Alicia added, "He said he was asked how many were in the group because a wager was placed at White's and the fellows wanted to know who won."

"Well, who won?" asked Meg.

Lawrence laughed and Alicia shook her head. "How would I know? I was not keeping count."

"Well I was," said Lawrence and I think at thirteen, we made a magnificent sight."

"Not according to Lord Summers," remarked Alicia. "He said I embarrassed him."

"More fool he," said Lawrence, "and so Kevin told him when the man confessed his outrage and how he chastised you for behaving less than a lady. You must not worry about whatever Summers said. You are well-liked by many and no man would taint your name by suggesting you acted anything but a lady. Summers was mad because he was not there and suffered the taunt he had not made the cut to join you. Give him time, his ego will soothe and he will apologize for his churlish manner."

"Churlish? More like impertinent," railed Meg. "Who is he to reprimand you? You are not betrothed to him and exactly where was he this morning?" asked Meg.

"He was training at Gentleman Jackson's," replied Alicia. "Mr. Donahue told me he showed poorly at his last bout and scheduled a private lesson with Jackson this morning."

"When did you see Mr. Donahue?" asked Meg.

Alicia blushed and answered, "He came to call after berating Summers. He said he wanted to assure me the man was an idiot and I should not credit anything Summers said."

"Well done," stated Lawrence.

"Indeed," agreed Meg and then frowned. "I guess I will have to forgive Summers and be cordial to him this evening unless you gave him his congé."

Alicia flushed again and explained, "Lord Summers will be late to the musicale this evening. I put him in another embarrassing situation by accepting Lady Hummingsburgh's invitation."

"How so?" asked Meg whose vexation was obvious.

"Apparently, he accepted Dumphrey's dinner invitation on our behalf," explained Alicia.

"Without asking you first?" inquired Meg.

Alicia bit her lip and then shook her head from side to side to indicate a "no" reply. She knew what Meg was thinking and agreed. She and Summers would not suit. He did not consider her wants or needs. While she did accept Lady Hummingsburgh's invitation, she did not do so for Summers because he had not granted his permission. Summers did not extend the same courtesy to her when he accepted Dumphrey's dinner invitation on their behalf. Alicia knew his manner foretold her future if she married Summers. The man would treat her as his property to do as he wished instead of as his partner.

"Alicia," asked Meg. "Are you sure you want to marry Lord Summers?"

"I do not know if I have a choice any longer."

"Of course, you do," quarreled Meg.

"I don't know if I can have what I want," confessed Alicia. "The only thing I know for sure is I want to go home. The problem is I no longer have a home."

"Nonsense," replied Meg. "What you need is a respite. No one said you have to marry this year. If you do not want to live in your papa's home and have no wish to live in town with my parents, then you will simply come home with me."

Meg turned and looked at her husband who readily agreed, "Of course Alicia. You always have a place with us."

"Of course," added Meg, "we cannot leave until Parliament closes, but we can remove ourselves for some country air. I am sure Anne will welcome us for a visit." Meg asked her husband, "What do you think Lawrence, will you ask Felton if we can come for a sev'night?"

"Your wish is my command, Meg," answered Lawrence.

"Feel better?" Meg asked Alicia.

Alicia smiled and said, "Yes, I believe I do."

The Atwood carriage came to a stop in front of the Hummingsburgh town home where every window curtain was pulled back to display the crush and elegance of a *ton* party. Lawrence quickly alighted from his carriage to help his wife step down onto the foot stool, expediently placed outside the carriage door by his footman, and onto the pavement. Once he assured Meg was sure-footed, he turned his attention to help Alicia make her exit. He watched the ladies straighten and smooth their skirts, before offering them his winged arms. The linked trio walked together up the front steps and into the illuminated home, where every wall sconce and candelabra burned bright.

The house was bursting with nobility, even though it was a small affair compared to a ball. The countess to ensure her event was a crush did not avail the use of her ballroom, but kept her party to her formal salons. To accommodate her guests, she opened the double doors separating two rooms and removed furniture to fit chairs for an audience of fifty which she could easily fill with family and close friends. Empty seats would not be remarked upon in tomorrow's parlours regarding her musicale.

Lawrence, Meg, and Alicia greeted their hostess and then moved forward with the herd of guests. The crowd split as some men made their way to the salon set up with card tables, while other gentlemen attentive to their wives or to the ladies they courted, headed to the salons where the musicale was held. Still, other guests roamed into the parlour, library, and dining room to search for either friends or snippets of gossip.

Meg took in the number of people flooding the rooms and pouted when they entered the music room to see all the seats occupied. Alicia was not concerned. She knew Lawrence would find a seat for his wife even if it meant removing a gentleman from one to obtain it. She was proven correct when Lawrence asked Meg where she desired to sit. Perplexed, Meg just stared at him. How could she answer when every seat was taken? Lawrence prodded her and asked, "Indulge me, Meg. What is your desire?"

Meg pointed to the aisle and adjoining seat in the middle row explaining how she might need an easy exit and how she did not want to be too close, nor too far, from the performers. Lawrence smiled and made his way to his wife's desired seat with an arrogance to be rivaled by none other than the Duke of Aubry.

Not one, but two gentleman were dethroned from their seats to ensure Alicia and Meg sat next to each other. Alicia saw the men were not pleased to leave their partners to whom they staked a claim, but had little choice when Lawrence questioned their gentlemen's code of conduct with a terse reprimand, "No doubt, you are unaware there are ladies standing or else you would have risen and relinquished your seats the moment you saw my lady wife and her cousin."

Both she and Meg smothered their smiles as not to offend the gentlemen when they gave up their seats to them. Lawrence ensured they were both settled comfortably, reminded Meg he was hers to command should she need anything and then went to stand at the back of the room. Lady Hummingsburgh's young daughter Catherine who just made her curtsey to the queen, opened the musicale playing a piece by Handel. She struggled with the musical composition and like someone climbing a hill beyond their skill, she began to slip and stumble with each measure. Her cheeky smile after each misstep soon charmed her audience to distraction. No longer did they listen to the music but watched her adorable and determined expressions to get through the piece. She did not disappoint her audience when she rose and blushed to the resounding applause she received. Alicia watched Lady Hummingsburgh rush to hug her daughter and thought the lady looked more relieved than Catherine to have her musical debut done and over.

The next three ladies performed adequately and then it was Priscilla's turn to play. Lady Hummingsburgh placed her last on the program as she was the most proficient of the pianists and no one wanted to play after her. Alicia did not notice when Kevin arrived, but she saw him approach the piano with Priscilla. He was most considerate helping her to take her seat and arrange her music on the piano. No other performer had a gentleman assist them, so the gallant exhibition spoke of Kevin's admiration and attachment to Priscilla. They looked amazing together.

A pang of regret quickly hit Alicia hard in her chest and she had no one to blame but herself. Priscilla's beauty, talent, and substantial dowry made her quite a prize and Alicia saw as she inspected the audience around her, there were a number of gentlemen unhappy with the American who held Priscilla's favor. These gentlemen had courted Priscilla and seeing one of the realm's jewels lost to a foreigner did not sit well with them.

Alicia looked at the couple on display and could not think of one reason why Kevin should not want Priscilla for his wife. The lady was a *diamond of the first water* and before Kevin took an interest in her, Alicia had called her "friend." Alicia had always admired Priscilla's boldness and the lady's ability to acquire whatever she set her mind upon. Kevin and Priscilla were well-suited in that regard and the revelation knocked the air from her lungs. She was dazed and while she waited for her natural breathing to return, she reflected on how her fears drove her down a path where only heartbreak and unhappiness now resided.

In fairness, she could not blame Summers. He was no different than any other nobleman who wanted marriage to gain a wife to serve his needs, increase his coffer, and produce his heir. Most young ladies were groomed and aspired from infancy to be such a wife but Alicia was tutored differently and her aspirations were different. She was not one to be dictated over, yet since coming to town she realized everything she did was to please a man she chose because he did not own her heart. She thought she could avoid heartbreak by marrying for convenience, but since joining the marriage mart she realized how unhappy she had become. Her plan was to avoid heartbreak; yet marrying a man who cared little for her own happiness seemed more of a recipe for heartbreak than losing the man she loved.

She guessed Summers first interest to woo her was because of the ridiculous bet placed at Whites. After all, he was a Corinthian and the idea of winning her favor, a lady known to reject suitors, was a challenge that spoke to his competitive nature. Even so, she believed he was sincere in his attentions to her during her father's hunt. She was liked by his peers and capturing her favor probably made him feel like he had bested them. His grandmother's requirement he wed to inherit her property, further motivated him to court her as she was his most expedient solution. However, since her father's hunt he was no longer the amiable and even-tempered gentleman she thought him to be. He was quite gallant and considerate of her basic needs, but critical of those attributes which marked her character.

In contrast, Kevin seemed to like everything about her, even those traits the *ton* called mannish. Perhaps, that was the reason why she was initially drawn to him and quickly grew comfortable in his company. From the beginning, she felt a companionship with him she had never felt with another man. She trusted him to share her life dream and allowed him liberties she never gave any other man, not even Summers, which should concern her. *Why hasn't Summers tried to kiss me? And why is it I never cared or desired his touch?*

Her dream of owning a horse breeding farm had encouraged her to accept Summer's courtship and to eventually accept his addresses. The irony was Kevin offered to help her realize her dream. She could have her dream and the man she loved, if fear did not drive her towards Summers and pushed Kevin to Priscilla.

She felt her anger rise envisioning Priscilla as the next Mrs. Donahue and then her body calmed when it occurred to her Priscilla might not want to marry beneath her station. Technically, Priscilla could retain her title of 'Lady,' but would she be happy living outside the *ton*? Alicia wondered if Priscilla aspired higher and if so, did that mean Priscilla would refuse Kevin's addresses? The notion lifted her spirits. Perhaps, she could continue to call Priscilla her friend, after all.

The movement of people coming to their feet broke Alicia from her thoughts. She realized she completely missed Priscilla's performance and quickly rose from her seat to join the rest of the audience in applause.

She blushed when Kevin left Priscilla with her adoring crowd to come greet Lawrence and make his bow to her and Meg. Her cheeks grew hotter when she saw him grin at her and had to bite her bottom lip from saying something far from kind. *The Rogue!* He knew he discomfited her and had the tenacity to laugh at her. She tried to think of a way to retaliate and would have thought she did the deed when his grin turned sour. Before she could ask him what was wrong, she felt Summers take her hand and brush a kiss over it. He said to her and to those with her, "I am sorry I am late, Honorable Alicia."

Meg was first to speak, "You would have been charmed by our hostess' daughter Lady Catherine and enthralled by Lady Priscilla, my lord. Both were remarkable performances though for different reasons."

"Then, I am doubly sorry to be late," replied Summers. He turned to Alicia and asked, "You did not wish to perform?"

Alicia dropped her jaw in stupefaction. *Does this man know me at all?* Before she could consider her quandary, Summers said, "Forgive me, I forgot you have no talent to display."

Mortified from the insult, she was ready to turn and walk away. Before she could, she heard Kevin say, "There you are wrong, Summers. Alicia is admired by anyone who has seen her on a horse. She is magnificent, owning grace and a skill that surpasses any rider."

Summers scowled and attempted to correct his blunder by saying, "I meant maidenly talent, Donahue."

Alicia gasped from the affront, but this time it was Lawrence who rose to her defense. "Again, you are wrong, Summers. Alicia is considered among her peers to be a consummate hostess. She is also admired by all for her amiable personality, gracious manner, and generosity."

Summers pressed his lips together in frustration. His nostrils flared as he breathed in to collect his wits. Alicia could see he was trying to see what he could say to ameliorate the situation and feeling sorry for him, intervened. Laughing, she said, "Thank you, my gallant knights. I believe you made your point and I do not think Lord Summers meant to offend."

"Indeed, not!" exclaimed Summers in horror.

"Come," commanded Meg to Alicia. "We are off to the retiring room. Perhaps, gentlemen, you will think of a suitable conversation for when we return."

Chapter Eighteen

It did not take long for Lawrence to secure an invitation from Lord Felton for his party. Lawrence once lived at Beaumont Manor and the earl kept his room maintained for whenever he and Meg wished to visit. Both the Marquis of Beaumont and the earl considered Lawrence a member of their family and for that reason, a response to his request was made with great speed. Lawrence received word he was more than welcome to visit and bring any guests for as long as he wished.

Normally, the hour long trip from London to Beaumont Manor was an easy ride, but Meg's condition made the journey intolerable for her. Even with the coach's springs, the abrupt turns and bumpy road was making her queasy. She tried not to give in to the nausea, nor worry Alicia by chatting incessantly, but her pallor revealed her attempts were far from successful.

Not since the day after the Richmond Park excursion did Meg feel so miserable. Had Lawrence known travelling by coach to Beaumont Manor would make his wife as ill as horseback riding, then he would undoubtedly have cancelled his trip. His fear for her health had driven him that day after the Richmond picnic to forbid Meg from riding horseback while in her condition. It was the only time Alicia remembered him using his authority over her cousin and the reason why she rode in the carriage with Meg instead of riding Cleo. She had assured Lawrence she would watch over his wife. Now, no doubt, once he learned of her suffering, Meg would be restricted from travelling afar, until she safely delivered.

The busy king's highway was not without its danger; especially for peers of the realm heralding their presence with shining and crested coaches. More than one nobleman had a story to tell of a bandit shouting "stand and deliver!" The stories, often exaggerated for the benefit of their audience, were a constant reminder for travelers to beware.

Lawrence brought two grooms to act as outriders. One servant rode in advance to ensure the road was clear and safe; free from a felled tree or other hindrance that could stop a coach and make their occupants vulnerable to bandits setting a trap. The other groom led Alicia's mare on a rope and followed the coach at a distance to keep the coach's dust out of his face. Lawrence did not expect any trouble since most highwaymen struck under the cloak of darkness and his small party was making their way to Beaumont Manor early in the day. He rode by the side of his carriage with his wife's comfort his only concern.

"I am sorry Charles could not join us," remarked Meg as she resettled and relaxed into the comfortable plush red leather squab.

Alicia's growing concern abated with Meg now at ease in her seat and her chatter reduced to a normal rate. Meg no longer looked like she was about to cast up her accounts, so Alicia held up her end of the conversation by explaining, "Lord Harry begged his company and Charles felt duty-bound to comply."

"That man is lucky to be alive!" exclaimed Meg, infuriated on her cousin's behalf.

"Indeed and lucky to have Charles for a friend," agreed Alicia. "Imagine if our cousin did not seek out Harry's father to inform him of the loan Harry took from Jones to pay his debts of honor. Harry would be soundly beaten for not coming up with the money by the due date. Harry thought he could rusticate until he was in funds again and dismissed Jones' deadline as bluster. More than likely, Harry put off his other creditors in the same way by withdrawing to the country, but Charles knew firsthand there was no escaping Jones' brutality. He told Harry about the beating of Squire Bigsby's son, but Harry dismissed the warning as a hum. Charles said Harry was more worried about missing his appointment with Hoby, our esteemed boot maker, than seeking refuge. In a panic for his friend, Charles tracked down the earl and told Belcrave of his son's impending danger. Thank goodness, the earl took immediate action."

"It is a wonder the earl gave the threat any credence," remarked Meg.

"Well, apparently there has been enough talk about Jones for the earl to heed the threat to his son. He might think Harry a coxcomb, but the boy, while not his heir is his spare. Besides, as much as the earl belittles Harry, I think he loves him. I don't think Belcrave would bring Harry along to so many of his hunts and activities if he had no regard for him."

"What will happen to Jones and his thugs?" asked Meg.

"They were found in the act of beating Harry in Green Park. Jones and his minion followed Harry from Hoby's up Picadilly Street and then pushed him into the park where one of Harry's friends tried to greet him. Harry brushed him off and his friend walked off in a huff. He must have questioned Harry's unusual behavior and his company, because he stopped Harry's father when he saw the earl riding down Picadilly. He quickly availed the earl of what he saw. The earl brought three stout footmen with him and they stopped his son's pummeling before Harry suffered too much. The earl had the foresight before galloping to Harry's rescue to send for a bow street inspector to follow in pursuit and make the arrest. The only good news is Jones and his accomplice will transport if not hang for brutalizing a nobleman."

"A deserving ending; especially after what they did to uncle and Squire Bigsby's son," commented Meg.

"Indeed," agreed Alicia. "I have to admit knowing Jones is removed from society gives me peace of mind. He terrified me."

"Well, he cannot hurt anyone any longer. I say good riddance to offal. Now, did I tell you Mr. Donahue will join us for a couple of days?" asked Meg.

Alicia's jaw dropped in astonishment. She thought to have a respite. She would hardly have any peace if she had to observe Kevin and Priscilla mooning over each other. She remembered to snap her mouth shut and quickly turned her head to look out the carriage window before Meg saw the pooling of moisture in her eyes. For some absurd reason, she felt like crying.

Meg touched Alicia's arm and said, "I thought it would please you to have his company, Alicia. I am sorry if I acted unwisely."

Alicia turned feeling guilty to concern her cousin. She put on her brightest smile and queried, "Not at all. I was just surprised. When do you expect Mr. Donahue and Lady Priscilla? Is her mama coming, as well?"

Meg chuckled and answered, "So that is what troubles you. No, silly. Priscilla was not invited, only Mr. Donahue."

Alicia grinned and then joined Meg in laughter.

"Oh, that felt good," gasped Alicia, "though I should not be so unkind. I like Priscilla. I just don't like the idea of her married to Kevin."

"Of course, you do not," stated Meg. "When are you going to accept you love the man?"

"I don't know what good it does when he loves Priscilla," rebutted Alicia.

"I doubt he loves her, but given no other choice he might open his heart to her," said Meg.

"I refused his suit, Meg, and I am practically betrothed to another," she reminded her cousin.

"Practically is of no consequence," said Meg. "Besides, a lady has the right to change her mind."

"I refused Kevin because I was afraid to fall in love with him and risk heartbreak should he die."

Meg chastised, "That tune grows weary, Cousin. I think it is a verse sung out of habit more than belief. Besides, death is not the only cause for heartbreak. Are you not suffering now? And your papa would never wish the years away he had with your mama to forgo the grief he suffered. His only wish would be she lived. You want a loveless marriage thinking it will subvert grief, but grief is suffered for a multitude of reasons. You should let go of your fear and open your heart before you lose the one man who accepts you for yourself."

Alicia's mouth formed an "o" and then she recalled how Charles always argued how she could have her pick of any gentleman. She never believed it. Men only wanted to be her friend, or *did I insist they be friends? Did I keep suitors at bay using friendship as my deterrent?* She had laughed when a gentleman tried to compliment or court her, insisting they were not serious. Not until she met Kevin did she let her guard down and let him get close enough to call her more than a friend. *Why? Because I was arrogant and thought I would never consider an American a suitable beau and because I soon discovered I enjoyed his company and his kisses. I trust him and through the attraction, teasing, laughing, arguing, friendship, and kisses, I instinctively knew he was the one I wanted to call my own.*

Her plan had been to marry a man she did not love to keep her heart safe. A marriage of convenience the British call it, when one married for benefit rather than love, but never did she consider the dilemma of marrying one man while being in love with another. Her unhappy state since resigning herself to marry Summers should have prompted her to ask some tough questions. *How do I prevent heartbreak when my heart is already engaged? How do I find happiness when I cannot share my joys? How do I feel safe when I cannot trust? How can I care about a future when I cannot have the one I want?*

"What you need to ask yourself, Alicia," asked Meg interrupting her cousin's thoughts "is whether your heart can withstand losing Kevin to another lady."

The idea brought Alicia such deep sorrow she couldn't speak. She never really envisioned a future without Kevin. He always hovered on the periphery. She just could not imagine not seeing him or knowing of him. Her forehead scrunched and her lips pressed into a pout as she recalled her misery during the months she did not see him. She knew her sad features were worrying her cousin, so she relaxed her furrowing brow and tried to look cheerful.

Her cheek tickled. Her hand brushed the annoyance and she almost laughed when she felt the moisture on her hand. She had cried. The cathartic release was just what she needed to unburden herself. She felt like the bold girl she was before her father's fall into destitution, the girl who knew her own mind and was capable of going after what she wanted. She asked Meg, more statement than question, "A lady does have the right to change her mind. Doesn't she?"

"Yes she does," replied a grinning Meg, quite pleased with breaking through Alicia's fears. Finally, she would see her cousin happy. "Now that is settled I feel hungry. Look in that basket under the coach seat and see if you can find me something to eat."

Alicia did as she was asked, foraging into a wicker basket before finding Meg a thick juicy meat pasty. The seasoned beef turnover was a specialty of Cook's. Meg no sooner devoured the pie when she insisted Alicia hand over another one to eat.

"Don't you think that a bit gluttonous, Meg?" asked Alicia.

"I am eating for two, Alicia. The second pasty is for me since my belly feels nigh empty."

Alicia watched Meg devour the second meat tart. She ate it so quickly Alicia was afraid her cousin was going to ask to eat another. She was about to ask if Meg wanted a little wine to wash down her meal when the coach violently jerked, forcefully throwing them forward and then back onto their seats. Alicia saw Meg's eyes widen in alarm from the hard impact of her body against her seat and feared Meg was injured. She rapped on the ceiling and then rolled down her side of the window to tell Lawrence to stop the coach.

No sooner did she return her focus on Meg than her cousin pushed the other coach door open and began to lean out. Alicia instinctively wrapped her arms around Meg's waist to keep her cousin from tumbling out of the still moving carriage. She pulled Meg's derriere firmly back onto the squab and held her cousin in place not realizing the reason behind Meg's rash behavior. To their horror, Meg convulsed and the remnants of Meg's lunch filled the coach with a sour stench.

The coachman slowed the gait of the two matched pairs as soon as he heard Alicia's raps, but stopping a traveling carriage took more time than bringing a mounted horse to an abrupt stop. Lawrence quickly dismounted his horse the minute the coach stopped and opened the door from which window Alicia called out to him. Alicia barely leapt out before Lawrence entered.

Alicia had to give Lawrence credit. Not one comment of revulsion did he make. He took his linen square from his coat pocket and brushed off Meg's lunch from her lap onto the floor. Then, he gently picked up Meg and carried her out of the carriage to the grassy mound away from the road. Alicia held her breath to keep her own stomach from retching and leaned into the carriage to pull the lap blanket from under the seat. She hurried after Lawrence and placed it on the ground where he stood with Meg cradled in his arms. Lawrence gently lowered himself onto the blanket to sit and care for his suffering wife.

Meg hid her face in her husband's coat and moaned. Alicia took out the laced-edged linen tucked up her sleeve and offered it to Lawrence for him to wipe Meg's face. "Are you better, Meg?" he asked.

Meg groaned. "I feel very dizzy and lightheaded. I do not think I can get in the carriage just yet. May I close my eyes for just a moment, husband?"

Lawrence grinned and replied, "Anything, my lady wife."

Alicia grinned at Lawrence and then went to check on her horse. She asked the brown-haired groom, not much older or taller than herself his name and when he replied his name was Joseph, she told him to seek his master for instructions. When the servant looked unsure of leaving his post, she informed him she would watch the three horses.

Joseph hurried to his lord and Alicia overheard the tasks set before him. The groom quickly went to help the coachman soothe and hold the team of horses in place until they settled. Then, poor Joseph had to clean the coach of Meg's expulsion. Alicia almost laughed when Lawrence gave Joseph his instructions to take care of his lady's mishap. Confused, Joseph asked, "what milord?"

Even from her distance, Alicia heard Meg groan, most likely from mortification when Lawrence exclaimed, "your nose will identify the mess before you see it!"

They just left the city limits and were on a deserted stretch of the king's highway. There would be conveyances and other travelers eventually, but essentially they were alone surrounded by nature. Alicia stared into the forestry flanking the road and a sense of unease washed over her. The oak and ash trees grew close to one another and were thick with rustling leaves. A number of indistinct sounds had her imagining all kinds of threats. Was it just nature's rodents rustling about the forest floor or something else? She quickly looked back to Lawrence for assurance but he also looked alarmed. Alicia hoped Meg felt better so they could be on their way.

She looked at the carriage wheels and wondered what they hit to cause it to jolt. Bending over for a better inspection, she saw the arm before she felt it wrap around her waist to jerk her tightly into the owner's body. The reins fell from her grip and she instinctively screamed and clawed at the filthy hand holding her snug. Well-trained, the horses did not bolt. Their hanging leather ribbons held them to a shuffling position. Alicia fought for release until she felt the cold nozzle of a pistol placed at her head. She immediately stopped fighting and felt the overwhelming sensation of losing consciousness.

She let her eyelids drop when the blackness closed in on her, but then a gun report startled her awake, thrumming her body with fear. Her eyes flashed open and her heart pounded loud as a warrior drum while she anxiously searched to see who was shot.

She saw the coachman sprawled belly down on the ground with his ridiculous and outdated blunderbuss by his side. His blood seeped from his body and pooled around him. Alicia felt sick but pushed down the fear causing her nausea to seek out Lawrence and Meg.

Lawrence stood in front of Meg who now sat on the blanket alone looking pale and afraid. Her arms were wrapped around her belly as if that simple act protected her baby. Alicia kept her eyes on Meg until another voice diverted her attention and she realized there was a second villain.

"What now, boss?" said the man who shot the coachman. The villain threw the smoking and useless gun to the ground having spent its bullet and powder. He looked familiar and Alicia blinked trying to recall him. The man holding her responded, "Get on the horse towing the mare."

Alicia recognized Jones' voice and began to shake.

"Ah," sighed Jones. "You remember me, lass. Good. I once told your father I would take you in lieu of payment. He took offense, the stupid man."

Alicia was afraid to move with the pistol pressed against her head, but once the gun was removed her eyes darted everywhere except where the coachman lay. She looked for Joseph and found him at the front of the team of horses doing his best to keep them calm. Unlike hunters who were trained to tolerate loud noises of yapping hounds and blowing bugles, the gun report frightened the coach team into wanting to bolt.

Alicia thought Joseph looked angry, but he was too far away and unarmed to do anything aside from save himself. He could easily jump onto one of the horses and ride off with the team. Jones only had one shot and she doubted he would use it on the groom. Jones was evil personified. He would kill whoever gave him the greatest advantage to escape and that person was Lawrence. She nearly blacked out again when she realized her error. Jones' greatest advantage was to shoot Meg because Lawrence would never chase Jones if he was busy trying to save his wife.

The idea Meg could die and not have her happy-ever-after enraged Alicia. Meg was right. There was more than one cause for heartbreak and Meg's death was one she never contemplated. Acting without thought, Alicia jerked her elbow and then drove it into Jones' stomach. The attack caused Jones to weaken his hold on her. In those brief seconds, she turned and drove herself into Jones, knocking them both to the ground. She knew he only fell because he was caught off guard, but the impact jolted the pistol from his hand.

Alicia was not strong enough to do anything but get away and run. She rolled off Jones and scrambled to stand and run as fast as she could, but Jones grabbed her skirt before she could escape. His speed and agility surprised her. He quickly jumped to his feet and wrapped his arms around her before Alicia had any chance of running. She fought valiantly, but Jones held her firm and then slapped her across the face when she refused to desist. Meg screamed.

"Leave her, Boss!" shouted his thug who picked up Jones' gun and held it at Lawrence. "Let's get out of here before another coach comes!"

Jones threw a dazed Alicia to the ground and jumped on Lawrence's horse. By the time, she turned over to look at the escaping villains, all she saw were two mounted figures and her beloved Cleo diminishing down the road. She fell back to the ground and passed out.

Chapter Nineteen

"Check her for injuries!" Meg's fearful voice resonated more like a screech than a shout. The moment Jones and his villain rode off, Lawrence ran as fast as he could to Alicia. His boots slapped the hard ground at a fast clip releasing puffs of gritty dirt in his wake. Fear marked his tight expression. Alicia had not moved since she fell to the ground.

He dropped to his knees when he reached her, uncaring of the sting from the ground's impact and looked for obvious cuts, bruises, and broken bones. He pressed his shaking fingers to her neck to check for a pulse and when he found her heartbeat steady, he asked, "Alicia, can you hear me?"

He placed his fingers behind her head to examine for an abrasion or bump when she didn't answer him. He no sooner pressed his fingers against her forehead when she groaned. Lawrence called out her name again.

Alicia's eyelids fluttered and after a few attempts, she finally opened them to reveal her light brown eyes. She whimpered and her pathetic sob prompted Lawrence to ask, "Are you terribly injured?"

She did a self-assessment of her aches and pains and rasped in voice strained from screaming, "Only bruised and sore." She looked dazed until she frantically inquired of Meg.

"She is fine," answered Lawrence in a calming voice to settle her. "She is just worried over you and our coachman. Can you move? I will see if my driver survived if you can walk to Meg."

More in command of her emotions and with her wits returned, she replied, "Yes, of course." Lawrence helped her to stand and steady herself before he released her. She tentatively asked if she could help, the whole time fearing he might take her up on her offer. She knew she would try to aid him if he needed her, but was afraid she might faint over the sight of the man's bloody body. Lawrence gave her a sympathetic refusal, almost as if he could read her mind and then he left her to assess his coachman's condition. Alicia hoped Tom was not dead.

Alicia held up her skirt and after one tentative step, ran to Meg and fell into her cousin's open arms. They both sobbed and looked for reassurances of each other's well-being by taking a quick inspection of one another. Satisfied, they were each fine under the circumstances, they stepped apart and turned their attention to the injured coachman. They began to tremble, fearing the worst for Tom and sympathizing with Lawrence for his grueling task.

Lawrence struggled to turn over his fourteen stone coachman. He pushed and suffered from having the body roll back at him a couple of times before he finally had Tom on his back. The bullet had entered high on Tom's shoulder and exited through his back. Tom's great livery coat was covered in blood, already thick and sticky from coagulation. The driver looked dead. His face was pale and his body stiff. His chest did not rise, nor did a grunt leave his lips as his body was pushed and prodded. Lawrence quickly placed his unsteady fingers on Tom's neck to search for a pulse and released a hearty sigh when a shallow beat thrummed.

He quickly pulled off his cravat, folded it into a square and pressed the swath of linen against the wound that still trickled a small amount of blood. His mind searched for the best way to get his coachman into his carriage without damaging Tom further and quickly determined he needed his groom's help. He called out to Alicia to relieve Joseph of settling his restless team of horses and to send the servant to him.

Once again, Alicia gathered up her skirt and started to run to where Joseph stood, until she saw Meg trying to keep pace at her side. She abruptly stopped and told Meg to stay put, but her cousin argued she was more than capable to assist. Meg explained any nausea she suffered was long gone, having been replaced with an earth shattering fear the moment Jones grabbed Alicia.

With no time to argue, they both rushed to handle the lead pair of horses.

Alicia grabbed the bridle of the left lead horse and told Joseph to help his master. Meg took hold of the right lead horse's bridle. The young and spirited team had been spooked by the gun report and were tossing their heads and shuffling their feet in distress. Alicia and Meg used soft words of encouragement and stroked down their long faces to calm them. The team's nervous state was affecting the seasoned second team who wanted to be released from their harnesses, having remained too long without grain or water to pacify them.

Both ladies continued to calm the horses with softly spoken words and were prepared to release their bridles should either lead horse bolt. They knew better than to hold onto a runaway team.

Lawrence and Joseph worked expediently to place the coachman into the carriage. Lawrence lifted him by the shoulders and backed into the carriage with his burden, while Joseph carried his legs. Tom was dead weight which made him exceedingly heavy to carry and maneuver. No easy feat, since the opening to the carriage was above stepping distance and Tom was like a tree trunk: round, solid, and heavy. The stool usually used to assist passengers to alight was too unstable for the purpose of wrestling a large man inside, so Lawrence and Joseph had quite a challenge to get the deed done.

They tried to be careful, but the poor man was jostled and banged just to get him partly inside. Their efforts were causing the carriage to rock. The coach had superior springs, but anything jiggling the harnesses, especially on an inexperienced and young team could provoke them to start. Lawrence voiced a heartfelt prayer petitioning for Meg and Alicia to hold his horses until he could release them from their duty.

He had his arms wrapped around Tom's chest and was wedged between Tom and the squabs when the noise of an approaching carriage resounded. Thundering hooves, rumbling wheels, and clanking bridles grew louder as the carriage approached. He struggled to free himself to get to the driver's perch to take a firm hold of the reins, but was stuck. Alicia and Meg would not be able to hold his team of horses. His matched pairs would want to step in time with the other horses when they passed.

He had no choice but to order his untried groom to drop Tom's legs and run to the driver's perch to take control of the reins. Then, he pushed and prodded Tom to break free of the hold his coachman's weight had on him. He had to leave a part of Tom's bum and legs sticking out one carriage door while he leapt out the other one. He raced to the front of his horses, vaulted onto the back of his left lead horse, grabbed the horse's reins and then leaned over and grabbed the reins of the right lead horse. He shouted for the ladies to step back and firmly held the reins just as a traveling coach and its outriders approached. It was Alicia's emotional shout that had him turning his head to look at the advancing rider.

Kevin practically flew off Maximilian before his thoroughbred even came to a complete stop and ran to where Alicia stood. The swelling redness of her cheek enraged him and he spoke with more force than tenderness when he cupped her face in his hands and asked, "What happened? Who did this to you? Where else are you injured?"

Alicia leaned her cheek into his palm and savored the warmth of his hand. She realized how much better she felt having him with her. She had no doubt Kevin would keep her safe. His presence calmed her and she had every confidence all would be well.

Kevin frowned at her when she did not reply to his questions. He asked again if is she was injured aside from her face, but before she could answer, Lawrence shouted at him. "Donahue! Can you give my groom a hand to hold these horses so I can see to my wife?"

His attention never wavered from Alicia, even though Lawrence sat bristling on his lead horse. They were close enough to hear his mumblings and she felt cherished to know she was the upmost importance to him. She assured him she was not suffering aside from some bruising. Satisfied, he kissed her forehead and with lightening speed raced to do Lawrence's bidding. She almost laughed seeing him scramble up to the driver's seat as quick as a squirrel up a tree trunk to adeptly take the four sets of reins from the groom. He looked strong, capable, and fearless as he stretched out his muscular right leg to place and secure his boot against the footboard. He looked more than ready to settle any hijinks the restless team delivered.

By now, the Deneham carriage was stopped, just ahead of the Atwood carriage and out from the coach stepped Baron Deneham.

Alicia exclaimed, "Papa!"

In seconds, her father was by her side, cupping the same part of her face Kevin had cherished. "My dear Alicia, what villain assaulted you?"

"It was Jones, Papa," choked Alicia, holding back tears as she continued, "His partner shot Coachman and they stole Cleo!"

Lawrence escorted Meg over to her parent's carriage once he was assured she was not injured or ill. He had work to do and knew Meg's parents would care for her while he saw to installing his coachman Tom in his own carriage and getting him some desperately needed medical attention. Sir Marcus immediately ordered two of his outriders to help his son-by-marriage place Tom in the viscount's carriage and then, ordered them to the driver's seat to relieve Kevin from holding the horses in check.

As soon as Kevin's feet hit the dirt, he went and asked Lawrence, "Is it true? Is that villain responsible for shooting Tom, assaulting Alicia, and stealing her horse?"

"Yes," he hissed angrily.

"How long since they left?"

Lawrence's eyes widened with understanding and replied, "Minutes." He turned to look at Sir Marcus, not sure who to address and asked, "I need your horse or the baron's, and someone to see my coachman gets medical attention."

Sir Marcus replied with an assured, "Done," and then snapped his fingers that brought forth a beautiful black stallion. Lawrence mounted the large barreled horse at the same time Kevin launched upon Maximilian. They galloped off before Meg or Alicia could stop them.

Sir Marcus took charge and told his two outriders perched on Atwood's driver's seat and Joseph to convey the coachman to the nearest town doctor. Joseph was instructed to stay with Tom and then send word to Beaumont Manor regarding the coachman's condition. His outriders were ordered to drive Atwood's carriage to Beaumont Manor after seeing the coachman and groom settled. Funds were distributed.

Alicia and Meg settled themselves in the Deneham carriage along with Alicia's father and Meg's parents. Sir Marcus instructed his coachman to make way for Beaumont Manor, the destination his daughter and niece were traveling before they were accosted. The carriage jerked forward as the horses started and jostled everyone until the wheels rolled at a marked speed. Alicia then turned and asked her father, "Papa, what are you doing here? Where is your new wife?"

The baron dismissed his daughter's inquiry and asked, "I am more concerned with your state, Alicia. Can you tell me what happened?"

Both Alicia's and Meg's emotions were stretched to their limits, so they could not check their eyes from watering or their noses from sniffling when they began to recall their frightening assault by Jones and his brute. Having Lawrence and Kevin leave without a word to her or Meg brought more emotions and worry to the forefront, causing Alicia to exclaim, "They have no weapons!"

Baron Deneham patted his daughter's shoulder. "Do not distress yourself, Daughter. It is no easy feat to shoot and hit a target from a moving horse, much less, at a moving horse. I doubt very much Jones would waste his bullet and I doubt your men will take any unnecessary risks."

Alicia looked at her father and pondered his words, "your men." *Does he think Kevin is my man?*

"Where is your wife, Papa?" Alicia asked again.

"Ah, my lady wife is most perceptive and thought I might like to spend some time alone with you before I make her presentation," he replied. "She awaits us in London. Sir Marcus and Alexandra offered to transport me to see you when I learned you left for Beaumont Manor."

The baron looked as though he just enjoyed a bowl of blancmange. His eyes were dreamy; he owned a foolish grin. Overall, he looked contented and happy. Alicia recognized the expression and exclaimed in disbelief, "You love her!"

Her father laughed and said, "Indeed, I do. I never thought I could ever love again, but Martha has my heart as no one has since your dear mama. Do not be angry with me, Daughter. I pray for your blessing of our union."

Alicia started to cry. She heard her father gasp, begging her to give Martha a chance. He praised his lady wife, listing all her virtues and explaining how much she wanted Alicia to accept her and call her a friend. Alicia's little hiccups of distress turned into hysterical chuckles. Her outburst completely silenced her father and everyone else in the carriage. Hesitantly, he patted Alicia's shoulder.

Alicia finally looked up at her astonished family and said, "No, no. I am all right and yes, Papa, I would love to call your new wife, "friend." Of course, you have my blessing."

"Then, Daughter, why the outburst?" asked Baron Deneham.

She confessed, "It has been a day of revelations, Papa. For years, I believed falling in love was not worth the grief we suffered after mama's passing."

Baron Deneham's eyes widened in surprise and he reflexively hugged his daughter. With upmost regret, he said, "Then, the fault is mine, Daughter. I should have blessed the years I had with your mama instead of damning a future without her. I thought you always understood it was from grief I spoke. I am sorry I never explained my sorrow better to you."

Alicia shyly asked, "You are not afraid, Papa, of suffering again?"

The baron's eyes showed his sympathy for his daughter's struggles. He put his arm around her shoulders and Alicia rested her head against him. He advised, "Alicia, if I worried about what the future held, my life would be overwrought with caution and temperance. I would hinder any chance for happiness because I would not trust in there being any. All my thoughts would be on what if, instead of what is. There are no guarantees in life, but happiness can abound when you cherish the joys, rather than worry over the possible sorrows. I loved your mama very much and am grateful we had sixteen years together. I never thought to love again. I did not need to love again. My life was full, but sometimes, when you least expect it, your heart knows better than your mind and nudges you to someone worthy of your love. A person who fills the void you did not even know existed and just like that, life becomes brighter, more colorful, and more joyful. I hope to talk to your young gentleman to ensure he understands how love is a gift to be cherished. I will not give my consent to your marriage if the man does not love you."

"Oh, no, Papa!" exclaimed Alicia. "I do not want to marry Lord Summers."

"Summers?" he questioned looking at his brother. "I thought you said she loved Mr. Donahue."

Everyone in the carriage laughed.

"I think you best explain this misunderstanding about Summers, Daughter," commanded her father.

"Well, until today," she answered, "I had convinced myself a marriage of convenience with Summers was my best chance for happiness."

"How so?" demanded her father.

Alicia blushed; embarrassed of the answer she was to give. "I believed a marriage without love would keep my heart safe from sorrow."

Baron Deneham hugged his daughter. "And now, how do you feel?"

Alicia looked at her aunt when a sniffle drew her attention and felt enormously guilty. She hated to disappoint her aunt, but she knew she could not marry Summers. She said to Alexandra, "I am sorry Aunt. I know you like Lord Summers, but I cannot marry him."

With a harrumph, she agreed, "Nor should you, Alicia, if your heart is not engaged."

Astonished, Alicia blinked her eyes in confusion. She argued, "But you like him. Why you promoted the match!"

"Only because I believed he was the one you wanted, but I should have known the minute I found you in Mr. Donahue's room and your subsequent odd behavior that he was the one you favored."

"What?!" bellowed the baron. "When were you in his room?"

Alicia blanched, her mouth forming an "o" in fright over what her papa thought. Thankfully, her aunt intervened.

"Do not let your hackles rise, Brother. The man was unconscious and completely unaware of her presence."

Alicia looked at her aunt who was not being truthful and received a discreet wink. She almost laughed out loud and had to keep her face diverted from her father, so he did not question her mirth.

"When was this, Alexandra?" he queried.

"It was after his injury at your hunt, Brother. You will remember he was unconscious and Felton called for his own doctor. Alicia, as lady of the manor dictated, looked upon him to ensure he had adequate care."

"Alexandra, I know you think you have hoodwinked me, but as long as Donahue does right by my daughter I will leave well-enough alone."

Oh, Lord, Alicia silently exclaimed.

Chapter Twenty

Beaumont Manor
May

Alicia struggled to lift one of her legs and then gave up trying. She was too fatigued to detangle herself from the bed sheets keeping her hostage. She lie awake in the same Green State Room assigned to her when she was here at Christmas, technically before Christmas since she, her aunt and uncle had spent the holiday with Summers. Once again, she stared at the green brocaded canopy, this time instead of worrying whether she should marry Summers, she worried over Kevin. *Where is he?*

Two days ago, the Earl and Countess of Felton graciously greeted Alicia and her family within the portico of their manor steps welcoming them to Beaumont Manor. Their arrival was not a surprise. A groom posted at the entrance to Beaumont's long drive, upon seeing the Deneham conveyance, raced back to the manor and informed his master of his guests' approach.

No sooner did the Deneham party alight from their traveling coach than they were brought into Beaumont's drawing room for refreshments. Anne saw Alicia's injured face and rumpled carriage dress before her husband and exclaimed with great concern, "My dear girl, what have you suffered?"

His wife's raised voice brought Felton to Alicia. He gently raised his large hand to Alicia's face and inspected it. His eyes held great sympathy and then anger. He immediately turned to Alicia's papa and uncle for answers. "Who is responsible for this travesty?"

Baron Deneham spoke first; regretful his family ever came to the villain's notice. "It was Jones," he said and offered no further description since Felton knew the criminal and his crimes. Deneham explained, "Atwood pulled his carriage over to see to Meg's comfort when Jones and his cohort attacked them. Jones' minion shot Tom Coachman and Jones assaulted Alicia."

"Jones?" asked Felton with raised brows. "I heard the ruffian was arrested."

"He was," interjected Alicia. "Harry's father saw it done." She voiced her revelation the moment it came to her. "Jones must have escaped. Now that I think of it, he did look dirty and shabby."

"Where is Atwood?" asked Felton. The young viscount was considered a family member and seeing his absence concerned him.

Alicia saw Meg shake her head, too overcome to answer, so she disclosed the rest of their harrowing story, pausing at intervals when her own emotions began to choke her discourse. Anne placed her arm around Alicia's shoulders for support and then looked over to where Alexandra held her daughter's hand. The worry for Lawrence and Kevin, while shared by all, was exponentially felt by the young ladies. They all hoped the gentlemen or a message regarding their well-being would soon arrive to alleviate their fears. Anne suggested the ladies retire to their rooms and get some much needed rest. As much as Alicia wanted to argue against leaving the vigil for Lawrence's and Kevin's arrival, she was beyond tired. She submitted to Anne's authoritative care and under the countess' direction was soon settled into a guest bed where she immediately fell asleep.

That was two nights ago, two nights of worry, distress, and waking up in a tangle of sheets after a sleepless night. Alicia pulled, shoved, and kicked to escape her cocooned sheet. She swiveled her legs over and off the bed to sit at its edge and took a moment to decide whether to summon a maid to help her dress. She decided to wear a simple round dress she could secure without assistance and once dressed, left her room to search out the rest of her family. She hoped news of Kevin and Lawrence had arrived, but upon entering the drawing room and seeing her cousin's grim expression and pallor, she did not need to ask.

She took a seat next to Meg and gave her cousin's hand a squeeze, before releasing it. The room was silent. No greetings were made, nor did anyone wish to speak of idle affairs or engage in amusements. They all waited, hoping for a message to arrive. After an hour passed and Meg left, Alicia decided to also retire to her room. She could not suffer the growing tension and decided she could worry just as easily in her room. She immediately took to her bed and eventually fell into a fretful slumber.

She dreamed of Kevin and while he was not injured in her dream, he stood out of her reach. She was shouting at him, but he could not hear her. In her dream, he kept yelling back, "What?" The more she tried to scream she loved him, the more his figure diminished. She woke in a panic with her heart racing and her cheeks wet with tears, afraid her worst fears were realized.

A maid helped her dress for a dinner she had no desire to eat. Her stomach churned with worry, so she ended up pushing the food around on her plate with her fork until it was removed. She was not the only one with a loss of appetite. Discussion topics died silently as her hosts attempted to distract their sober party from worry. Felton signaled his lady wife to stand and lead the ladies to their drawing room when no one touched the dessert placed before them.

Alicia begrudgingly followed Anne and complained, "I don't know why we must excuse ourselves and leave the men to their port. I want to hear what they plan to do to find Lawrence and Mr. Donahue."

Anne waited until they were in the drawing room to answer Alicia. Her footman set up her mahogany tea table near her chair, while a maid set a tray with her

Sévres porcelain tea service upon it. She motioned her guests to take a seat and recommended Meg make herself comfortable by reclining on the camelback sofa. Alexandra encouraged her daughter to comply and when it looked like Meg might argue, she quietly reminded Meg she needed to think of her baby.

Meg did as she was told, while Alicia accepted Anne's soft reprimand, "I believe my lord husband, Honorable Alicia, thought to see to our comfort when he signaled me dinner was concluded."

"I beg your pardon, my lady," she said.

"Duly accepted," replied Anne. "Now rest easy, I will hunt them down if they do not join us...what do you think, Alexandra, fifteen minutes?"

Alexandra grinned. She was placing a pillow under Meg's feet to elevate them to ease the swelling she noted. She agreed, "Fifteen minutes is plenty of time for them to finish their libations and for us to enjoy a small respite. We will need great fortitude for the coming hours and nothing helps better than a soothing cup of tea. Why don't you pour, Anne, and I will pass the cups around. I see you have a smaller pot brewing, something special for my Meg?"

"Indeed, our good cook brewed the herbal concoction she made me drink when I was enceinte. I found it very beneficial. The tea calmed my stomach and freshened my breath," she laughed. "Which reminds me, Honorable Alicia, how is the bruise on your face? Did the poultice Cook make help? The swelling looks reduced."

"Yes, thank you, my lady," replied Alicia, remembering the maid who brought up the poultice with the cook's compliments and who helped her disrobe for bed. "Please give my thanks to Cook. I apologize for being remiss in not extending my gratitude sooner."

"Nonsense," replied Anne. "You have enough on your mind and my good cook is very sensible."

Alexandra gave Meg the mint tea and watched with everyone else as her daughter blew at the steaming brew before taking a sip. The tea agreed with Meg for she quickly took another drink. Numerous sighs were heard when the warm brew brought color to Meg's complexion and improved her countenance.

Alicia's own anxiety kept her in motion meandering around the room. She kept checking the long case clock to see when the requisite fifteen minutes ended, while Anne and Alexandra distracted Meg from her worries with anecdotes about common friends they knew.

Eyeing the clock, Alicia immediately rejoined the ladies when the time elapsed and asked, "Well, my lady?"

Anne smiled at her impertinent guest, then stood and pulled the bell cord to summon her butler. When her servant appeared, she inquired the location of the gentlemen and learned they were in the library reviewing regional maps. Meg barely got to her feet to fall in line with the others to march to the library when Felton walked into the room followed by Deneham and Sir Marcus.

The ladies practically opened their mouths in chorus with questions. Felton raised his hand in response to halt their queries and then quickly explained how he, Deneham, and Sir Marcus marked out various quadrants on a regional map to coordinate a methodical search. Felton and Deneham would join a number of his servants to search for Lawrence and Kevin. They would begin where the gentlemen were last seen and work their way out to the various quadrants, each team reporting back to the manor with their finds. Felton explained Sir Marcus would coordinate the search from the manor, assigning new quadrants to investigate if the men were not found and pass on the pertinent information to the searchers. Finished with his explanation, Felton suggested they all retire to get their much needed rest for he and his men would leave at dawn.

The gentlemen herded the women like sheep towards the double parlour doors when the doors unexpectedly swung open. Gasps and nervous exclamations exploded. There at the door's threshold was a gape-mouthed Lawrence, surprised at their outcry. He did not have a moment to apologize for his abrupt entrance when his wife barreled into his chest, causing him to step back to save them both from falling over. He no sooner caught his balance than Meg began to pat his body to check for injuries. First, she patted his shoulders and then his arms and chest, and then she did the process again before wrapping him up with her arms. The couple hugged and then broke apart to ask each other if they were well. Then, they wrapped their arms around each other again for another hug. Lawrence quickly brought Meg to his side and wrapped his arm protectively around her shoulder when everyone converged upon them to exclaim how happy they were to see him safe and sound. The clumsy, boisterous and affectionate welcome had everyone grinning and laughing in delight.

Alicia extricated herself from her family and looked for Kevin. She guessed he was seeing to Maximilian's care when he failed to appear. It did not bother her he sought his horse's comfort before his own, but in this instance, she wished he handed the responsibility off to one of Beaumont's grooms. The marquis employed sufficient staff and Maximilian would come to no harm under their ministrations. She felt a pang of envy knowing Lawrence's concern for Meg superseded everything else, even the care of his horse. Meg came first above all else and that kind of love was worthy of admiration.

Where is he? Kevin's tardiness made her anxious and until he entered the room she could not relax. She was overwrought with both relief and exaltation and wished she could release her pent-up energy by greeting Kevin as affectionately as Meg did with Lawrence, but she could not. They were neither married nor betrothed, and any amorous display would be unseemly. For all she knew, he already paid his addresses to Priscilla and wouldn't that be a fine mess to love a man who loved another.

What is keeping him? The vision of Kevin pampering Maximilian, instead of just seeing to his immediate needs vexed her and she was determined to give Kevin a less than warm greeting when he did grace her with his appearance.

She walked the perimeter of the room, working on what she would say to Kevin when Lawrence stepped out of his cocoon of well-wishers. She thought he looked severe as if he carried a great burden. Her heart started to pound when she saw him make his way to her and she began to shake, worried he conveyed dire news regarding Kevin. Her distress was seen by all and her father charged forward. He wrapped his arm around her and held her snuggly against him. Alicia fought the unconsciousness pulling on her.

"I am charged to inform you, Honorable Alicia," Lawrence began soberly, "that Mr. Donahue is delayed. He learned Lord Summers is making his way to you to request an interview with your father and begs you not to accept his lordship's addresses, that is, until he has the opportunity to present his own."

Alicia's jaw dropped in astonishment and the pull to faint diminished the moment she heard Kevin was delayed. Not wounded, nor dead, but delayed. *"Mr. Donahue is delayed...asks you not to accept his lordship's addresses..."* This declaration was far from what she expected and her fear turned into a simmering and noticeable fury. Her father feeling her body tense, quickly released her and stepped back to see her once pale face crimson in anger.

His removal of support and scrutiny reminded Alicia she had an audience. She quickly closed her gaping mouth and pressed her lips together to keep from taking her ire out on Lawrence who was not at fault. No, the man responsible for the multitude of emotions she suffered was absent and not available to receive a most deserving rant. Her anger fumed, but unlike a tea kettle, she had no outlet to vent her steam, except silently.

The audacity of the man! I am worried beyond reason and he chooses not to return to ease my fears. Instead, he asks me to heel like a dog. I am supposed to tell Summers, thank you, my lord, but I cannot accept your addresses because Mr. Donahue might make one of his own. Why the rogue hasn't even courted me and he expects me to accept him. She would have vented on in silence if the notion Kevin's absence might be due to an injury did not enter her mind. Her anger mildly appeased, she quickly and guiltily asked Lawrence, "Is Mr. Donahue hurt?"

Lawrence laughed, "No, not at all. In fact, his heroism is worthy of a ballad which I will share, now I have completed my duty to you."

Alicia was not thinking heroically of Kevin, nor remembering how she did not want to marry Summers. She was angry. She was finally ready to reach for a happily-ever-after, but it was hard to have one when the man she loved did not present himself. A vision of kicking him in the shin made her feel better. She held on to the image of

Kevin hopping around on one foot while she waited to hear Lawrence's tale.

A number of questions were made before Lawrence could begin and Felton stepped forward to suggest, "If you allow Atwood to speak I am sure he will provide an explanation to answer all our questions."

Lawrence grinned and thanked his host. "I will begin and tell you both villains are dead, so you may rest easy." When the baron began to ask how they died, Lawrence raised his hand to silence the man and said, "I ask for your patience. Trust me, I will reveal all."

"When we left the scene of our attack to chase after Jones and his minion, we discovered we were not far behind them thanks to my missing groom Walt. He was riding point guard when we started our journey and was making his way back to us when he recognized our horses. With pistol in hand, he immediately challenged the thieves by asking them what they were doing with his master's horses. Jones tried to talk his way around Walt, but my groom is street smart and did not hesitate to fire when Jones raised his pistol. Walt said Jones' was pulling on my horse's bit, worrying his mouth and making him anxious. It was no surprise the gun report frightened my horse into rearing. Jones lost his pistol when he tried to hold onto his seat. Without a weapon, he kicked his heels and raced off, leaving his cohort alone and unprotected."

"Turns out, Walt's shot whizzed by Jones and hit Jones' thug with enough force to knock him off his seat. The bullet did not kill him, but the rock he hit his head on did. Walt was trying to hold and secure three horses when we approached."

"Walt shouted Jones was just ahead and we raced on. We came upon Jones fairly quickly. I feared the villain had injured my horse since he was being held to a walk. It was then I realized we had no weapons. I turned to tell Donahue and dropped my jaw in amazement. Our American friend was unraveling a lasso while he rode. I watched him widen the loop and whirl it above his head as we chased Jones. That villain heard us pounding the dirt behind him and heeled my stallion to get going, but by then it was too late. Donahue leaned forward and with a flick of his wrist, threw the lariat and it flew out and over Jones' head. Donahue pulled and closed the loop around Jones' body and dragged that scoundrel right off my horse onto the ground. In one motion, he brought Maximilian to an abrupt halt and dismounted. Then, he grabbed a dazed Jones up from the ground by the collar and planted a facer on him. Donahue told him the punch was for assaulting Honorable Alicia and then he hit Jones again. That punch he said was for the beating he took at Deneham Manor. Then, he hog tied Jones like the American authors write about in their western novels."

Felton was the first to ask what everyone wanted to know, "What happened to Jones?"

"Well, we took him to the local magistrate, cautioning the man of Jones' villainy and recent escape. The judge carelessly said Jones would hang for his actions and the remark infuriated Jones. Only Jones' hands were bound and when he spied a pistol on the judge's desk he ran forward to grab it. The judge reached the gun first and shot Jones point blank."

"But where is Mr. Donahue?" demanded Alicia.

"Yes, where is Mr. Donahue, Atwood?" queried Baron Deneham.

"All I can tell you is he was delayed and begs your forbearance. He follows in a couple of days."

Chapter Twenty-One

"Well, Cleo, What am I to do?"

Alicia stood next to her mare in her horse's stall with one hand at the top of her horse's back, the other midair holding a brush. She was seeking her own counsel, even though she spoke to her horse. She asked her question and while her mind contemplated an answer, she brushed her mare's body with another stroke. The action comforted her. She rested her forehead against Cleo's flank and breathed in the stable's earthy scent of horse, leather, wood, and hay.

She lifted her head and apologized to Cleo for not seeing her sooner. Last night, she had not paid attention to Lawrence's news of retrieving Cleo and his own horses. She was too worried and then angered over Kevin's absence. Her guilt had brought her to the stables at dawn to see how her mare fared. She nuzzled Cleo's hide and then grinned when her clever mare snorted and shook her head as if disabusing her need to apologize.

Alicia ran the brush over Cleo's body again. She was tired of worrying. The issue was not whether she loved Kevin. That was settled. What plagued her was whether he loved her.

She knew he cared for her. She felt it in his touch and in his kisses. He looked at her in a way that made her feel special and important. She never feared anything when she was in his company. She enjoyed being with him, unless he did something to provoke her, but even then, she preferred his company more than anyone else's.

Kevin's message said he "wanted the opportunity to present his own addresses to her." He wanted her to refuse Summers. Well, unknown to him, she was already going to decline his lordship's offer. What she wanted to know was why Kevin wanted to marry her.

Isn't he courting Priscilla and if not, what happened? Could he be a fickle man? Perhaps, he is competing with Summers?

It was known to be done. The aristocrats made all kinds of foolish bets. Some even lost their homes on what they believed to be a winning hand at cards.

Maybe, I am simply the means to his end?

He had spoken of his dreams, wrote it all down in a letter to her explaining how one day he would own a piece of land, breed horses, and marry the woman he loved.

How do I know the woman he loves is me? If I was that woman wouldn't he have told me by now? Wouldn't he have waylaid Summers' pursuit of me, instead of becoming his best friend and exclaiming the man's virtues? It is all so provoking, but if I was going to be honest, the thing disturbing me the most, is why am I not first in his thoughts as he is in mine? Why did he not return to me after the whole Jones ordeal as Lawrence did for Meg? Where is he?

Her weariness and insecurities plagued her into thinking Kevin was only interested in the business partnership he once offered her when they first met. After all, her breeding acumen and popularity among those gentlemen who purchased thoroughbreds, would single her out as a great asset to any man who wanted to succeed in the business of breeding horses.

Her head hurt with all the questions bombarding her mind. She decided it was time to return to the manor and have a nap. Nothing would be settled by continuously asking the same questions to which she could not answer. She finished brushing Cleo and promised her horse she would return later for a ride.

She headed up the staircase to her guest suite and met Meg halfway as her cousin descended the stairs. They each stopped and looked at each other and then to Alicia's horror, Meg became teary-eyed and pulled her into a sorrowful hug. Alicia felt her own eyes well up with moisture knowing her sadness was worrying those who loved her. Yet, Meg's countenance owned more sympathy than concern and it occurred to Alicia her cousin might know something about Kevin's absence. She stepped out of Meg's hold, but kept her hand on her cousin's arm to make sure she could not escape her inquiry.

"Where is he, Meg? And don't tell me you don't know. Lawrence left him somewhere and since you constantly remind me the two of you do not keep secrets from one another, then you must know something!" She pleaded, "Please tell me. I would rather know and deal with reality than weary myself with the unknown."

"Come to your room, Alicia," commanded Meg. "You will not like what I impart, but I caution you to wait to hear Mr. Donahue's account before you think the worst of him. Lawrence believes Mr. Donahue has a satisfactory explanation."

Alicia's hackles rose. Was she wrong regarding Kevin's character? Her heart said no, but she had a feeling she was going to feel quite provoked with whatever Meg told her. Alicia let Meg pull her into the Green State Room and over to the canopied bed where they both sat down on the feathered mattress and turned their bodies to look at one another.

"Well?" prodded Alicia, disengaging herself from Meg's hand.

"According to my husband," started Meg. "Both he and Mr. Donahue decided to break their fast before returning to Beaumont Manor." Meg paused and then said, "It is reasonable, Alicia. They must have been exhausted after all the business with Jones."

Alicia agreed and with annoyance said, "Of course, Meg. I am not going to begrudge the man his meal or rest. What I want to know is why he did not return with Lawrence!"

"Of course," replied Meg before continuing. "Well, you see, it was during their meal the Earl of Luxingfield entered the tavern with a number of his cronies. That is how Lawrence referred to them, but I expect the gentlemen were all peers of the realm for why wouldn't they be?"

Meg paused again, almost as if she expected Alicia to agree, but continued when Alicia gave her a steely-eyed glare indicating she was about to lose patience. "Well, anyway, Luxingfield saw Mr. Donahue and Lawrence and invited them to engage in a card party. Lawrence refused."

"But not Mr. Donahue," stated Alicia in a voice sounding more like a question than a statement.

"Well, Lawrence made a point of telling me Mr. Donahue did hesitate before he accepted Luxingfield's invitation. Lawrence did not think Mr. Donahue wanted to go, since he went all silent, almost as if he was thrashing it out in his mind. Lawrence said once he made up his mind to go, he bobbed his head in agreement. Then, he asked Lawrence to relay the message you heard."

"But where is this card party? Was it there at the tavern where they ate?"

"No, Lawrence watched them leave. He thinks Luxingfield has a hunting lodge near, but he is not sure if they went there."

Alicia asked, "Why would they go to a hunting lodge for a card game and how would Lawrence know of it? Lawrence does not follow the hounds, nor have I ever heard of a hunt Luxingfield hosts? How is this lodge used if not for hunts?"

Meg raised her shoulders, feigning ignorance.

Alicia squinted her eyes in thought and then asked, "Were there ladies who made up this party of Luxingfield's cronies?"

Meg replied, "Funny, I asked Lawrence the same thing."

"And what did Lawrence say?" asked a peeved Alicia.

Meg answered, "Definitely no ladies." Meg pressed her lips together as if keeping any further words from coming out.

Alicia's anger peaked. She replied, "Got it, no ladies. What of women, Meg? Were there women in Luxingfield's party?"

"Well, they did not arrive with any, but it seems some of the men in the party pulled two of the better looking bar maids to accompany them. Lawrence said the publican was not happy."

The silence following, weighed heavily between them. Neither spoke or moved until Alicia released a heavy sigh and said, "Well, that is it, then."

"What is it, Alicia?" asked Meg, whose confusion revealed itself in the line creasing between her eyes.

"The end of waiting for a happy-ever-after," she replied sadly, though her sorrow did not last long before pride took over. Alicia's anger spewed out like a geyser and she raged, in words full of vigor and determination, "I will not indulge anymore in the 'what ifs.' I am making myself sick and I am too proud to suffer over a man who does not want me!"

"But Alicia," encouraged Meg in a soft voice. "His message proves he wants you. He said he wants to pay his addresses to you."

"Why, Meg? Not once has he professed a love for me. How do I know he doesn't love Priscilla? How do I know he is marrying me because she won't have him?"

"Oh," grinned Meg. "I know the answer to that worry."

Surprised, Alicia asked, "What do you mean, Meg?"

"Well, it will come out eventually, so I might as well confess, but I beg you not to be too mad!"

"I am already mad. Now tell me what you know!"

"Well, the three of us sort of plotted," confessed Meg.

Alicia asked, "Who?"

"Well," answered Meg. "Technically, it would be five if we include the Countess of Felton and Lady Priscilla."

"Meg, you are severely trying my patience. Stop stalling and tell me all."

"Mr. Donahue confided to Lawrence and me how you would not have him because you feared you might fall in love with him. I kind of thought you were halfway there; especially, the way you couldn't stop talking about him and broke all protocol to write to him all the time. It was actually Lawrence's idea, but I am the one who put the plan into action...with Anne's help of course."

"Meg," simpered Alicia. "My head hurts. Can you please tell me what you are talking about with as few words as possible?"

"We thought to make you jealous. We wanted to show you there was more than one way to lose someone you loved and while you could not control losing your mama, we hoped you would realize you could do something about losing Mr. Donahue," she explained.

"Jealous?" squeaked Alicia. "Do you mean to tell me you all plotted to make me jealous over Priscilla and Mr. Donahue?"

"Yes," confessed Meg. "And before you get so angry you can't see straight, just remember it worked. If Mr. Donahue had not started paying attention to Priscilla and if Priscilla had not favored Mr. Donahue, you would still be determined to marry Summers."

"You are sure Priscilla was just acting? They looked quite taken with one another. There is no affection whatsoever between the two of them?"

"None whatsoever," replied Meg. "Priscilla was happy to help because she likes you and said it sounded like fun. Mr. Donahue was just as determined to try anything to win your hand."

"But why did he promote a match between me and Lord Summers?"

"Did he?" asked Meg.

"Oh, I don't know anything anymore, except he has not confessed to love me!" exclaimed Alicia.

"Well," offered Meg. "You will just have to ask him, won't you? Do not lose your confidence, Alicia. Did you not just tell me you had too much pride to suffer over a man who did not want you? Well, what if the man wants you? Have you enough pride to believe you are all a man could want?"

Alicia laughed. "Oh Meg, I don't know what I would do without you. All right then. I shall wait to hear what Mr. Donahue has to say for himself. After all, what do I have to lose?"

"Nothing," replied Meg. "I expect the man is all yours to win."

"We shall see." replied Alicia.

Chapter Twenty-Two

Alicia opened her door to one of Beaumont's maids. The upper servant handed her a folded note and informed, "From the baron, Honorable Alicia. I am to tell you not to go downstairs until you see him."

The maid curtseyed and left. Alicia quickly unfolded and read the note which summoned her without delay. She reached back with her hand to close her room's door, and then hurried down the hall to her father's assigned suite. Her brow wrinkled in discernment over what possibly transpired to demand she present herself without explanation. She could not think of anything she did to deserve a scold, since to her recollection those were the only times he summoned her without reason.

Concerned, she did not bother to knock nor wait to be admitted, but walked right into her father's room. The baron was sitting at an elaborate Louis XV writing table situated near a white paned window framed in rich *garter-blue* velveteen tier curtains topped with a tasseled valance. The ostentatious *bureau á cylindre* spoke of a period of splendor. The roll top desk was adorned with gilded bronze and veneered marquetry of various woods, forming flowers and other delicate pictures as did the rest of the furniture in the room. The baron's guest suite was slightly larger than her room but with similar appointments. The high white plastered ceiling was decorated in the Neo-classical style with crown moulding and circular medallions. The walls were covered in blue Damask silk marbled with veins of a darker blue and the floor was covered with a blue rug patterned with rows of gold fleur-de-lis. The blue bed cover and other blue upholsteries also bore the pattern of fleur-de-lis.

Her father was working on some correspondence, looking rather lordly until her abrupt entry drew his attention. His expression softened at seeing her.

Anxious, she blurted, "What is it, Papa?"

"Ah, Alicia," replied the baron when his daughter entered his room. "I see you received my message. Good of you to come as bid." The baron assessed his daughter's countenance and frowned at seeing her looking sad. Her eyes were dull and heavy lidded, her complexion pale, and her mouth was turned down as if she carried the weight of the world.

"Papa," prodded Alicia. "The maid who delivered your message implied your summons was of the upmost importance. Is something wrong? And why would I not come as bid?"

The baron grinned before replying, "Alicia, are you so out of character you do not remember seeing to your own wishes first before my own?"

"Papa," her lips almost turned up in a grin when she said, "I am no longer ten years old. Of course, I will come as bid."

The baron chuckled. Alicia had learnt a valuable lesson the day she ignored the summons to her father's study, choosing to take her mare out for a ride instead of attending to his wishes. Learning of her impertinence, he went after her. She had thought to outrace him when she saw him galloping towards her, but was no match for his thoroughbred. He came upon her like a hawk swooping down on its prey and literally pulled her off her horse. He brought her home for a very stern scolding. Alicia's riding privileges were taken away for a week and she never dared to ignore his summons again.

"I thought you might like a word with Summers before I spoke with him. I hate the idea of refusing his suit when he has reason to believe otherwise. Unless, dear daughter, you changed your mind and wish to receive his addresses."

"He is here?" asked Alicia.

"He sent his card up with his request to speak to me written on the back of it. I instructed Beaumont's butler to show him into the drawing room and see to his comfort. I summoned you to ensure your wishes have not changed."

Alicia shook her head from side to side to inform her father she had not changed her mind. Even though Kevin's message warned her Summers was on his way, learning the man was now downstairs upset her. She was not ready to receive him. In retiring to Beaumont Manor, a part of her hoped she would not have to deal with Summers' impending offer of marriage. The thought of now giving the man his congé at this late date in their courtship seemed cruel and thoughtless. He had responded to her flirtation because he needed to marry in haste and because she seemed receptive to his attentions. The fact she wanted a marriage of convenience only made her more desirable in his eyes. Summers was far from ready to settle down and the idea of having a wife with no wish to curtail his activities was more than he could have hoped.

He had courted her in earnest, even though his attentions lacked the warmer side of a man wooing a lady. He had never attempted to embrace or kiss her, but then Alicia never desired or suggested she was agreeable to that kind of response from him. In fairness to Summers, he probably thought she was too shy or prim to engage in such behavior before marriage. Kevin on the other hand, took several liberties. The memory of those kisses and how she boldly returned them, made her cheeks warm in embarrassment and her mouth turn up in pleasure.

Regardless of how she felt about Summers, she could not complain he played her false. He made his intentions clear from the beginning and courted her faithfully from the moment they arrived in London. He squired her about town and they were seen everywhere together. His singular attachment to her was remarked upon in drawing rooms throughout Mayfair. His comments made in the company of others implied Alicia was part of his future and since she did not disabuse the notion she had brought the man up to scratch, everyone anticipated their betrothal. After all, it was common knowledge Alicia, along with her aunt and uncle, had spent the Christmas holiday with Summers and his family. It was also known Summers needed to marry in order to comply with his grandmother's wishes to inherit.

Alicia's guilt weighed heavy on her knowing she had plenty of opportunities to inform Summers she had changed her mind about marrying him. She could have informed him after she toured his grandmother's property or when she met his family. She could have broken his courtship of her whenever he called upon her in town, but instead she let him believe she would accept his addresses.

Her stomach tightened. She dreaded confronting and informing Summers she would not marry him. She wished she had not turned to him when she feared she was falling in love with Kevin.

"It has been four days, Alicia," stated the baron, breaking into her silent regrets. She blinked her eyes in confusion and then looked at her father attentively for further explanation.

The baron saw her confusion and explained "Mr. Donahue has not sent any kind of communication regarding his intentions for you. Are you sure you want to refuse Summers?"

Resolute in her response, she said, "I cannot marry Summers. Do not look so worried, Papa. I will not be sorry, even if Mr. Donahue decided we do not suit. I will speak with his lordship and inform the man of my change of heart, though truthfully my heart was never engaged."

"You will be kinder, Alicia?" asked her father.

Alicia laughed and replied, "Of course, but I do not think Summers will suffer. Ours was to be a marriage of convenience, after all."

"Never the less," reprimanded her father. "A man's pride is no little thing to dismiss. Summers was honorable in his intentions to you and while he might consider your union a marriage of convenience, that does not mean his feelings were not engaged. His pride, if not his heart will indeed suffer when you refuse him. I caution you to reject him with compassion because of those feelings."

Alicia felt duly chastised and nodded her head in agreement to her father's warning, saying, "I will decline his offer of marriage with due sympathy, Papa. I know my refusal will set back his expectations, but I cannot marry a man just so he can inherit some property."

"Nor should you," responded her father. "Your happiness is my greatest concern, not his expectations."

Alicia kissed her father on the cheek and welcomed the warmth his arms brought as he wrapped her up in a hug. He held her tightly for a moment and she heard him say softly, "You have no need to marry, Alicia.

You may live with me. Martha assured me she would welcome you with love."

Alicia wanted to cry. She pushed herself out of her father's arms and said, "Thank you, Papa. And Martha too! I am eager to meet your generous wife and if Mr. Donahue does not come up to scratch, it pleases me to know I still have a place I may call home. I finally understand what you tried to tell me about hearth and home. I very much want to marry for love and have a home and children I can call my own. If Mr. Donahue proves to be lacking in wit to know the prize he has in me, then more fool him, or maybe I am the foolish one for giving my heart away to someone undeserving. Do not worry about me. I will come about. For now, I must gather my fortitude and speak with Lord Summers. He deserves better than to marry a lady whose heart belongs to another."

"You will do well, Alicia," stated the baron. "Your generous heart will guide you in what to say. Send for me if you need me to intervene."

"I should change before I meet him," remarked Alicia as she looked at her skirt and smoothed down the wrinkles. She was wearing an old sprig muslin day dress worn more for comfort in the home than for public display.

"I think not, Alicia," cautioned the baron, "unless you wish to mislead the man. He will think you dressed to impress him if you take time on your toilette."

Alicia's eyes widened and then she grinned at her father. She asked, "Have you always been so wise, Papa?"

The baron laughed. "Not in all things. But I was young once and remember a thing or two."

Alicia gave her father another hug and then left him to make her way to the drawing room. She thought of the common phrase "we do not suit" generally used to break a courtship and found it utterly inappropriate, even if the phrase applied. As friends, she and Summers were quite compatible with similar interests regarding horses and hunts, but in marriage she knew they would clash. She could not abide to be treated like a fragile flower or a lady with no wit, and Summers knew no other way to treat a lady. He had been taught to use his authority over his wife, while she was raised to have authority. Now, she felt a need to apologize for misleading him and delaying his quest to meet his grandmother's demands.

She entered the drawing room cautiously, pulling her shoulders back and lifting her chin to give herself confidence. She was working out what to say to Summers, something compassionate as her father recommended, yet precise. She did not want to repeat herself or have to convince Summers her rejection was earnest. He was a handsome man with expectations, whom aside from Alicia, would win the hand of any lady in the marriage mart. Her father was right to say his pride would be hurt by her refusal, especially if her rejection became a parlour *on dit*. An injured man could become quite discourteous. She hoped he would not rant at her, deserving of it or not.

The confidence she mustered quickly diminished when Summers rose to his feet from where he sat and strode enthusiastically towards her. She might fear she was under attack if he did not look so happy to see her. She pushed her arms out, her hands open and fingers spread wide to stop him when she realized his intent was to hug her. Summers was oblivious to her wishes and embraced her so snuggly he practically squeezed the breath from her body. Her feet left the floor and she thought Summers was going to twirl her around, the way her father did when she was a child. She was speechless, lightheaded, and dumbstruck.

Summers never behaved as a man in love. His inclinations were to be polite and gallant in her company. It was the primary reason she never felt pressured to end their courtship for he never pressed her to be more than a friend. He was good company until he began to treat her as a possession rather than a person.

"Honorable Alicia," Summers whispered into her ear. "You are supposed to wait until I speak with your father, but it pleases me to see you are as anxious as I am to begin our future together."

Alicia could feel his smile; his face was pressed against her cheekbone. She also felt the strength of his fit body. His arms were strong, his shoulders broad, his chest solid, but unlike Kevin's embrace where she felt all warm, ardent, and dreamy, Summer's hold left her feeling uncomfortable. She wanted nothing more than to be released from his hold. She pushed on his shoulders to no avail. The man was practically giddy with anticipation and had no clue the lady in his arms did not want to be held.

She opened her mouth to demand he put her down, but every time she uttered "my lord," he interrupted her with his joyful chuckles. It was as if he was lost at sea and had finally found land. Summers was so engaged in his excitement he was not paying her any attention.

He moved his head back to speak directly to her face though he did not release her. He said, "You must be wondering how I knew your father was here or even you for that matter. I admit I was a bit put out at first to learn you left town without word to me, but when I learned your father was with you it all seemed fortuitous."

"My lord," croaked Alicia again. "If you will release me, I will say what needs to be said."

"I suggest you heed the lady, Summers," said a voice Alicia recognized all too well. Both she and Summers turned toward the man who spoke. Alicia closed her eyes in disbelief, before opening them to see Kevin entering the drawing room and striding towards them. Summers finally allowed her to stand on her own, though he kept an arm around her shoulder when Kevin joined them. She could tell that act of possession by Summers did not please Kevin.

"Ah, Donahue," expressed a gleeful and oblivious Summers. "You are in time to congratulate me."

Kevin looked at Alicia and said, "Am I?"

Alicia shook her head in the negative which did not go unnoticed by Summers. The man looked at Alicia and then Kevin. He released Alicia and took a step back to look into her face. He remembered she had something to disclose and asked, "What is it that needs to be said, Honorable Alicia."

"Perhaps, Mr. Donahue," remarked Alicia to Kevin, "you would permit me a moment with Lord Summers?"

Kevin strode over to the other side of the room but did not leave. He took a watchful stance. He might not be listening to their words, but she and Summers were under his scrutiny. Both men looked impatient, wore frowns, and stood with their arms crossed over their chests. Summers returned Kevin's hard look with one of his own before turning his attention to Alicia. She thought it would serve them both right if she just walked out of the room and let them deal with the situation themselves, but knew she would only create a larger mess to deal with if she did.

She asked Summers to take a seat on the sofa with her and needed to cajole him a bit to get him to acquiesce. She saw Kevin raise his brows when Summers sat right next to her and quickly resituated herself to create some space between herself and Summers by turning her body to face him.

"My lord," she began, struggling for the words that would give least injury. She paused too long because Summers intervened rather testily, "Are you or are you not going to marry me?"

"Not," replied Alicia with sympathy.

Summers' frown lines bore deeper into his skin bringing his eyebrows to near touching. He looked at Kevin and then back to her. Astonished, his eyes opened wide at the revelation. He asked, "You are going to marry him?"

Alicia sighed and replied, "I expect I will."

Summers' frown softened and he said almost with a chuckle, "It sounds as though Donahue's suit is no more desirable than my own. Are you sure you will not have me?"

"You deserve better, my lord," she explained. "Do not think I do not appreciate you and what you were willing to offer me, but I am ashamed to say I did you a great disservice to agree to a marriage of convenience when my heart was already engaged to another man."

"How, when?" queried a puzzled Summers.

Alicia searched deep into her mind for the answer. Her upper teeth scraped her bottom lip as she puzzled out the truth and when it settled upon her, she grinned and said, "From the beginning."

The reply held little meaning for Summers. He shook his head in disbelief and said, "You will forgive me if I do not congratulate your Mr. Donahue."

"Of course," she replied. "My lord, will you forgive me for misleading you."

Summers stood and helped Alicia to rise; an impish grin marked his face as if he thought of some type of revenge to bestow. Thankfully, he must have rethought his intentions for all he did was take her hand and place a kiss on the back of it. Regardless, by the sound of Kevin's growl the affectation made a direct hit, drawing a full-faced smile from Summers. He quickly sobered and leaned towards her to admit, "You most likely spared us both from grief, so no forgiveness is necessary."

Alicia saw Kevin advance toward them and feared a brouhaha, but luckily Summers saw her concern and stepped back. He took his leave without a backward glance, though he undoubtedly heard Kevin rant, "What the devil did he say?"

Chapter Twenty-Three

"That is none of your affair," replied Alicia, provoked at being at the end of Kevin's interrogation, especially when he should be the one explaining himself.

Her dam of worries poured forth with all her emotions and like a runaway carriage, she expelled a diatribe without rein to what she said. "Where were you, Kevin? Do you have any idea how concerned I have been? First, I feared for your safety. Then, Lawrence returns and relays your message I refuse Summers. He tells me nothing of your whereabouts or what keeps you from me. I have been miserable. I no sooner accept I love you and then your life is in jeopardy and my worst fears are being realized."

Kevin wrapped her up in his arms and wearing a grin which did nothing to soothe Alicia asked, "You were miserable?"

Alicia's eyes widened and then her face crimsoned in anger. "You rogue; you dare gloat at my expense!" Alicia was about to swing back her leg and kick him in the shin as she once silently threatened when he confessed, "I was miserable, too! I was scared out of my wits when I entered and saw you wrapped in Summers' arms. My heart stopped beating until you denied his claim."

She pushed out of his arms and pressed him again to answer, "Where have you been?"

"Seeing to our future, Alicia," Kevin replied heatedly, responding in kind to her temper. "I could not offer you with less than Summers."

Confused, Alicia placed her fists on her hips and asked more calmly, "What are you talking about?"

"I gained us some property where we can build our horse breeding farm. It is not far from here, nor from Newmarket. It needs work but together I believe we can accomplish anything," he explained.

Alicia dropped her arms to her side. Her temper diminished by his revelation. She asked, "You speak as if I am to be your partner?"

"Of course," Kevin replied. "In all things."

"Is this to be a marriage of convenience?" she cautiously asked.

"It is what you always wanted."

"I am not sure you are convenient," she replied tartly, "nor am I sure we suit. You have not courted me."

"Ah, dear heart, I have courted you since the moment we met and now I am ready to pay my addresses to you, once I speak with your father."

She argued, "When did you court me? I think I would have known?"

"Actually, I believe you began our courtship the moment you snuck into my room at your father's home."

"Indeed not!" exclaimed Alicia. Embarrassed her presence in his room suggested she behaved improperly. She retorted, "It was my duty as mistress of the manor to see to your care. I did not sneak." With a touch of mischievous delight, she recalled, "My own aunt knew of my presence."

Kevin laughed and recalled for her. "Actually, I have no need to court you. I only need to confess to your father of our clandestine meetings and he would demand we marry."

Alicia's eyes widened at the threat. Kevin immediately stepped forward and wrapped her in a tight hug. He apologized for his unkind remarks.

Alicia pushed out of his embrace again to clarify, "You would not force our marriage?"

"Never," responded Kevin. "I want your happiness even if it means my own sorrow."

"Is that why you promoted a match between Summers and me?"

Kevin rolled his eyes and ran his hand through his hair in exasperation. He argued, "Alicia, I never promoted a match between the two of you. I distinctly remember telling you in one of my letters."

"Well, you did not disrupt his courtship of me. You actually liked him well-enough to become his friend."

"Who said I did not cause the man an inconvenience or two? I believe you took offense when I first switched our places at dinner. If I did anything, such as keep him from your company by scheduling appointments for him, I would never say."

"You are the reason why he often sent his regrets? How could that be when you were always where he should have been?"

"We can speak of specifics later. First, tell me why you are unsure of me? Why do you feel the need of a courtship when our hearts are already engaged to one another?"

"Are they? You never once shared what is in your heart."

"Neither have you, but I do not doubt you love me. It is in your being. I see it in your look and feel it in your touch. Your thoughts are my own and visions of my future have you by my side. Am I the only one to know we were made for each other and are better together than apart?"

"All you say resonates with me and my heart readily accepts it to be true, but my mind wants the words, Kevin. Why haven't you told me I am the woman you love?"

"Ah," sighed Kevin. "Alicia, I believe I fell in love with you the moment you snubbed your nose at me at Tattersall's. I thought you were a termagant, a beautiful and bold lady whom I wanted to meet. I quickly learned how smart, talented, and mischievous you were when I stayed at your father's home. You immediately touched my heart with your caring nature and intrigued me with your competitive spirit. I saw in you my helpmeet, someone with whom I could share my life and grow a family. My dreams are more meaningful because I am striving for us and not just me. I love you, Alicia. I tell you now, but I told you before. Did you not read the letter I wrote of my big dream?"

"Of course, I did. I read all your letters more than once. You never singled me out, Kevin. You just said you wanted to marry a woman you loved. How was I supposed to know it was me? For a while, it was Priscilla."

Kevin's jaw dropped and Alicia gave herself away when she chuckled. He closed his mouth and shook his head. "You minx," he scolded. "You know very well my courtship of Priscilla was a ruse. Why tease me, especially when I have been steadfast in my affection and pursuit of you."

"Using Priscilla to make me jealous was most unkind, Kevin," she argued. "You should have told me you loved me."

"And have you running for the hills? Alicia, you are rewriting history. You had no wish to marry for love and any hint of what was blossoming between us scared you into Summers' arms. I was not going to chance you marrying the man without benefit of courtship just to keep yourself from loving me."

Alicia took Kevin's words to heart and knew he was right. She still wished he said he loved her without being prompted. Her forlorn look made Kevin sigh and command, "Go! Go get the letter I wrote."

Alicia almost argued he had no authority to order her about, but his stern expression prompted her to turn and race from the drawing room to do as he bid. Alicia passed her father on the stairs.

The baron exclaimed, "Alicia! I understand Mr. Donahue has finally come."

Alicia shouted, "Drawing room," without a hitch in her step and continued on her way to her suite, while her father chuckled and descended the staircase to search out his future son-by-marriage.

It took Alicia only a few moments to retrieve the letter Kevin wanted. All his missives were tied together with a red ribbon and hidden deep in a highboy drawer. She always kept the letters with her no matter where she traveled. She liked to read them to feel close to Kevin, but they were her private indulgence and she knew she risked scandal if her indiscretion was uncovered. Maidens were not allowed to receive mail from men, aside from a father or brother. If they did and it became known, then their virtue was speculated upon in polite society which often led to their ruin.

She returned to the drawing room and asked Kevin when she did not see her father, "Did Papa come and greet you?"

Kevin smiled at Alicia's confusion and explained, "The baron and I had a very successful interview. He is quite happy I love and cherish his daughter. He worried over your unique interests and talents. I assured him I am in admiration of them and feel lucky to find a lady who values horse breeding as much as I do. I also assured him I am now a landowner with expectations to keep his daughter in the style she is accustomed. After which, I asked for your hand in marriage."

"What did he say?" Alicia asked.

"He gave me permission to pay my addresses to you, but said it was your decision to make."

Alicia nodded, knowing the decision was always hers to make. Little did she realize when she was doing her best to discourage Kevin, she was already halfway in love with him. He sparked her interest and caused within her a sensation of feelings that surpassed friendship. Yet, they were indeed friends, owning a compatibility that made whatever they did or discuss greater because they did it together.

She responded to him the first time she saw him. At Tattersall's, he angered her. During the hunt, he provoked her. In his injured sleep, he intrigued her and in his wakened state, he excited her. No one before Kevin had ever made her heart race or her insides toss about as if she swallowed a dozen butterflies.

She should have known Kevin was more than just a friend for she had never shared her dreams with anyone aside from Meg and Charles, nor had she ever confessed her fears to anyone but family. From the beginning, she knew she could trust him and be herself with him. She never had to be less than she was, nor subdue her personality to please him. Kevin liked her and she preferred his company to all others.

They shared a dream and often seemed to be of one mind. He listened to her, challenged her and made her feel good, happy, even when he provoked her. He was always in her thoughts, and she always saw him in her future. In hindsight, she felt silly it took his pretend courtship of Priscilla to make her recognize how much she loved him. He said he knew she loved him and that words were unnecessary, but she wanted to hear the words. He said he told her in a letter which provoked her. *Does he think I am incapable of reading?* As much as she wanted to be proven wrong, she also wanted to be proven right.

"Here," she said, and then waited while he opened the letter and began to read out loud.

Alicia,

My grand-da was a big believer in dreams. Even after he was pressgang into the Royal Navy, he never gave up believing he would one day have a piece of land with a wife he loved by his side.

To this day, I can hear his voice with his Irish lilt telling me, "You Dream Big Kevin. Anything less is just a notion that is easily forgotten."

Are you resolute to marry Summers and let go of your dream? It would take a dream bigger than the one I *have to give it up. I plan to breed horses and race the best of them. I am going to find a nice piece of grazing land, build me a house and stable, and then marry <u>The Woman I Love</u>, a woman who is not afraid of hard work and who has a lot of faith. A smart, strong, capable, and determined lady who will stand by my side in good times and bad, and who shares my dream as if it was hers from the beginning.*

I'll not waver and hopefully someday, you will see me successful. I'll write and continue to share my trials and successes with you, unless you inform me differently. Take care of yourself and be the termagant I know you to be. With your permission, I will call on you when I get to London.

Kevin

Kevin returned the opened letter to Alicia with a look that bespoke, "I told you." Alicia quickly rebutted, "You said you were going to marry the woman you love. You did not say you were going to marry me!"

Kevin rolled his eyes and directed Alicia to look at the letter. He said, "Read me the first underlined word in the letter."

Alicia read through the letter quickly and found the word "You" underlined. She looked up from the letter and recited, "You."

Kevin grinned and said, "Exactly."

Alicia looked confused and before she could ask what Kevin meant, he prodded, "Go on. Find the next underlined word."

Alicia returned her eyes to the paper and quickly understood the letter Kevin wrote had a coded message embedded. She found the other underlined words and read them silently. When she failed to read the words aloud, Kevin prodded, "Well, when put together, what do the underlined words say?"

Alicia's face broke into a broad smile and then she recited, "You are the woman I love." Alicia was so full of joy. She was about to ramble how she did not know and how she had no idea there was a hidden message in the letter when she recalled she still did not know where Kevin had been. She also remembered he left the tavern in the company of the Earl of Luxingfield and two barmaids. Her jovial face quickly turned angry. She knew Kevin saw her mood change for he was girding himself for her onslaught.

"Where have you been, Kevin? And don't say you were seeing to our future unless you can explain how two bar maids assisted you in acquiring your new land."

Kevin chuckled, but before he could reply, the drawing room doors opened and Meg and Lawrence walked in.

Lawrence apologized, "Sorry, Donahue. I could not keep my lady wife from entering."

Kevin smirked and jested, "Coming in or falling in. How much did you hear?"

"Enough to know Meg felt compelled to be at hand to comfort Alicia."

Meg grimaced, "I did tell Alicia you would have a perfectly reasonable explanation for joining a party with barmaids."

"And so I do," grinned Kevin. "In answer to your question, Alicia, the barmaids did assist us in acquiring our property. I said ours and I meant it. For months, Luxingfield has been dangling some land of his I want to buy."

Alicia interrupted, "Why?"

"Because," replied Kevin, "he wants Maximilian. He has been trying to buy my thoroughbred ever since he saw him on the field at the hunt where I met him. I refused his offer, but he thought he could persuade me to risk Maximilian for the title of some land for which he has no use, but he knows I covet. Well, I finally agreed to play for it."

"Why play now? Maximilian was not worth the risk."

"You are worth the risk, Alicia. Besides my dreams are diminished without you at my side, so when Luxingfield entered that tavern and asked me to play, I agreed. I knew Summers was on his way here to pay his addresses and I wanted to offer you as much as he."

Alicia shook her head in disbelief and then reminded him, "You told me to refuse him. He was never an issue."

"Never the less, I want what you want and you want to own a breeding farm. I have seen our property. It is prime grazing land and suitable for our needs."

Alicia was ready to hug Kevin until she remembered the bar maids. She sternly asked, "Explain the barmaids."

Kevin grinned and said, "Well, I don't think they need an explanation, other than to say they were helpful in distracting Luxingfield. By the time he realized the hand he held might not beat my own, he already anteed up too much money to fold. He thought to outbid me with the title to his property, but between my winnings and Maximilian I was able to meet his bid. My hand won. I not only walked away with a bushel of money, but a fine piece of property to boot."

Alicia's mouth gaped. She had not expected a reasonable explanation. Kevin tapped her mouth shut and then kissed her pursed lips. She did not like being caught with her mouth open or having attention drawn to it. She was about to make that clear to him except his kiss caused the same warm sensation that overcame her every time he held and kissed her. She became dreamy-eyed and it took her a moment to understand what Kevin was up to when he dropped to one knee.

She blinked a couple times, before her eyes widened. Holding her hand in his, he asked, "Honorable Alicia. I love you. I want to spend my life with you and share all of its joys and sorrows with you. I am not fool enough to believe we will not have any pitfalls, but I know with you by my side we can overcome and achieve anything. Will you do me the great honor of marrying me?"

Meg gasped, "Oh Alicia, How perfectly romantic."

Alicia and Kevin laughed in unison and then Alicia pulled Kevin to his feet. He raised a brow, silently prodding her to answer his proposal. He got more than he asked for when she wrapped her arms around his neck and kissed him soundly before saying, "Yes."

Kevin pulled back and asked to confirm her answer, "Yes, to marrying me?"

Alicia smiled and answered, "Yes, to loving you. Yes, to being your helpmeet. Yes, to being your partner in all things. Yes, I will marry you." Then, Alicia kissed him again and this time, Kevin kissed her back. They never even heard Meg and Lawrence leave the drawing room or knew they were alone until they ended their kiss.

Alicia sighed, "Oh my!"

Kevin grinned and looking at her flushed face said, "Oh my, indeed." Then, he pulled his once very reluctant lady back into his arms and kissed her again.

Acknowledgements

Thank you, Alicia Floyd, for your editing talents and on point suggestions. As always, your sideline remarks are duly appreciated. I especially enjoy your sidebar "ha-ha" and happy face when something in the story makes you laugh or smile.

Thank you, Christina Brusaca, for orchestrating the book cover's photo shoot with amazing grace and keeping the endeavor fun and productive, especially for my daughter who is this book's featured model. You have a great skill at directing a scene and framing in the perfect image.

Thank you, Debby Ring, for being my "go to" girl regarding everything I need to know about horses. If you don't have an answer for me, then you know someone who does.

A special thanks for my loving husband Larry, my amazing children and grandchildren, and my ever-inspiring parents for their continued support and encouragement.

About the Author

Teresa Sweeney is a Golden Leaf Award winner for her novel *Only A Captain Will Do* and Golden Quill finalist for her novel *The Reluctant Viscount*. She takes great pleasure penning historical romance novels focusing on the charm, wit, and banter of courtship.

She is a wife and mother of four adult children. She dotes on her six grandchildren and is looking forward to welcoming a new grandbaby. She loves to read, write, and a myriad of other pursuits where she can use her creativity and imagination. Visit her website www.teresa-sweeney.com for the latest information on her novels.